August's Heat

A Larry Macklin Mystery-Book 10

A. E. Howe

Books in the Larry Macklin Mystery Series:

November's Past
(Book 1)

December's Secrets
(Book 2)

January's Betrayal
(Book 3)

February's Regrets
(Book 4)

March's Luck
(Book 5)

April's Desires
(Book 6)

May's Danger
(Book 7)

June's Trouble's
(Book 8)

July's Trials
(Book 9)

August's Heat
(Book 10

DEDICATION

For all the staff and volunteers that keep
local theatre alive across the country.

CHAPTER ONE

I was shocked awake shortly after one on Tuesday morning by the sound of Will Smith singing "Men in Black" and to Cara hitting me with a pillow, begging me to make it stop. I groaned and groped around in the dark for my phone, knowing it was dispatch. I was on call and should have just slept on the couch, but I'd hoped that a Monday night would be quiet. No such luck.

"What was that?" Cara mumbled.

"Darlene got ahold of my phone the other day and screwed around with my ringtones. Sorry."

"Not the song."

"Oh, it's a body. I gotta go." I fumbled around in the dark for my clothes and took them into the bathroom before turning on a light.

"Bye," Cara said, covering her face with my pillow.

Half an hour later, I was staring down at the body of a man sprawled across the front hallway of a house in town, a dime-sized hole in the middle of his forehead.

"The man that called it in is sitting in my car," Deputy Julio Ortiz said.

"Good, keep him there until I can talk to him." I stifled a yawn.

"What kind of revolver is that?" Julio asked, his usual light accent just a bit thicker in his excitement.

"Old and foreign," I said. "What's his name?" I guessed the man's age to be somewhere in his late fifties or early sixties.

"Conrad Higgins. This is his house. I pulled up his DMV records, but I haven't checked his pockets for a wallet."

"Good. There'll be plenty of time to rummage through his pockets after we get pictures and Darzi's folks have examined the body. Speaking of pictures, is crime scene on the way?"

"Yes. I asked for Shantel or Marcus."

"Perfect. They aren't going to appreciate getting up in the middle of the night, but then neither did I."

"Sorry, but…" Julio pointed at the body.

"I know. That's why I'm on call. And this one looks like it could get complicated."

"Old man like this, who'd want to shoot him? When I cleared the house, nothing looked out of place. I don't think this is a robbery."

"That's not the kind of gun most robbers carry," I said, hearing a car pull up outside. "Let's clear out so the techs can do their thing."

When we stepped out onto the porch, Marcus Brown was trudging up the walkway to the house, carrying his camera and shouldering a large bag. Marcus and Shantel Williams comprised our best crime scene team, but tonight he was alone.

"Shantel's out of town and no one else would answer their phone. I'll need some help."

"Julio, stay out here and hold back the coroner's assistants until Marcus is through."

I saw the disappointment on his face. Julio had gotten it into his head that he wanted to move out of patrol and into criminal investigations. But two in the morning, with a fresh body and a case that looked like it was going to be more involved than a drive-by shooting, wasn't the time to start.

"While you're waiting, work with dispatch and see if you can come up with the next of kin," I finally said, throwing him a small bone so that he could still feel like he was part of the investigation.

"Where do you want to start?" Marcus asked me when I came back into the house.

"Start with the rooms on the left side of the hall and go clockwise. I want the whole house filmed and photographed. If this is going to be a who-done-it, then there's no telling what's important and what isn't. We'll do the downstairs first."

While Marcus took photographs, I followed him through the house with the video camera and got a good look at the place. It was a nice old Craftsman, probably built before World War II, and was full of antiques.

"Bunch of this stuff looks valuable," Marcus said as he took pictures in the office.

"I doubt this is a robbery gone bad. The one shot to the head looks very professional," I said thoughtfully.

"Big old revolver."

"It's not one I'm familiar with."

"You think the gun means something?"

"Looking at all these antiques, I'm guessing that it's his gun. Maybe he heard a sound, grabbed the gun and came to investigate. Then the intruder took it away from him and shot him." I doubted that theory as soon as I heard it come out of my mouth. "Of course, he's dressed in street clothes so he obviously wasn't in bed yet. And one shot to the forehead seems a little on point for an intruder. I'd be curious to know how complicated that particular gun is to fire. Some old revolvers are single-action and require you to cock the hammer before you can pull the trigger."

"Maybe the old man cocked it before it was taken away from him," Marcus suggested, then pointed at a spot where he wanted me to lay a yardstick down next to some stains on the carpet.

"Most single-actions have a light trigger. If he'd cocked it and someone tried to take it away, odds are it would have gone off. But I doubt he'd have been shot in the forehead. With a struggle like that, you'd expect the shot to go into the stomach or an appendage, or even up through the chin or neck." The more I thought about the scene, the more intriguing it was.

Julio called on the radio to let me know that the coroner's van had arrived. "Let's clear them a path," I told Marcus. The sooner they could get in and take the victim's temperature and check for other physical signs like lividity, the more accurate Dr. Darzi's official time of death would be.

The two assistants were both women.

"I'm Linda and this is Ann, one of our lowly interns," the first one said, nodding toward the other. They looked like they could have been sisters. Linda was a bit older and had broader shoulders, but both were just over five feet tall and had dark hair. Each of them carried a large black bag with "Coroner" stenciled on the side.

"I know that look. Yes, we're strong enough to lift a body. Okay, most bodies," Linda continued lightly. "Wow, right in the forehead. Nice shot."

She had been talking so fast that I hadn't had a chance to introduce myself. Finally I was able to say, "I'm Deputy Larry Macklin."

"Yep, I figured," Linda said without taking her eyes off of the body as she examined it from head to foot. She kneeled down and carefully lifted the head and felt the back of the skull. "Exit wound in the rear. Let's lay some plastic out and roll him over onto it. Go ahead and unbuckle his belt and pants. Once we have him on his stomach, we'll need to get them down so we can take his temperature," she instructed Ann.

I decided that I didn't need to watch any more. Lifeless bodies are a cold reminder of the indignities that await us in death. I left the foyer and found Marcus in the kitchen.

"I don't need any help with this or filming the outside,

but I *will* need someone to help me collect evidence. I called dispatch and told them to kick someone out of bed and send them over here."

"I'll be outside," I told him and walked out, averting my eyes as I passed the two women still examining the body.

I found the man who'd reported the body sitting in Julio's car and looking a little irritated. He was in his early sixties and wearing a robe and tennis shoes. I introduced myself and handed him one of my cards.

"Jason Harmon. I'd give you one of my cards, but…" He indicated the robe.

"Would you like to talk here or at your house?" Making a witness feel comfortable and in control helped encourage them to take their time and give full and complete answers.

"My house would be great," he said, stepping out of the patrol car and heading toward the house next door. Like most of the houses in the neighborhood, his two-story Colonial sat back from the road on a large lot. Lights burned in two of the windows.

"I wouldn't have heard anything if we weren't having trouble with our air conditioning," Mr. Harmon said as he led me into the dining room.

"Start about ten minutes before you noticed that something was wrong. Where were you?"

"In bed. I swear, now that I'm getting long in the tooth I can't manage to sleep through the night. I got up and went to the bathroom, then decided I wanted a glass of water."

"Where's your bedroom?"

"Upstairs. I came down to the kitchen for the water. We've got a water cooler. The city water is awful. Anyway, like I said, I came downstairs, then I heard something outside when I got to the bottom of the stairs."

"Something…? Can you be any more specific?"

"Not really. I was kind of just cruising. You know, not fully awake. I wouldn't have heard anything if I hadn't had some of the windows open downstairs. Guess I won't be doing that anymore. I've been getting estimates. At first I thought I'd just replace the heat pump outside, but then all the guys who came out said I'd save a lot of money in the long run if I replaced the duct work too. These old houses... So I put a window air conditioner in our bedroom, figuring it's going to take a while to get everything fixed." He shook his head.

In my experience, most witnesses would rush through their story to get to the exciting part where they discovered the body. I often had to drag them back to the other details. By comparison, Mr. Harmon was in quite a conversational mood.

"So you don't know what you heard?" I asked to get him back on track.

"That's right. Maybe voices? Whatever it was, it made me wake up all the way. So I went over to the window to listen and that's when I thought I heard someone yell. A second later, I heard the gunshot."

"What did the person yell?"

Mr. Harmon pursed his lips and narrowed his eyes. After a moment, he said, "Maybe 'No!' or 'Don't!' Something like that."

"Male or female voice?"

"Male, for sure."

"Was it Mr. Higgins?"

"I don't know. It was shouted, so it was hard to distinguish," he said reasonably.

"Did you know Mr. Higgins well?"

"Sort of. We've been neighbors since my wife and I moved here ten years ago, but we don't socialize with him. Just over-the-fence stuff. I did buy a lawnmower from him a while back. That was a mistake."

"A mistake?"

"Yeah. Well, long story, but he kind of cheated me on that one."

"You mentioned your wife. You're married?"

"Nineteen years. Second wife."

"Is she here?"

"No, she's in Tennessee with her kids. End of summer vacation."

"No one else is in the house?"

"Just my girlfriend." He saw that I wasn't laughing. "Only kidding," he said lamely.

"You said that Mr. Higgins cheated you?" I wanted more details about that comment.

"It wasn't a big deal. Just a good lesson. Talk to other folks in the neighborhood. Higgins managed to screw over most of them at one time or another. The joke around here is that his name should be Conman Higgins, not Conrad. Honestly, when I saw him lying there on the floor, the first thing that came to my mind was that he'd finally cheated the wrong guy."

"Okay, let's go back to the point where you heard the gunshot."

"Right, right. I do a little shooting, so I know what a gun sounds like. It was probably stupid of me, but after the shot I opened the front door and listened. I heard a door slam over at Higgins's place, so I looked that way and saw a man running away from the house. He went down the walk and turned right."

"Are you sure it was a man?"

Mr. Harmon thought for a moment. "No, but that was my impression."

"What else did you notice about the person?"

"Hard to say. It was pretty dark and he was wearing dark clothes, maybe a hoodie. Possibly jeans. All dark, even the shoes. Since he turned and ran the other way, I didn't get a look at the face." He paused, looking past me. "I'm trying to think if there was anything else. I can't believe I saw a murderer. On our street. Wow, what the hell was I thinking leaving our windows open?"

"What did you do after you saw the person running away?"

"It was all so weird. I guess I felt compelled to go check on Higgins. Sounds stupid since I didn't even like the guy that much, but the whole scene was so out of the ordinary. The guy is a jerk, but you never hear any noise coming from his place. No loud sounds, arguments, TV, music, nothing in ten years. But now there's a gunshot and someone running away from the house in the wee hours of the morning. Anyway, I went outside thinking I'd walk down the sidewalk far enough to see if there was a light on in Higgins's house. There was, and I could see that the front door was open. That's when I realized that I must have heard his screen door slamming shut."

"And?" I prompted.

"I just kept walking. Next thing I knew, I was on the porch looking into his house. I could smell gunpowder and see some smoke. I think the smoke was what caused me to open the door and go in." He paused and I thought I would have to nudge him again, but finally he went on. "You know what's strange? I didn't call for Higgins. I think I knew at that point that something really bad had happened. I walked in far enough to see him lying on the floor with that hole in his head." He stopped talking and, for the first time, looked really upset.

"Did you go over to the body?"

"No. I reached for my cell phone, but when I realized I didn't have it on me, I kind of panicked. I ran all the way back to my house and called 911."

Mr. Harmon didn't have much to add to his story. After a few more questions, I told him I'd let him know if I needed any more information, and not to talk to anyone about what he'd seen. Of course, I knew that he would anyway. No one in Adams County could keep a secret for more than five minutes.

CHAPTER TWO

Back outside, I looked around and saw that the lights were on in the house across the street. Two faces, a man and a woman, stared out at me through a front room window. The owners of the house obviously weren't used to seeing flashing blue lights in their neighborhood, but they were too polite to come across the street and stare. I looked at my watch. It was only two-thirty, but if they were up anyway…

"I'm going to talk to them," I told Julio, who waved me over to the side of his car.

"I found a Facebook page for Higgins and a link to his website," he said, showing me his phone. "He buys and sells antiques, specializing in military weapons."

"Great. Let me know what other information you get out of it." I walked away, thinking that Dad had better find a place for Julio in investigations before he started looking at other agencies. The young deputy clearly had the itch to do more than work patrol.

The faces at the window looked confused as they saw me walking toward them. Finally the man left the window and opened the door.

"What's going on?" he asked before I'd even reached the porch.

"There's been some trouble across the street," I said cryptically. "I'd like to talk with you all, if you don't mind."

I could see curiosity eating at the man. It finally won. "Sure, come on in." He turned back into the house. "Tracy, a cop wants to talk to us!" he shouted as I followed him into the living room.

Tracy was a petite woman, barely five feet tall. She was wearing a robe and nervously playing with the ties.

"Can I get you something?" she asked. "We have iced tea, water, milk…"

"He doesn't want anything to drink. He's here to ask us questions," her husband said dismissively.

"I'm Deputy Larry Macklin with the Adams County Sheriff's Office… and you all are?"

"I'm Ed Landers and this is my wife, Tracy," he said quickly, as if he was answering questions in a quiz.

"What woke you all up tonight?"

"All the ruckus outside," Ed said, and then must have realized from the look on my face that it wasn't much of an answer. "I woke up when I heard cars pulling up outside. I opened my eyes and saw the lights flashing through the curtains. That got my curiosity going. We hear sirens from time to time, but we don't normally see the lights outside our house."

"And you?" I said to Tracy.

"Ed woke me up. I sleep pretty soundly. He shook me and said that there were cops outside and that he was getting up."

"Neither of you heard anything before that?"

"Like what?" Ed asked.

"Anything," I said, not wanting to put ideas into their heads.

He looked thoughtful and shared a glance with his wife. "No, I don't think so. I'm pretty sure the cop cars pulling up is what woke me up. What happened over there?"

"We're still trying to figure that out," I answered evasively. "Are you all friends with Conrad Higgins?"

"The guy across the street?" Ed asked and I nodded. "Nah. I've talked to him a few times, but that's it. He had a beautiful 1936 Rolls Royce for a couple of months. Man, was that a beautiful car. I managed to talk him into starting it for me once, but as soon as he found out I wasn't interested in buying it, he gave me the brush off. Came across as sort of a jerk."

"Ed," Tracy admonished him.

"Well, he did. I said that I wished I had the money for something like that and, right away, he turned the engine off, closed the hood and said he ought to charge me for the gas he wasted. Total assh... jerk." Ed still sounded stung by Higgins's rejection.

"When was this?"

"Two, three years ago. I haven't said a word to him since. Trust me, he doesn't have a lot of friends in the neighborhood. Hell, Clint was even considering reporting him to the county."

"Ed, don't be gossiping."

"Well, it's the truth."

"What did he want to report him for?"

"Running a business out of his house. Like the car. He buys and sells antiques. Everybody knows it. And Clint says it's dangerous. Higgins advertises stuff for sale on the Internet. Who knows who might come into the neighborhood? Is that what happened? Did someone rob him?"

"He's been killed, hasn't he?" Tracy said, putting her hand up to her mouth in surprise.

I guess I didn't have my poker face on because Ed's eyes got wide. "Damn!" he exclaimed.

"Who else in the neighborhood had problems with Mr. Higgins?"

"You can't... What I said about Clint, it wasn't anything like a big deal. And I never had any real issues with Higgins." Ed was backpedaling as fast as he could.

"I'm not here to accuse anybody of anything. I just need

15

to find out how Higgins got along with his neighbors."

"Then I guess the cat's out of the bag. Look, nobody liked the guy. I could name half a dozen people who walked away from him feeling cheated. But I don't know anyone who'd…" He paused.

"What?"

"Nothing," he said unconvincingly.

"You thought of someone who had a serious problem with Higgins, didn't you?"

"I don't want to say," Ed insisted stubbornly.

"Not the way this works," I told him.

"That's what you get for running your mouth," Tracy said, giving him a look.

"I know there was some bad blood between Higgins and Faith Osborne. Nothing else."

"What caused it?"

"I… Okay, geez. Look, I don't know the whole story, but what I heard was that Higgins bought some of Faith's mother's jewelry. Her mother, Dot, died about four years ago over at the Magnolia Ridge Nursing Home. The trouble with Higgins started about a year before she died. Dot had a bunch of heirloom jewelry and Higgins offered to look at it and give her some idea of what it was worth. He wound up buying it for next to nothing. One of the pieces, a ring or something, turned out to be worth almost six figures. When Faith found out, she was fit to be tied. She sued him, but since there had never been a formal agreement for him to appraise the pieces, he was just a buyer and she was just a seller. Bottom line, he was a jerk, but he hadn't done anything illegal. Ever since then, Faith has called him a crook whenever and wherever she can."

"I'm guessing he didn't like that very much."

"He sued her for defamation or some such and won a small settlement."

"Which made Faith even madder?"

"Ballistic," Ed confirmed.

"Where does Faith live?"

"To the right, four doors down from Higgins on his side of the street."

I thought about how Mr. Harmon had reported seeing someone running from the house. Did that mean whoever killed Higgins lived nearby? I noticed Tracy shaking her head.

"You don't agree with your husband?"

"It's ridiculous," Tracy said, eyeing Ed to see if he was going to give her a hard time for contradicting him. He just rolled his eyes. "Faith gets a bit… angry, but it's all just talk."

"Is Faith married?"

"Divorced."

"Did either of you see anyone walking around the neighborhood tonight?"

Ed thought for a minute. "There are a lot of walkers in this neighborhood. I saw… Look, I'm really not pointing fingers, but I did see Faith walking her dog around eleven. But then, I see her most nights. I also saw Mr. Hollis around ten. He always takes a walk after dinner, and I try to avoid him like the plague. If he gets to talking to you, you'll never escape."

"What were you doing when you saw them?" I thought it a little odd that Ed had been outside of his house that late himself.

"I'm a pharmaceutical rep. Before I go to bed, I usually arrange the boxes in my car for the next day. I'm not a morning person. I want to be able to go out, get in my car and head to my first stop without having to think too much. So I'm in and out of the house quite a bit and usually wave to whoever is walking by."

I didn't get anything else useful from them, so I headed back across the street. Linda and Ann were standing outside, waiting for me. Illuminated by the blue lights from Julio's car, they were leaning against the hood of their van.

"We're ready to move the body, but this guy said we had to wait for your okay," Linda said with a smile, nodding toward Julio. She took a swig from a bottle of water. "How can it be so hot in the middle of the night?"

"What's your best guess at the time of death?"

"Considering the air temperature, the body hadn't cooled off that much. In fact, if he hadn't had a hole in his head, he could have theoretically still been alive. No lividity to speak of, so I'd say not much more than an hour before we got here. I'll turn in all of our numbers to Dr. Darzi and he'll give you the official estimate." Linda grabbed one end of the stretcher and they headed back into the house.

I looked at my watch and saw that it was a little after four. Even though she was a notorious early riser, it was still too early to text my partner, Darlene Marks. I decided to walk around the house to look for anything out of the ordinary.

There weren't any signs of a break-in. Most of the windows had been painted shut over the years and you would have had to bust through a couple layers of paint to get them open. Luckily, Higgins had kept the house in good shape. It was hard to investigate a crime if the crime scene was already a mess before the event occurred. But here everything looked normal.

A car was parked in front of the garage. It was an old '70s Chevrolet pickup in very good condition. It had an antique tag and chrome rims. *Sporty*, I thought.

I gave up after an hour and sat down in my car to wait for sunrise. I must have dozed off, because the next thing I knew there was a loud thumping on the door.

"Hey, we aren't paying you to sleep!" a familiar voice shouted at me. I looked up and saw my dad staring at me through the open window.

"I'm not going to school today," I joked, sitting up.

"You always were a pain in the butt to get out of bed."

"What are you doing here at this hour?" I asked, glancing at my watch to see that it was only six-thirty.

"I'm going to the Calhoun Business Association's monthly breakfast in an hour."

"Shaking babies and kissing hands, huh?" Dad was

running for reelection as sheriff in November.

"I think I'm in pretty good shape, but I don't want to take anything for granted. Speaking of which, has Chief Maxwell come snooping around the scene yet?" Charles Maxwell, Calhoun's chief of police, was Dad's only serious opponent in the election.

"No, he seems to be staying clear. Dispatch gave the call to Julio." Technically, since the murder had happened within the city limits, the Calhoun Police Department would have had jurisdiction. But since the department was so small, the sheriff's office handled most major crimes.

"Good. I'm impressed that he hasn't let the election interfere with his judgment."

"He's not an idiot. It wouldn't do him any good to try and take over an investigation that his people aren't qualified to handle and that his department doesn't have the resources to examine properly."

"I think he may be having problems raising money."

"You've done a great job for the county. The only people rooting for Maxwell are folks you've pissed off."

"Me, piss anyone off?" he said, a mischievous spark in his green eyes.

"Probably even a few within our own ranks."

Dad frowned slightly. "That may not be a joke. I can think of two deputies that are probably acting as spies for Maxwell."

I knew exactly who he was talking about. He'd reprimanded one deputy for coming in to work physically exhausted after repeated warnings that he couldn't work sixty hours off-duty along with his regular shift. Another deputy had been caught passing food and cigarettes to a prisoner at the jail who happened to be his ex-girlfriend. Dad had given that one a week's suspension without pay, which most of the rest of us thought was lenient.

I got out of the car and stretched. "Why do you have the van?" I asked, noticing the battered old van plastered with "Re-Elect Ted Macklin" stickers.

Dad didn't answer, but walked over to the van and pointed through the side window. I looked in and saw a dead Angus bull sprawled in the back. Actually, it was Mauser, Dad's one-hundred-and-ninety-pound, black-and-white monster of a Great Dane. The only sign that he was alive was the gentle up and down motion of his chest and the occasional puff of breath out of his droopy flews.

"How did you get him out of bed at this time of the morning?"

"Same way I used to get *your* lazy ass out of bed. I pulled him out. Jamie couldn't make it today," Dad said, referring to Mauser's usual babysitter. "So I just decided to bring him along. He'll be a hit at the breakfast." He was right. Mauser was one of Dad's most effective public relations tools.

"You know, people are really just laughing at you for having a dog like that."

Mauser must have heard me, raising his head for just a minute and glaring at me before falling back onto his pillow.

"Let 'em laugh as long as they vote for me. What have you got here?" Dad asked, all business now.

I filled him in on the murder scene.

"Higgins was a piece of work," was his only comment before taking off for the breakfast.

As I watched the van drive away, my phone rang. It was Darlene.

"Morning, sunshine!" she said.

"Stop it! You know I'm not a morning person," I responded, grinning in spite of myself. Darlene's energetic personality had taken some getting used to, but I had to admit that I enjoyed working with her. "I was just about to call you."

"I woke up and heard Julio on the scanner. There was a murder on Washington Avenue?"

"Bullet hole to the forehead. The victim is a guy named Conrad Higgins."

"I'm on my way," she interrupted before I had a chance to elaborate on the case. Surprised, I looked at my phone.

Darlene was always gung-ho, but this seemed a bit much even for her.

The coroner's van was gone when I walked back up to the house, but Marcus was still hard at work. He'd finally been joined by Charlie Walton, one of our younger techs. Julio was sitting in his car and hopped out when he saw me.

"I've got water and some energy bars if you need them," he said.

"I'm good, thanks. You get off in an hour?"

"Yeah, but I'd like to stay on and help with the investigation."

"Sure, why not. We'll need help canvassing the neighborhood when people are up and moving about. We don't want to give them a chance to leave for work before we talk to them. Darlene's on her way."

Half an hour later, she pulled up behind my car and got out, looking a little less put-together than usual.

"I hurried over here," she said by way of explanation. "Have they taken the body?"

"A couple hours ago. You seem very excited by this case."

"I was with Higgins last night." My mind immediately went places it shouldn't and Darlene gave me a poke in the ribs when she saw the expression on my face. "Get your mind out of the gutter, cupcake. He gave a talk to the Adams County Historical Society. I was there."

"What time did he leave?"

"Around ten. When was he killed?"

"Just before one."

"This his house?"

"Yep."

"Where's his car?" she asked and my stomach lurched.

"I figured he drove the truck," I said, pointing at the old Chevrolet.

"That truck might be his, but it wasn't what he was driving last night. I helped him carry some of his guns out to his car after the talk."

"Guns?"

"He was giving a talk on historical firearms, pre-World War II. He was driving a grey Honda CR-V. I'd say 2014 or '15."

I looked up and down the street. No CR-Vs. And there had been nothing in Higgins's garage except some metal and wood-working equipment.

"Son of a..." I shook my head and called dispatch, asking them to put out a BOLO on the Honda with a note to call me if it was found.

"Killer take it?" Darlene asked.

"We have a witness who saw a person fleeing the scene on foot shortly after the shot was fired," I said, kicking myself for not checking the DMV records earlier for any other vehicles owned by Higgins. If the killer *had* taken the car, then he had a few hours' head start on us now.

"Interesting. Guess I can see why you didn't think Higgins's car would be missing."

Still pissed at myself, I filled her in on what little we knew and pointed out the houses where I'd already conducted interviews.

"So the folks in the house on that side didn't wake up?" she asked, indicating a brick home with decorative wooden trim. The windows were still dark.

"If they did, then they never turned on their lights. Or they'd turned them off by the time I got here."

"Makes me want to talk to them," Darlene said. She had a point. With all the lights and activity near their house, it seemed odd that they hadn't been as curious as other residents in the neighborhood.

"It's almost seven. I think we can start knocking on doors." Of course, I could have gone up and down the street last night and woken people up, but dragging people out of bed in the middle of the night wasn't the best way to ensure willing cooperation.

We headed straight for the brick house.

"Pete was there too," Darlene mentioned.

"At the talk? Why didn't I get the memo?" I asked, though I wasn't that surprised. Pete Henley was my ex-partner and the department's primary firearms instructor. I knew he had an interest in all things that went boom.

"Too intellectual for you, kiddo," she joked.

"Thanks, Einstein," I tossed back as we climbed the steps to the front door. I knocked authoritatively. Nothing. I repeated the knock, but still received no response. We were walking away when a car pulled into the driveway.

A young man in his early twenties slowly got out of the car. Darlene and I had stopped walking and stood between him and his house.

"You live here?" I asked, pointing over my shoulder.

"Yeah, what's going on?"

"I'm Deputy Macklin and this is Deputy Marks. We'd like to ask you a few questions."

"Something happen over at the Higgins house?" the man asked, looking back and forth between us and the house next door.

"We're investigating," I said elusively. "You are?"

"Boyd Long."

"You live here?"

"Yes."

"By yourself?"

"No, my parents live here too."

"Where are they?"

"Panama City. They're on vacation." He kept glancing next door.

"Where have you been?"

"Work." He wasn't volunteering any information. *Is this his normal attitude or is he purposely trying to hold back information?* I wondered.

"Let's lay some groundwork here, kid," Darlene said, stepping in closer and crowding Boyd. "A man's been murdered next door. We don't have time to play fifty questions. When my partner or I ask a question, then we'd like you to give us a full answer. Understand?" She drilled him with a hard stare, her face only a foot from his. His eyes darted to mine, looking for help, but I ignored him. Finally he nodded and Darlene stepped back. "So, fill us in on what you did last night, starting at about ten o'clock."

"I left for work around eight. I grabbed a double meal at the Express Burgers and got to work at the Supersave at nine. I worked until six this morning. Hung out for a while with some co-workers, then came home." He looked at Darlene to see if his answers met with her approval.

"The Supersave closes at eleven on weekdays," I pointed out.

"I restock the shelves and unload trucks. Me and a couple other guys. Bob's our supervisor."

The Supersave was less than two miles from his house, an easy run. I thought for a minute, then decided not to ask him about any breaks he may have taken. We could cover all that ground if he started to look like a real suspect.

"Have you noticed anything unusual going on next door over the last couple of days?" Darlene asked.

"Noooo. I don't think so," Boyd said slowly. "Like what?"

"New folks hanging around. Maybe Mr. Higgins doing something unusual. The house or yard looking different. Strange cars. Anything like that."

"There's always people coming over to his house. Some of the neighbors are pretty ticked that he's been running a business out of his house, but hey, it's like everybody sells stuff on the Internet these days. My mom still talks about department stores like that's a thing." He rolled his eyes to show how out of touch he thought his mother was.

"What did he sell?"

"Cars, sometimes. He's had some really cool ones over there. When I was a kid, I used to hope my folks would buy me one someday."

"He sell anything else?"

"A bunch of old junk." He paused, then glanced at Darlene and added, "And guns."

"Did you know him well?" I asked.

"I guess. I mean, I'd say hi when I saw him, or ask about some of the cars. But it was like I wasn't important enough to talk to. He'd answer my questions, but it was like he didn't want to."

"That's the only interaction you ever had with him? Asking him about the cars?"

"Pretty much. When I was younger, he asked me to mow his lawn once. I did and then he didn't want to pay me. Said we hadn't agreed on the price. Dad was pissed."

"What did your dad do?"

"He went over there. I was just a kid, maybe ten, and I was crying 'cause he wouldn't pay me. Dad stalked next door and, when he came back, he gave me twenty-five dollars. He said that Higgins had paid, but that I wasn't ever to do any work for him again. Thinking about it later, I was pretty sure that Dad had just paid me the money. I know they never tried to be friendly with him again."

We asked a few more questions, then thanked Boyd for his help and headed back next door.

CHAPTER THREE

"Higgins doesn't seem like someone you'd want to buy a used car from," I said when we were back in his front yard. "Had you met him before last night?"

"Nope. Albert had recruited him for the meeting. He's the society president, you know. He arranges most of the speakers. Which brings up something I need to tell you about. Just before the meeting started, I saw Albert and Higgins talking pretty heatedly. I thought I was going to have to go over and find out what it was all about, but Eddie beat me to it. He got between them and seemed to smooth everything over."

"Let me get this straight," I said, stopping and staring at Darlene. "You, Pete, Albert Griffin and Eddie Thompson, my occasional informant, were all at a lecture given by our victim a couple hours before he ended up on his back with a large-caliber hole in his head?"

"That about sums it up," she said, sounding smug.

"I ought to lock you all up as material witnesses," I joked, shaking my head. More seriously, I continued, "What do you think about the altercation between Griffin and Higgins? Was it a fight or just a discussion that got a little intense?"

"Albert looked upset, while Higgins seemed more

aggressive. You know Albert, he's about as mean as a guinea pig, so I had the other guy pegged as the troublemaker. My guess is that Higgins said something that upset Albert and then wouldn't take it back. Knowing what we do about Higgins, it probably had to do with money. The historical society sometimes gives speakers a small stipend. Maybe that's what it was about."

"And Eddie's part in this?"

"He came over and talked, mostly to Albert. Looked like he was trying to calm him down. He gave Higgins a couple of hard looks, but then there were nods all around. A couple minutes later, Albert asked everyone to have a seat and the talk got started."

"Higgins talked about guns?"

"Antique guns. He brought in about eight or nine different ones. Four rifles and as many handguns. He also had a slide show."

"Where was the lecture?"

"We use a room at the library."

Inside the house, we found Marcus and Charlie carefully probing a hole in the wall.

"The bullet is lodged in a stud," Marcus told me. "We're going to have to chip a pretty big hole in the wall to get it out without damaging it. Get me the reciprocating saw," he said to Charlie, who turned and headed out to the van.

A rough outline of the body had been drawn on the floor.

"Do we have a good trajectory for the bullet?" I asked Marcus.

"I measured and photographed a string from the hole in the wall to our victim at the approximate height where it would have entered his forehead. Then I ran it as far as I could to the opposite wall." He pointed to a spot on an interior wall about eight feet from the body. The front door was ten feet from the spot where the trajectory would trace back to the wall.

"So the shooter was fully inside the hall when he shot

Higgins," I said.

"He most likely knew the killer," Darlene said thoughtfully, looking at the pictures of the body that I'd taken with my phone. "I'd say Higgins didn't try to run or to avoid the person with the gun."

"Maybe he didn't believe the person would shoot him," I said.

"The guy seems to have gotten into scraps all the time. I guess he misjudged the situation this time." Darlene took her time examining the hallway and front rooms. "Lot of stuff to steal."

"There's a huge safe in the wall in the office," Marcus added.

"Really?" I'd been through the house at least twice and hadn't seen it.

"We just found it about an hour ago. It was covered by a wall panel that swung out. It's locked."

"We need to find his next of kin before we start drilling into the safe," I said.

"It's big enough to have a body or two inside."

"Thanks for that thought," I told him and excused myself, heading outside to see if Julio had had any luck in his online search for relatives.

"I've found a couple of possibilities," Julio said, tapping on the keys of the laptop in his patrol car. "I'm running them down now. His personal pages are all about the business. The sites don't have comments or posts from others."

"I bet they don't. From what we've heard so far, he was a crook of the first order. I doubt he wanted to share any comments he received."

"Here's a possible brother, Earl Higgins, living in North Carolina. He's the right age and originally from here."

"Conrad Higgins was a native?"

"This was his parents' home. He moved back here when his father died ten years ago. His mother died three years ago. I'm messaging the possible brother."

"Thanks, Julio. Darlene and I are going to start canvassing the neighborhood." People were beginning to emerge from their houses to collect the paper or get some morning exercise and most seemed very interested in what we were doing.

I saw a woman coming down the street with a French Bulldog tugging on his leash in front of her. I had planned to get Darlene before starting interviews, but the woman made eye contact so I walked on over to her.

"Morning," I greeted her as the Frenchie trotted up and started sniffing my legs.

"That's Melvin. He's harmless," the woman said. She was in her mid-fifties, with dark hair and a full figure that filled out her walking shorts and T-shirt. Everything about her suggested a natural perkiness. "What's going on at Higgins's place?"

"I'm Deputy Larry Macklin. You are?"

"Very nice and a little saucy," she said with a wink, then she noticed my expression. "Sorry. Just a little fun. Nobody has a sense of humor anymore. I'm Bernadette Santos. I live two blocks that way." She pointed off to the east.

"Do you know Mr. Higgins?"

"Afraid so. We've had a somewhat tumultuous relationship with the man."

"We?"

"The Grove Theatre. I'm their artistic director. On occasion, Mr. Higgins has provided us with set dressing or props for our shows. But it's usually a pain in the ass to get anything from him. He always wants to charge us an arm and a leg and we have to get into these long, drawn-out negotiations. The man is a jerk but, just occasionally, I think I've seen his better nature buried under all the Ebenezer Scrooge exterior. Is he okay?"

"Do you know if he has any next of kin?" I asked, since this was the first person I'd run across who seemed to think there was a human side to Conrad Higgins.

"He's never mentioned anyone. His father died a number

of years ago and his mother passed away a few years back. Even when his mother was alive, he didn't talk about her very much. And he's never mentioned any brothers or sisters. From your question, I'm guessing that something bad has happened to him."

"I'm afraid he's been killed."

Bernadette didn't react the way I thought she might. Instead of gasping in surprise, she just shook her head. "Can't go through life picking on everyone and not expect someone to punch back. Have you talked to anyone else about him?"

"I have."

"Then you've gotten an earful already. Not many... Almost no one liked him."

"What about you?"

"I have a place in my heart for villains. Always my favorite part in any production. And he was a most excellent Simon Legree. I always thought it was a shame that he didn't have a huge mustache to twirl."

"That bad?"

"If I was seen talking to him, for the next day or two I'd have people warning me not to deal with him. Total strangers, sometimes."

"Can you think of anyone in particular who had a grudge against Higgins?"

"No... Well, maybe."

"Maybe?"

"I think you'll hear it from more people than me. Faith Osborne had a very public feud with Conrad. He bested her twice."

"So I've heard. She must have been pretty upset over that?"

"Faith is not the type of woman who's used to losing an argument. But I think the lawsuit took the wind out of her sails. I haven't heard her say anything else about him since she lost the libel suit. Faith and I are good friends. I really tried to get the two of them to work out their differences, but there was just too much bad blood. Our friendship almost fell apart because I wouldn't ban Higgins from the theatre. Faith and I finally patched things up. Agreed to disagree."

"I see. Can you think of anyone else?"

"No one who stands out in the crowd. You'll find a bunch of people who disliked him and felt like he'd cheated them in one way or another."

I got her information, gave her one of my cards and then rounded up Darlene. I called dispatch to ask for another deputy to guard the crime scene while Julio helped us canvass the neighborhood. They told me that all our available deputies were tied up at a large accident scene, but they'd send over a Calhoun police officer. Once he arrived, I gave Darlene and Julio the names of the folks I'd already interviewed, then we split up the remaining ten houses within a block of Higgins's house. I made sure that Faith Osborne was on my list.

I was planning to head directly to her house, but then I saw a man walking out to his car at the first of the two houses I had to pass on my way. I sighed. No sense wasting an opportunity.

"What's going on over there?" Andre Shaw asked after the usual introductions. His caramel-colored skin was highlighted by his light tan suit and crisp white shirt. He leaned against his newer model BMW as we talked.

"We're in the process of figuring that out."

"That's cop-speak for 'something bad has happened, but we want to ask questions, not answer them'. That's cool." He looked at his watch. "I've got about half an hour that I can spare." Glancing at my face, he added, "Though, if it's important, I can make more time. I'm not trying to avoid talking to you. Just have to open the bank. I'm the branch manager."

"It shouldn't take too long," I assured him. "Were you home last night from, say, ten on?"

"Yes. I got home around seven. Ate. Did the social media

thing. Watched a little TV and went to bed."

"Anyone else live here?"

"My two children stay with me on the weekend, but no one was with me last night. Do I need an alibi?" He smiled.

"No. We're just trying to get an idea of all potential witnesses."

"Okay, humor me. I figure that if y'all are going door to door talking to people, then something pretty bad has happened. Let me guess. Someone beat the hell out of Higgins. Or did they vandalize his house?"

I decided to see what kind of reaction I would get from him. "Higgins is dead. Odds are he was killed."

Andre raised his eyebrows and started to say something, but changed his mind.

"Did you hear anything last night?"

His expression grew serious as he thought about my question. "I woke up once. I might have heard something, but with the air conditioner running, I couldn't be sure."

"When was this?"

"I looked at the clock. It was about a quarter to one. Do you all have any idea who did it?"

"We're working on a couple of leads," I lied. "Have you seen anything else in the last week or so that struck you as odd? Maybe a car you didn't recognize or someone hanging out in the neighborhood?"

"No, I haven't seen anything out of place in the neighborhood." He paused. "But I *did* see something at the bank on Friday." He hesitated again. "We keep our depositors' business confidential. However, seeing that our client is dead, and that there's the possibility he was killed..."

"I can tell you that it's more than a possibility. It's a probability. Anything you can tell us that might help catch the killer would be serving your community and your customer."

He nodded. "Higgins was in the bank on Friday morning. He's one of a small handful of problem customers. He has a substantial amount of money on deposit with us, and his parents were good customers for many years, so we treat him with a certain amount of… care."

"What do you mean by 'problem customer'?"

"He's been argumentative with our tellers, and he even got into a heated discussion with one of our associates a few years back. There have also been a few occasions when he's gotten into fights with other customers. I've given orders that I'm to be notified any time he comes in. I don't always serve him, but I make sure that the person who does is… sensitive to his personality.

"Point being, I was told that he was in the bank last Friday and I got up to greet him. When I walked out into the lobby, he was standing by the door at the back of the bank that leads out into the parking lot. There was a young man with him. They were talking with their heads close together. I started toward them and Higgins came forward, leaving the other man by the door. Higgins made a couple of transactions, including taking nine thousand dollars in cash out of his account. This wasn't unusual. If you've looked into him at all, then you know that he wheels and deals in all kinds of merchandise. He told me once that having cash on hand could make the difference between making a deal or having it fall through."

"Did you recognize the man he was with?"

"No. What's odd is that I've never seen Higgins come in with anyone else. I'm not even sure I've ever seen him hold a conversation where he wasn't arguing."

"They looked like they were on friendly terms?"

"I would have said that they were confiding in each other, or maybe conspiring. For one crazy second, I thought they might be planning to rob the bank. It looked that… odd. Especially when he walked away from the man like he didn't want me to have the chance of meeting him."

"What did this man look like?"

"In his early twenties, probably. Dark hair. Slender build. He never looked at me. That was another thing that seemed odd. He was always looking around, but never making eye contact with anyone. Maybe that's another reason I got the impression they were casing the bank."

"What was he wearing?"

"Nothing that stood out. Maybe cargo pants or Dockers. Polo shirt or a button-down. Didn't scream workman or businessman."

"Can you pull the CCTV footage?"

"Let's see… This is Tuesday. Yes, we should still have it. I'll get my IT guy on it."

"I'd like to send our IT guy to talk to your IT guy about it," I said.

"Crazy world. The computer geeks are becoming our oracles."

"I think they're the high priests to the computer oracles."

"There you go." He laughed.

We swapped contact information and I walked to the next house.

CHAPTER FOUR

No one was home next door, so I headed for Faith Osborne's. Hers was one of the largest houses on the block. It was a two-story Victorian that was well tended, but a couple years past due for a paint job. I knocked and almost jumped back when there was a loud thud against the narrow glass window that framed the door. A black-and-tan face peered out at me from waist level.

"Cleo, give me some room," said a voice from the other side of the door.

A tall woman wearing jeans and a blouse opened the door and smiled at me. "You'll have to excuse her. She has to check out any company that comes to visit." A fawn Great Dane stood behind her. The animal would have seemed large to me if I hadn't been used to my father's overgrown lummox. I guessed that Cleo weighed about one-hundred-and-sixty, some thirty pounds less than Mauser.

"I assume you're a deputy. Hope you don't mind me asking for your ID?" the woman said with a heavy Southern accent.

I pulled out my badge and gave her plenty of time to scrutinize it. "I'm Deputy Macklin. Are you Faith Osborne?"

"I most certainly am. Come on in." She had to body-

35

block Cleo so that I could get through the door. "You better just let Cleopatra give you the once-over. She'll leave you alone as soon as you pass inspection."

I let Cleo sniff my hands and feet and finally received her approval as she leaned heavily against my legs. "She's beautiful," I told Faith.

"When I finally got around to kicking my deadbeat husband to the curb, I decided I needed some real companionship. I got her as a puppy five years ago. You're a big sweetie," she said to the dog, who looked up at her with big brown eyes before trotting off into the living room to flop down on a large pillow bed.

"I know why you're here," Faith continued. "I got a text from a neighbor this morning. I hope you don't expect me to cry crocodile tears for that... No, I won't call him names. But I also won't pretend to be sorry that he won't be cheating people in our town anymore."

"I've heard about your feud with Mr. Higgins."

"Of course. It wasn't exactly a secret."

"I'd like to hear your side of the story."

"Then you might as well sit down." She pointed to a couch in the living room and she sat down across from me in a chair that was close enough to Cleo's bed that she could let her hand drop down to pet the dog's head as she talked.

"I met Conman Higgins when my mother was in the nursing home. Mom wasn't that out of it, but she had moments when she would get confused and very forgetful. I was still working full-time and just felt like she'd be better off at Magnolia Ridge where they had activities and someone to look after her all the time. And she liked it. I could have moved her in here, I guess, but, truth be told, we never got along. Wow! It's been years and I'm still trying to rationalize it to myself. 'Guilt sticks like sap' was one of my mom's favorite sayings. She sure hit that one on the head."

"About Higgins..." I prompted.

"I saw him in the halls of the nursing home at first, and I figured he had a relative staying there. I said hi, like you do.

We even swapped small talk a couple of times. Turned out he volunteered there. The home has a lot of volunteers— people who play music for the residents or who bring their dogs. I go there once or twice a week myself to lead a stretching class. Higgins would give regular talks on different subjects. I didn't think too much about it.

"After a while, he started visiting my mother. He'd bring her magazines and books. I actually wondered at first if he wasn't doing it to meet me. Boy howdy, was I misguided! At some point, he convinced my mother to let him appraise her jewelry, or at least that's what I thought. He'd told me he ran a successful antiques business and I'd looked him up on the Internet… seemed legit. Long and short of it is, he bought the jewelry off of her. Though *stole it* is more the truth. I tried to fight him, but Mom was still alive and, like I said, she and I didn't always see things the same way. I think she was flattered by his attention. Well, she took his side, so there wasn't anything I could do. Even when I did some research and showed Mom how much the pieces had really been worth, she wouldn't hear a bad word against him."

"So you sued him?"

"I did after Mom died. I tried it on the grounds of undue influence. Trouble was, she and I had argued about it enough that there were plenty of witnesses who heard her say she wanted him to have the jewelry. Then he counter-sued me for slander." Faith's face reflected the anger she still felt.

"And he won."

"I had to pay him ten thousand dollars in damages and court costs," she said flatly.

"When was this?"

"The judgment was two years ago. I'll go ahead and answer your next question. No, I didn't kill him. And, yes, you can find lots of folks who heard me say I'd like to kill him. I'm hot-blooded, as my mother used to say. But truth be told, it's all just sound and fury." She seemed sincere.

"Have you had any contact with Higgins since the court

case?"

"Yes. I let loose with some of that sound and fury at him one day in the Supersave. I don't doubt you'll hear about it eventually. He was in front of me in the express lane and had quite a few items over the limit. Somewhat under my breath, I said that once a cheater, always a cheater. He turned to me and asked if I'd like to have another round in court. I told him he could go to hell and that I hoped he choked to death on that ten thousand dollars. Well… things got very verbal until the manager came over and asked both of us to leave before he called the police."

"And this was?"

She sighed. "Last fall. The man just got my goat, that's all. I'm not the only one. I hope you know that. Everyone who met him eventually came to the same conclusion. The man was a crook of the first order." Her voice was edging higher, but she caught herself and brought it back down to a normal tone. "I was in the right. He was asked to leave Magnolia Ridge and not to come back only a few months after the incident with my mother."

"Where were you last night?" I asked, cutting to the chase.

"I was home all evening after eight. I watched a movie, texted some friends and posted some pictures of Cleo on Facebook." She still sounded worked up from discussing Higgins.

"What time did you go to bed?"

"I took Cleo for a walk about eleven and went to bed as soon as we got back to the house. I guess it was around eleven-thirty."

"Where'd you go on your walk?" I asked, eliciting another sigh from Faith.

"I went down a couple of blocks and did a circle. Yes, I walked by Higgins's house."

"Did you look over at his house?"

"Yes. I can't help myself."

"Did you see him?"

"No. If I had seen him, I would have avoided him. Especially at night. I'll tell you something else. This won't make me look more innocent, but it's the truth. I thought the man could be dangerous. A couple of times when we were locking horns over the jewelry, I saw a look in his eyes. He wanted to hurt me. That's all I'll say. My point being, if I'd seen him, I wouldn't have wanted to get into an argument with him when no one else was around."

I let that go for now. "What did you see last night? Were his lights on? Were there any cars in his driveway?"

She looked thoughtful. "The lights were on. I think there were a couple cars in the driveway, but I can't be sure about that."

"Did you see anyone around the house?"

"No. I would remember that. Like I said, I wanted to avoid running into him in the proverbial dark alley."

"Did you meet anyone else on your walk?"

"No."

"See anyone?"

"Yes. I saw one of Higgins's neighbors, Ed Landers."

"What was he doing?"

"Putting something in his car, looked like."

"Did he see you?"

"I think so."

"You didn't see anyone else?"

"No."

"Any cars?"

"Nothing specific. There are usually a few cars when we take our walk, but unless they're unusual in some way, I wouldn't remember. The ones that are booming their music so loud that it hurts my fillings, now those I remember."

We talked for a few more minutes, and I told her we'd need a formal statement from her in a day or two. As she walked me to the door, she said, "You don't remember me, do you?"

The question was so odd that I looked at her more closely. There was maybe something familiar about her, but I couldn't be sure.

She smiled gently. "Can't blame you. I've aged a bit since then. I knew your mother, Jo. I was at the funeral. I'm very sorry."

I felt my heart ache a little at being taken back to that day eleven years earlier. "I don't... I was in a bit of a... fog that day."

"I saw you a few other times too when you were about this high." She held her hand beside her waist.

"How did you know Mom?" I asked.

"We were good friends in high school. We were the brainy, boring ones, I'm afraid. Worked on the yearbook and all that kind of stuff. People used to kid us, saying that she was the sweet one and I was the sour one. I hate to admit it, but there was a lot of truth there. Unfortunately, I got married and moved up to Maryland. We kept in touch with letters and phone calls and I visited once or twice, but I was the busy wife of an up-and-coming lawyer. Talk about a waste of time. Anyway, I'm glad to see you. She'd be very proud of you and your father."

Cleo chose that moment to come over and lean against Faith protectively. She gave me a look as if to say: *Weren't you on your way out?* "It's funny, but it's partly because of your mother that I've got Cleo. I always loved visiting the Great Danes at her house. Then later she'd send me pictures of y'all's Great Danes."

I felt a bit overwhelmed at the wave of memories and emotions she was causing. "Thank you. It means a lot to me that she's still remembered," I said honestly.

"I've seen your dad around with that big puppy of his. Sometime I'd like to meet..."

"Mauser."

"That's right, Mauser."

"When you come in to give your statement, maybe we can arrange for Mauser to be there," I said and shook her hand.

Back at the house, I ran into Marcus in the office. Before leaving the room, he handed me a letter that he'd found from Higgins's lawyer, Franklin Beck. I knew the man and it didn't surprise me... He and Higgins were birds of a feather. I gave him a call.

"I'd told him to tone it down. I said he'd either end up in jail or on a slab. No satisfaction in being right," Beck said wistfully. I thought of pots and kettles, knowing that Beck had had his own run-ins with the Florida Bar Association.

"We need to notify his next of kin. We think we've found a brother who lives in Boone, North Carolina. Does that sound right? Or do you know of another relative?"

"No, the brother is Higgins's closest family. I'll give him a call."

"I'd rather you wait at least a day. We'd prefer to make the notification."

"Of course. There'll be lots of work to do," Beck said, and I could almost hear the money symbols swirling around in his head.

"Can you tell me who benefits from his will?"

"You know I can't do that. If you had a warrant... Or if the brother gives his permission. Though I guess I can go ahead and say that his brother is the main beneficiary."

"One last thing." I'd saved the best for last. "Do you have the combination to the safe in his house?"

"It might be in his papers."

"Check. I'll give it a couple of hours, but before the day is over we'll need to open that safe. I'd rather not have to damage it." *I'd also rather not have the department be charged a hefty fee from a locksmith*, I thought.

"I'll look and get back to you."

"We'll be in touch," I said, not minding if it sounded like a threat. The man had sued the sheriff's office several times. One client had had a legitimate complaint, but the others had all been clients he'd hunted up and solicited to file a lawsuit.

As I hung up, Darlene and Julio came back into the house and joined me in the office. "How did your interviews go?" I asked.

Darlene looked at her notes. "Two of the houses didn't have anyone at home. At the third, the guy was home but not awake. Once he got done being pissed that I'd woken him up, he did remember that he saw Higgins in his driveway around eleven. The witness was coming home from a visit with his kids in Tallahassee. He said he always looks toward Higgins's house when he drives by because he likes to spit in its direction."

"So, not a fan, huh?"

"Higgins sold him some paintings that turned out to be worthless. He said he learned from talking to other people that had also been swindled that Higgins was very good at figuring out what people were interested in, but didn't know much about, then taking advantage of them."

"And I'm sure he used the primary tool of all con artists: greed."

"No doubt. He sure left a lot of bruised egos around here."

"This Higgins should have learned not to crap in his own bed," Julio interjected.

"What did you find?" I asked him.

"One person had just moved into the neighborhood. He didn't see nothin', hear nothin' or know nothin'. Another young couple hadn't had a run-in with Higgins themselves, but they'd heard all the gossip and were happy to talk about it. But they didn't see or hear a thing last night."

"Anything else?"

"The last was the jackpot, sort of. The man didn't see anything, but the woman says she saw the CR-V drive away. Only problem is, she's not sure when. She has insomnia so she was up reading. Heard a car and saw that it was Higgins's."

"She's sure it was his?"

"Very sure. They sold it to him. And guess what? They

think they got gipped. Believe he used some phony Bluebook numbers and argued them down. According to her, they lost about a thousand dollars on the deal. Every time she sees the car, it pisses her off. So, yeah, she knew it was that car. But she didn't know who was driving it and she's not sure on the time. She knows it was after midnight and before she saw the blue lights flashing in the window."

"If the CR-V was taken by the killer and the guns were still in the car, or if he took items from the safe, then maybe the motive was robbery," Darlene said.

"But if the killer was the person that the neighbor saw fleeing on foot, then it's unlikely that robbery was the reason. Even if they came back for the CR-V and the guns, why leave everything else?"

"Maybe they took a handful of stuff and didn't want to risk another trip," Darlene suggested.

"Possible. At this point, anything is possible. We've got a whole neighborhood full of suspects. Which means we need to make sure that our witnesses aren't really suspects who are giving us false and misleading information."

Julio's phone rang. He had a brief exchange with the caller, then held the phone out to me.

"Earl Higgins?" I asked.

Julio nodded as I took the phone.

"This is Deputy Larry Macklin with the Adams County Sheriff's Office. Are you the brother of Conrad Higgins?"

"What's he done now?"

"I'm afraid we have bad news. Your brother was found dead in his home this morning."

"Really?" The man sounded more surprised than grief-stricken. "Are you sure it's him?"

"Pretty sure. Looks like him, in his house. That seems like an odd question to ask," I said.

"My brother was an odd man. Trust me, officer. I'd double-check everything. I think when you look into his past you'll discover that he has a history of fraud. Faking his own death would not be beyond him. I'm surprised he hasn't tried it before." The man sounded irritated as much as anything.

"As his next of kin, we could use some help."

"I don't even know if he has me as the executor on his will or what. I'm sorry. I know that I don't sound like I care. The sad truth is, I don't. My brother was not a nice guy. We grew up together, lived in the same house, had the same parents. Why he was the way his was, I don't know, but long ago I got used to the thought that we would never be friends. And through the years, I've realized I don't care about him at all."

"But he did come home and take care of your parents. Do we have that right?" I was trying to puzzle out their relationship.

"And that is the great irony. Both of my parents cared more for him than they did for me." There was silence for a moment. "Okay, that might be too much, but they certainly had a strange affection for him. Conrad caused them no end of grief, but if he didn't show up for a family function, then they were crushed. Me? Meh." All the pain of a dysfunctional family was evident in his voice

"Still, he was a human being and someone murdered him. I would appreciate your help," I encouraged him. If there wasn't any brotherly love left, maybe I could plead to his humanity.

"I believe in law and order. I also appreciate the hard job that law enforcement officers have. And believe me, if you have to sort through all of the people that wanted Conrad dead, you're going to have a very hard job. Fine, what do you need from me?" He was all business now.

"Contact your brother's lawyer and find out if you are the executor of the estate. The sooner we can get some of that information, the better. I take it we have your permission to search his property?"

"Yes, of course."

"Do you have the number to the safe?"

"I might. That safe was put in by our father. When he

had it, the combination was his wedding date: ten, nineteen, fifty-five. Of course, my brother might have changed it, but the safe was a custom job and it probably would have been hard and costly to find someone to work on it. My brother never did anything that was hard or costly," he said dryly.

"I have to ask: where were you last night?"

"Where I am now. Boone, North Carolina. I teach at Appalachian State University."

"Are you planning to come down here?"

"I guess that depends on what the lawyer has to say. I'll need his number, by the way."

"I'll text it to you. Get in touch with me if you think of anything else that might help."

CHAPTER FIVE

"I've got some numbers if you want to give the safe a try," I said to Darlene and Julio.

It took us four tries to get the right number of rotations between the numbers, then the safe opened with a satisfying *clunk*.

"Wow!" Darlene exclaimed, looking at the six-by-six-foot interior of the safe. It was filled with antique guns, watches, coins and jewelry.

"Takes your breath away," I agreed.

"That's a lot of guns. And a lot a jewelry," Julio said. His jaw hung open.

"I don't know if the guns he had last night are in here or not," Darlene said. "There must be almost two hundred."

She was right. Most of the guns dated from World War II or earlier and there was a whole section dedicated to Colt single-action revolvers.

"You think anyone has an inventory of all of this?" asked a voice from behind us. We all turned to see Pete Henley, his three-hundred-pound frame blocking the doorway. He came the rest of the way in to get a closer look at the guns.

"You were at the talk last night?" I asked him.

"I was. Of course, I was interested in the subject, but I

was also interested in the man. I've had a couple of my range buddies tell me to steer clear of him. Particularly on the older guns."

"Why?"

"Apparently, he had a tendency to fake them. There are some pretty good reproductions being made in Italy and imported by half a dozen different companies. Now, if you take one in good condition, almost anyone with a little bit of knowledge can tell you the difference between an original and a reproduction. But you can take a repro, get rid of the modern stamps and put on some halfway decent fake inspection stamps, switch out some parts for original parts and then batter it up. For instance, peeing on it and then burying it for a couple of weeks puts a nice patina on the metal. Next thing you know, you have what looks like a rough original. You've taken a five-hundred-dollar gun and turned it into a two-thousand-dollar gun."

"Not a bad markup."

"And if you're a good liar and put the right serial numbers on it, you can make it even more valuable."

"How?" Julio asked.

"Colt, Remington, all the big manufacturers kept good records of the serial numbers of their guns and who they were sold to. For example, they have a pretty good idea which single-actions were used by the Seventh Cavalry at the Battle of Little Big Horn. Those guns are highly sought after. And there are a bunch of fakes kicking around." Pete craned his neck into the safe, trying to get a look at as many of the guns as he could without touching anything.

"From everything we've heard about Higgins, that is exactly the type of scam he would pull," I said.

"I'm amazed he was never arrested," Julio said.

"A good conman stays just on the line between morally reprehensible and outright illegal," Darlene said.

"How many calls for service involved Higgins?" I asked Julio. He'd called dispatch earlier to check the records.

"His name came up in twenty-four calls for service at

different locations in the county since our new system went in five years ago."

"I'll check with Beth in records and see if we can find out how many times Higgins's name comes up in reports. I'm thinking we'll be looking at more than double that number." For every arrest, there are dozens of calls for service and reports written up.

"How many times did he call himself?" Darlene asked.

"There were four where the reporting address was this house. Vandalism and a couple assaults."

"Interesting. We need to pull those reports, especially the assaults. That would give us some suspects who were willing to break the law," I said.

Marcus came into the room and stared at the open safe. "Wow!" he said.

"That's the word of the day," Darlene said.

"Double wow. Fingerprinting and logging all of that is going to be a bitch."

"Did you get any prints off of the safe?"

"No, wiped clean."

"Our bad guy might or might not have even found the safe, but…" I said, sympathizing with Marcus.

"I'll call Charlie back out."

"Getting an expert to examine all of the items could be illuminating too," Pete said. "Finding out how many items are fake versus real could tell you something."

"If it doesn't help us find the killer, it might at least help the prosecution establish motive when we have the murderer in court," I said, knowing how much Dad was going to enjoy paying an expert to appraise a safe full of antiques.

"You might actually need two people. A gun guy might not be able to tell you anything about the jewels and coins and vice versa," Pete said.

"Thanks, Pete. Dad will love that suggestion. Don't you have your own cases to work?"

"I just thought I'd check in and see how you all were doing. I knew you would be lost without me. Also, I wanted to let you know that I sorted out the morning reports already and put a couple on each of your desks," Pete said with a smile.

"Ouch! And I bet you gave us the best ones," Darlene said.

"Only the best for you," Pete said with a smile, and we both shot him a bird. "Fine, I know when I'm not wanted. Have fun with your who-done-it." He waved and headed for the door.

"I'm going over to talk with Albert Griffin and find out what the disagreement was about last night," I said to Darlene.

"Good idea. I'll see to warrants for Higgins's phone and financial records."

"I'll double-check the homes where we didn't get a response when we canvassed earlier," Julio said.

"And I'll spend the next five hours going through the safe," Marcus sighed, walking back into the room with an armload of evidence bags and tags.

Albert Griffin had rented out an apartment above his garage to Eddie Thompson, my confidential informant. Though, now that he was clean, Eddie wasn't particularly informative anymore. Still, I couldn't begrudge either one of them the change in their lives. Mr. Griffin had seemed happier with someone around to help him out with the harder chores involved in keeping an old house in good repair. For his part, Eddie seemed to enjoy having an older male role model who wasn't an asshole. His own father and grandfather had been deep into the drug trade and had become very abusive to him when they had learned that he was a crossdresser.

I knocked on the front door of the old Victorian house.

"Come on around back," I heard Eddie call from the side of the house. Curious, I walked back to find Eddie in the azalea bushes, wrestling with a Virginia creeper that was attempting to take over the old house.

"Yard work. I'm impressed."

"You should be," Eddie said, blowing sweat off his nose. "My sponsor says that hard, physical work helps keep a recovering addict from spending all their time navel-gazing."

"How's Seth doing?" Eddie's sponsor, Seth Craig, had been kidnapped and tortured last month.

"He's doing better than I would be. He's home. I think his biggest problem right now is that his mother is being over-protective."

"Understandable. She knows she beat the odds getting him back."

"I gotta take a break," Eddie said, climbing out of the azaleas and dragging the vines he'd pulled off of the house.

"So is the hard work helping?" I asked.

He paused. "I hate to admit it, but yeah." He looked up at the house. "It's really weird, but this place feels more like home to me than my own house ever did."

"Mr. Griffin's a nice guy. Remember what I told you about not screwing him over," I said.

"You didn't need to say that." Eddie looked genuinely hurt.

"I know you've got a good heart. I wouldn't have worked with you if I didn't think so. But you're also an addict. Recovering or not," I pointed out.

Eddie looked down at the ground, his lips pursed. "Fair enough. I really do think that I can stay clean."

"And I'll do what I can to help," I said, feeling brotherly. "Hey, I'm here 'cause I want to ask you about last night."

"What about it?" Eddie sounded puzzled

"You went to a meeting of the historical society?"

"Yeah, I helped Albert take in his stuff and arrange the chairs. The talk was kind of interesting. Why?"

"What did you think of Higgins?"

Eddie's face darkened. "That asshole tried to blackmail Albert. I don't know if blackmail's really the right word. But Albert had agreed to pay the guy, like, twenty-five bucks as a stip... sti... little bit of money for doing the talk. But when we were all set up, he told Albert that he'd need a hundred dollars. What a jerk." Eddie was shaking his head angrily.

"Did Mr. Griffin pay him the hundred dollars?"

"Hell, no! Albert didn't know what to do. The historical society hadn't ever paid anyone anything like that, but he felt stuck. When I got over to them, he was getting ready to pay the guy out of his own pocket, but I put a stop to that."

"How?"

Eddie's eyes danced all over the place, trying to keep from meeting mine.

"Okay... Well, you probably aren't going to like this, but I was pissed. I couldn't let that jerk take advantage of Albert." Eddie stopped like he thought I'd just leave it there.

"What did you do?" I asked sternly.

Eddie sighed, still not looking at me. "I told him I worked for the sheriff's office and that I'd see him in jail before we'd pay him a dime more than what he'd agreed to."

I wanted to be angry, but I couldn't really blame him. "You don't work for the sheriff's office," I reminded him. "Impersonating a law enforcement officer is a serious crime."

"I never said I was a cop. I told him exactly what I just said. I know I don't actually work for the sheriff's office, but you do pay me sometimes."

"Technically. What about the part where you said you'd throw him in jail?"

"I never said that. I said I'd *see* him in jail. Doesn't mean I'd be the one to put him in it," Eddie said self-righteously, finally meeting my eyes as he defended himself.

I held up my hands in surrender, trying hard to hide a grin. "I give up. Let's just say you were skirting the edges of the law. Did Higgins accept that?"

"Funny, for a minute I thought he was going to just turn and walk out. But then he kind of shrugged and said, 'Whatever.'"

I had a good idea why Higgins had wanted to do the talk regardless of what he got paid. Thinking about what Pete had said, I figured that Higgins had planned on working the room looking for marks. What better place than a historical society meeting to find older, and possibly gullible, people to peddle over-priced, and possibly fake, antiques to?

"Did he report me?" Eddie asked.

"No. He's dead," I said bluntly.

Eddie's eyes went wide. "Seriously?"

"I need to ask Mr. Griffin some questions. Is he inside?"

"I'll show you."

"Okay, but I want to talk to him alone. And don't blurt out that Higgins is dead until after I've questioned him."

"You don't think that Albert had anything to do with this Higgins guy dying, do you?" Eddie said incredulously, and then realized that I hadn't told him how he'd died. "Was he murdered?"

"Enough. I need to talk to Mr. Griffin."

Eddie took me in the back door and we found Mr. Griffin in his office working on a magazine article. He told us all in one breath that the article was about shade tobacco farming in north Florida and its economic and social effects on the growers and harvesters. I shooed Eddie back to the kitchen.

"I heard about your problem with the speaker at last night's meeting," I said.

Mr. Griffin gestured to a seat by his desk. I sat down and Brutus, one of the house's many resident felines, immediately jumped up in my lap and began to chew on my hand.

"Brutus has taken quite a liking to Eddie," Mr. Griffin said proudly. Brutus looked at me with stern, and slightly crazed, yellow eyes. It had been surprising how quickly Eddie, who was afraid of cats, had been won over by the big, black bruiser.

"I couldn't understand it. We had an agreement. Higgins knew that. Some people." Mr. Griffin shook his head sadly, seemingly both surprised and disappointed at the number of jerks in the world. "That Eddie, though…" He continued to shake his head, but was smiling now. "He set that guy straight. I hope Eddie isn't in trouble. Is that why you came by? 'Cause he was just helping me out."

"Eddie's not in trouble. Had you ever met Higgins before the meeting or did you set it up by phone?"

"I met him at the library. I was checking out a book on nineteenth-century bank notes. You know, back in those days everybody printed currency. Banks, railroads. We had a local bank that had a couple different currency printings." Mr. Griffin stopped himself. "You don't care about that. Anyway, when I was at the counter, Higgins was also standing there ready to check out. He asked me if I was interested in early banknotes. I told him I was particularly interested in ones printed in the Big Bend area. He said he was a dealer and that sometimes he had some for sale. He said if I told him what I was interested in, he would keep an eye out for them. I invited him to come to the historical society meeting. This was a couple of months ago. He showed up at the next one and then offered to give a talk on historical firearms."

"Did you all talk any other time?"

"We talked on the phone twice, I think." He narrowed his eyes in concentration. "Yes, twice. Just to finalize the arrangements for the meeting. And we came to a very specific agreement on the amount of his stipend." This last was said with much indignation.

"Did you notice anything different or strange about his behavior last night?"

"When he started trying to change the terms of our agreement, he got very aggressive."

"Anything else?"

"It was odd. Once Eddie laid down the law concerning the payment, Higgins went back to being his congenial self. Like he could turn the attitude on and off like a faucet. When I worked at the library I also freelanced for the paper from time to time, and I interviewed a few people like that. They would use physical and emotional intimidation to press their viewpoints. It was usually a sign of a weak argument."

"Were there any other strangers at the meeting?"

"We did have a few more people than normal in attendance. Everyone is fascinated by weapons. Your friend Pete was there. And you can ask Darlene. She was there too."

"Did you see Higgins talking to anyone at the meeting?"

"A couple people came up afterward and asked questions about the guns, and I saw him hand out some cards. I think all of those people were regulars. Afterward, Darlene helped him carry his guns and props out to his car."

I had to ask the next question whether I liked it or not. "Did you see Eddie talking to him after the altercation over the fee?"

"No. Eddie stuck pretty close to me. Mumbled a lot about Higgins being an... A-hole."

"Do you know where Higgins lived?" I asked, wondering if Mr. Griffin would pick up on the past tense.

"Lived? As in doesn't live there anymore? Or as in doesn't *live* anymore?" he asked.

"Higgins was found dead in his house early this morning."

Mr. Griffin sat back with his eyes wide. "No kidding. Well, ain't that a kick in the pants? I understand why you're here now. I'm not sure what I can tell you. Except for him trying to railroad me, everything seemed pretty normal last night. I wish I could help you out," he said sincerely.

"Last night, did Higgins seem preoccupied with his phone? Check it more than usual? Seem to be writing a lot of texts?"

"These days, everybody seems obsessed with their cell phones. But I don't think I saw Higgins even pull his out. I did notice that your friend Pete checked his every five minutes."

"For Pete, his phone is like an electronic umbilical cord to his wife and daughters." I got up. "If you think of anything else, give me a call."

"I will. Higgins said his family has been in the county for a while. I'll go through my private newspaper morgue and see if they're mentioned anywhere." When the local paper had shut down, Mr. Griffin had moved all of their back issues to his place.

"Let me know if you find anything."

I was amazed to see Eddie back at the vines as I headed out of the house. Now he had an assistant. A young orange tabby chased the vines as Eddie dragged them over to a pile of yard debris.

"Thanks for helping him out," I said.

"We're helping each other out," Eddie said, looking a little embarrassed by the sentiment.

CHAPTER SIX

As soon as I sat down in the car, I realized I was starving. I checked in with Cara, who hadn't yet taken her own lunch break, and told her I'd be right there. She was helping an old man take his cat's crate out to the car when I pulled into the parking lot of the veterinary clinic.

"Where to?" I asked once she was in the car.

"There's a new café downtown. The Tasty 'Wich or something. Dr. Barnhill said it was good."

"Sounds a little suggestive, but I'm game," I said with a wink.

The route from the clinic to the courthouse square would take us past the spot where, a month earlier, an explosion had killed a colleague and nearly killed me. I was still haunted by the memory, but I refused to drive out of my way to avoid the site. I was determined not to let the act of a maniac determine where I went in my own town.

"I didn't think about—" Cara started to say as we approached the spot, scorch marks still evident on the pavement.

"Don't. Half of me wants to stare and obsess on that spot while the other half of me never wants to see it again. But I can't live like that." Cara reached over and put her hand on my arm. I made myself turn and smile. "It's getting better," I said, not knowing if I was lying or not.

Once we were seated in the café with our sandwiches, Cara looked at me. "You must be exhausted."

"I managed to grab a quick nap in the car this morning."

"Any chance you'll be able to make it home early?"

"Probably. So far we don't have any hot leads. Though a I did meet another Great Dane this morning. Her name's Cleo."

"Miss Cleopatra, Queen of the Clinic, we call her," Cara said with a big smile. "She's my second favorite Great Dane. Maybe my third favorite pooch after Alvin and Mauser. She's very sweet."

"That was my impression. A world away from the black-and-white menace."

"You love that big dog," she chastised me.

"Yeah, I suppose," I admitted reluctantly.

"Miss Cleo does hold herself in a much more dignified manner than Mauser. But then, she *is* a girl."

"Okay, that is a very sexist remark," I kidded her.

"Hey, look at us. I'm refined and you're a barbarian," she said with a laugh.

"You wish," I said, smirking obnoxiously and causing her to laugh harder. "Okay, calm down. People are staring. Seriously, since you know Cleo, what do you think of her owner?"

"Oh, the investigator is back. Let me think. She's nice. Dotes on Cleo, which is always endearing. Other than that, she does what Dr. Barnwell tells her to whenever Cleo has an issue, which puts her in the top twenty-five percentile of clients. I'd say I like her."

"Have you ever seen her angry or upset?"

"Is she a suspect?"

"Just answer the question, ma'am."

"She did get a little pissy about a charge on her bill once, but turned out she was right. She was just a little snarly about it with Gayle. They called me out of the back and I was able to clear it up. Just a miscommunication, really." Cara shrugged. "I did get the feeling that if she thought she'd been wronged, she wouldn't back down."

After I dropped Cara back off at the vet, I wandered into the sheriff's office to check email and my inbox. Then I headed down to the records department.

"Look who the cat dragged in," Beth Miller said. She was our head records clerk and the best baker in the office. Almost every day she brought in muffins, cookies or something equally waist-expanding. "You're too late for the goodies today. Half of patrol came in about two hours ago and cleaned me out."

"My luck. But, honestly, that was only half the reason I came down here. I could use your help."

"I'm all ears."

"I need any records that mention Conrad Higgins," I said and saw her immediately tense up.

"What's that rat done now?" Beth was one of the most easygoing people I knew. For her to have this reaction to Higgins, he had to have stomped on her toes pretty hard.

"Sometime last night he fell on his back with a bullet hole in his forehead," I said dryly.

"Couldn't have happened to a nicer guy."

"Little touchy when it comes to Mr. Higgins?"

"He and his lawyer probably get more copies of reports than any other two people in the county," she said, then added: "By far."

"And, let me guess, they aren't the easiest people to deal with," I said, and could actually see her face turning red.

"I swear my blood pressure goes up forty points whenever I see one of those two... jerks." It was obvious that wasn't the word she wanted to use. "They'll come in here and demand that their copies be made right then and there. And that Higgins, he'd try and cheat me out of the five cents a copy that we charge. So forgive me if I'm not prostrate with grief that he took a bullet," she finished, looking at me hard. *A reminder never to get on her bad side*, I thought.

"I try never to bother you unless I have to."

"Don't be silly. You're no bother." She paused. "Because you're polite and you wait your turn." She wagged her finger at me.

"Yes, ma'am. I'll wait quietly and politely at my desk," I said lightly and headed for the door.

I sat down at my desk and immediately felt my lack of sleep catch up with me. I struggled to get a start on writing my preliminary reports, but I had to fight the urge to lay my head down on the desk. Half an hour later, Darlene came to my rescue.

"Wake up. I see those eyelids drooping," she said with a toothpick hanging half out of her mouth.

"I could have called you in at two this morning when I realized it was a homicide," I told her.

"And I'd have been there with bells on." She grabbed her desk chair and wheeled it over to me. "Let's see where we are and where we're headed."

I grabbed a pen and yellow legal pad. Seeing the blank paper, Darlene grinned. "Looks like we're still solidly at square one."

"Yep. I don't think the motive was robbery, but I can't be sure."

"There was a lot of valuable stuff lying around that house," Darlene said.

"But most of the items were antiques that could easily be identified. Maybe the bad guy didn't want to get caught with something that could be traced back to the crime."

"So he stole the car and whatever was in it?"

"Or something else from the house. Remember that the banker said Higgins pulled out nine thousand dollars in cash a few days ago. He also said that it wasn't unusual, so there could have been tens of thousands of dollars in the house. Cash is the perfect thing to steal," I said, arguing against my intuition.

"I can't quarrel with any of that. Unfortunately, Higgins

was very secretive. We may never know what's missing or not missing from that house."

"Speaking of the bank." I picked up the phone and buzzed Lionel West, our IT guy. I'd already talked to him earlier about getting the video from the bank.

"I got what I could, but I don't think you're going to be happy," he said. "But come on down if you want."

Lionel's office looked like someone had gutted a dozen laptops and computers in some weird, electronic massacre. Darlene and I had to clear away various spare parts in order to use a couple of chairs.

"Either they got lucky, or they knew where to stand to be outside the camera's field of vision," Lionel said, pointing to a monitor where we could see three different camera angles inside the bank.

"How could the cameras not have picked them up?" I asked, knowing that the bank was properly paranoid about security.

"It's not that your two suspects don't show up on the video. They just never give you a clear shot of the younger guy's face. Here, watch." The first image started to move on the screen. "See, they come in together with Higgins in front, partly blocking the second man. Also, the second man keeps his face turned down and to the left, away from the camera. This camera loses them just inside the door. Here's the second one. See how it fails to capture that one corner of the bank just inside the door? You can see Higgins walking around… and there's the manager going over to talk to him. They're clearly shown and get picked up by the third camera when they go over to a teller window."

"There isn't another camera that could pick up that one spot?" Darlene said, sounding incredulous.

"No. I didn't go through all of their cameras, but from what I saw, that is one of the only spots in the bank other than under desks and counters that's not covered by cameras."

"What are the odds?" I thought out loud.

Lionel pointed to the screen again. "Here they are leaving. You get a nice image of the second guy's back. His hand. Maybe a wristwatch. Seems a little odd that he's wearing a long-sleeve shirt."

"Yeah, it is. The temperature on Friday started out at seventy degrees and it was ninety-eight or thereabouts for a high."

"Hiding a tattoo?" Darlene asked.

"Maybe. But looking at the big picture, if you're so paranoid about being caught on film, then why would you go into a bank to begin with?" I asked.

"Because you don't trust the guy getting the cash," Darlene suggested.

"Very possibly. Knowing the type of businessman that Higgins was, I wouldn't trust him either. And this guy," I pointed to the back of the second man leaving the bank, "could have been a crook himself. Higgins probably dealt with shady characters on occasion. Another thing we need to check is if any of the valuables in his house are on stolen property inventories."

"I don't think he dealt in stolen goods. That would be over a line that he seemed to work hard to edge up to but not cross," Darlene said.

"You've got a point, but we should still check. And I'll be interested to see the reports that Beth pulls up. Getting a look at the full range of activities that Higgins participated in should be illuminating."

"We've got half the town down as suspects now," Darlene said.

"That's the problem. Everything we do seems to enlarge the pool of suspects instead of narrowing it down."

"On the plus side, we don't want to focus in too fast."

"No danger of that. We'll just follow the evidence wherever it leads us."

"However *far* it leads us," Darlene said grimly.

"I'll enhance the video as much as I can," Lionel offered, "but there really isn't much in the images. Even if they were as sharp as a movie, what would you get from it?"

"What about the parking lot? Did you check those cameras?" I asked.

"Yep, but they must have walked in from somewhere else. Maybe parked on the street." He pulled up another video. It was just possible to see two heads moving alongside the building. "They stayed close to the building until they got to the door. I'm not a detective, but I'd swear they knew where the cameras were and were working hard to avoid them."

"Does look that way. But why?" Darlene said.

"And this was several days before the murder. It might have nothing to do with his death. We know that Higgins was constantly working different scams. Which reminds me, did you get his computer and phone from Marcus?" I asked Lionel.

"Yep." He pointed to an evidence bag and box.

"If you could expedite them, that'd be great."

"Should be able to start work on them this afternoon. Then we'll really see how paranoid he was."

Darlene and I left Lionel to his electronic abattoir. Back at my desk, I called Dr. Darzi and found out that he'd scheduled Higgins's autopsy for ten o'clock on Wednesday morning. I told him either Darlene or I would be in attendance.

"My preliminary assessment is that the man died of a bullet wound to the head," Darzi said, deadpan.

"You were made for Vaudeville," I told him.

"It's a gift," he said and hung up.

"Go home and get some sleep," Darlene told me.

I didn't argue with her. On the way home, I made a quick stop by Higgins's house, where I found Marcus and Charlie just finishing up with the items in the safe.

"I got it all, thanks," Marcus said sarcastically as he loaded the last evidence bags into the van.

"Your work ethic is admirable," I told him and got the finger.

At home, I shared a pizza with Cara, then headed to bed before the sun was all the way down.

On Wednesday, my first stop was the evidence room to pick up the keys to Higgins's house. I found Marcus still eating his breakfast.

"I hope you're happy with yourself. I was here until nine o'clock cataloging all of that stuff," he told me as he worked his way through a greasy egg-and-bacon sandwich from Express Burgers.

"I really do appreciate all your effort," I said, feeling a little guilty knowing that, with Shantel on vacation, his workload was heavy even without the Higgins case.

"Not to mention that the place was hell to fingerprint. It was like a murder had happened in the Smithsonian or something."

"I promise only to investigate murders if they happen to people who believe in minimalist decorating. You're done with the keys?" I asked, grinning as Marcus handed them to me before I'd stopped talking.

I wanted to look at the house again without any distractions so that I could think things through. Most cases have an obvious suspect or, at most, a couple of suspects. In those circumstances, the difficult part is not getting locked in on one theory and suspect. But here, the case was wide open. Practically everyone in the neighborhood had a motive. Maybe not a good one, but these days it didn't take much.

A familiar car was parked in front of the house.

"Great minds," I said to Darlene, who was standing in the driveway and staring at the front of the house.

"I called Marcus and he said you were on your way here, so I figured I'd let the keys deliver themselves."

"Whatcha thinkin'?" I asked.

"Good question. Was this a premeditated killing? That's my first question. Or could someone who hated him have just been walking or driving by, saw an opportunity and attacked him?"

"His car is missing. Could your average, run-of-the-mill bad guy have been walking by, seen him unloading the car, and decided that it was a good night for a car-jacking?"

"Possibly."

"It could be very enticing," I reasoned. "A middle-aged guy, alone late at night, with a car full of guns. What bad guy wouldn't be tempted? But then how does the murder weapon fit in? I'm assuming that none of the guns at the talk were loaded."

"Absolutely not," Darlene said emphatically. "I checked them all and I'm pretty sure that Pete did too."

"So how could an antique gun get loaded and fired by a transient bad guy? I'm pretty sure that particular model doesn't use a standard cartridge. Not a round that some guy on the street is going to have in his pocket."

"It would have had to be loaded already."

"Did he have that gun at the talk?"

"I believe so. Or one that was very similar. Pete would know better."

"Let's assume it was. Could Higgins have loaded it for protection before unloading the car?" I asked,

"It's possible, but it would be an unlikely choice. The man had a bunch of guns to choose from. Why would he pick one that might not be very reliable?"

"Might be another question for Pete. Even if the murder was premeditated, we have to get over the hurdle of why that particular gun was loaded."

"Finding that car would make me feel better."

"Bound to help. Let's go in," I said.

Once inside the front door, I noticed a hall table that had a small, oily spot on it. I called Marcus. "Did you take a sample of the oil?" I asked after describing where the table was.

"I did," he answered and gave me the evidence reference number.

"Is it on the way to the lab?"

"It's on the way, but they're pretty jammed up. It's summer barbeque season. Lots of late-night parties with people getting rowdy and stabbing and shooting each other. The guys at the lab told me that they're weeks behind. I couldn't come up with a reason for a rush on this stuff."

"Not until we have a suspect. But push this to the front of the line," I requested and hung up.

"Smells like gun oil," Darlene said, sniffing the table.

"My thoughts exactly. Maybe our murder weapon was lying on this table. No more than ten feet inside the door and in a direct line to where the body was found."

"Someone comes in, picks up the gun and shoots him. That doesn't sound premeditated."

"Not to us, but I'm pretty sure that the prosecutor could make a case for first-degree murder." As far as the law is concerned, a suspect only has to decide to commit the murder a few minutes, or even seconds, before they stab, shoot or bludgeon the victim to death. If they made the conscious decision to kill before they struck the first blow, then it is considered premeditated.

We started walking through the house. Every room was full of furniture and knickknacks, making the house feel like a giant antiques store. The master bedroom was on the ground floor and was clearly where Higgins slept. His clothes were in the closet and personal items filled the dresser and nightstands. The bed was a huge four-poster that was much too big for the room. One of the posters still bore an old paper price tag, showing that the bed had once been marked for sale at twenty-five hundred dollars.

"This must have been his mother's," Darlene said as we walked into the next room. "An old woman's clothes, a walker, prescription drug bottles years out of date." After a pause, she added, "I sure wish there was some option between getting old and being dead."

Upstairs we found another bedroom filled with a jumble of furniture, but not much in the way of personal items. The house was old enough that this room didn't even have a closet. Instead, a large Edwardian wardrobe stood in the corner. I opened it as Darlene checked out the nightstand by the twin bed.

"This is interesting," I said, looking at a couple shirts and a pair of jeans hung up in the wardrobe. "Who do you think these belong to?"

"Probably the same person who owns this," she said, holding up a USB charger and a cable.

Inside a dresser, I found a few pairs of underwear, socks and cargo pants. The sizes matched the clothes in the wardrobe.

"These are new, and I'd say they belong to a young man... or at least someone thin."

"This shirt has an interesting logo. Slovenly Records?" Darlene said, holding up a T-shirt. She took a picture of it. "Maybe I can find out something about the shirt which might tell us something about the guy who owns it."

"Man, you really are a detective. What would I do without you?" I said with smile. She gave me a hooded glare and I quickly moved on. "So it looks like there was a young guy living with Higgins. Makes you wonder what their relationship was."

"Higgins hasn't ever been married."

"Boyfriend, maybe. Though that's kind of a stereotype for an antiques dealer."

"Just because it's a stereotype doesn't mean it isn't true," Darlene said.

"Maybe Lionel will be able to give us something from Higgins's computer."

"What did we do before computers and phones? People put their whole lives on those things."

"It definitely helps when you find that the wife had searched for sources of cyanide on the Internet two days before her husband keeled over. Before electronic data, there was just a whole bunch more footwork to do."

"My feet get enough work as it is," Darlene said,

thumping her size eights on the hardwood floor.

"I wonder if the houseguest is our guy in the bank video?"

Darlene just shrugged.

"He wasn't getting his mail here," I said, going through a stack of letters and junk mail once we were back downstairs.

"Nothing in any of the garbage cans either."

I called Marcus again. "Did you pick up any fingerprints or palm prints in the guestroom upstairs?"

"You *do* know that we're the crime scene department for *all* of the investigators and deputies working for the sheriff's office, right?" he asked.

"Yes. And you're doing a wonderful job of covering for Shantel. She'd be glad to know that you're giving me hell for taking up so much of your time," I joked. I really did miss Shantel's barbs.

"Just so you know. Okay, looking at the notes and the map, we definitely picked up some prints in that room."

"I would really, really appreciate it if you took some of your valuable time and compared those prints to Mr. Higgins's," I said.

"That's a better attitude. I'll see what I can do and get back to you."

"There was a witness that saw someone running from the house, right?" Darlene asked.

"Yeah, Mr. Harmon from next door. Maybe whoever our live-in is got scared and ran off when the shooting started."

"Or he did the shooting. Domestics are number one on the motive hit parade."

"Maybe we'll get lucky and his prints will be on file. Who's going to the autopsy?" I asked.

"Not a lot of mystery involved with this one, but maybe Darzi will find something of interest."

"Rock, paper, scissors?"

"Do it," she said and won with paper to my rock.

"Your choice."

"I always like to see a Darzi slice-and-dice."

"You should take video of this one. Enough people hated Higgins that you could probably sell copies," I said laconically.

CHAPTER SEVEN

When I got back to the office, I saw a tall man walking up to the door. Something about him was oddly familiar. He was dressed in a polo shirt and slacks and had grey hair that was retreating from his forehead. I held the door for him while trying to figure out where I knew him from.

"I'm looking for Deputy Macklin," he said when he reached the front desk. Dill Kirby, our semi-retired, sometime desk sergeant, raised his eyebrows and looked over the man's shoulder at me.

"I'm Larry Macklin. How can I help you?"

The man turned around. "I'm Earl Higgins. You're investigating my brother's death."

Aha! I thought. *That explains why you look so familiar.*

Once in the conference room, Earl said, "After talking with my brother's lawyer, it seemed like the easiest thing to do was to come down and deal with all of this directly. Better now during summer session than getting stuck trying to come down here in the fall when I have a full schedule."

"You teach college, right?"

"Yes."

"I haven't talked to Mr. Beck since I talked to you. Did he tell you who the beneficiary of your brother's will is?"

"I'm the sole beneficiary," he said flatly. "I'll be curious to see how much trouble I've inherited."

"You and your brother didn't get along. Can you elaborate on that?"

"How much time do you have? If you've talked to anyone who had anything to do with him, then you already know that the man was a jerk. A conman, for sure. I don't think I'd go so far as to call him evil. I'm not even sure if I believe in that concept, but I'd say he was certainly a psychopath. Runs in the family."

"We couldn't find any documentation that would suggest he was ever married. Did he have any girlfriends?"

"He tried dating a bit when he was in high school, but he gave it up. Honestly, I think he quit once he realized that if you take a girl out on a date, she usually expects you to pay. Once when he was in college, he told me that it was a lot cheaper to rent a woman for an hour than to date one."

"Did he have any boyfriends?" I asked, watching Earl's reaction. He looked thoughtful for a minute before answering.

"I don't think so. But like I said, he was a psychopath. Using people for personal gain was his thing. If he thought money could result, I don't think he'd hesitate for a moment to be whatever he had to be to get close to someone in order to take advantage of them." I don't think I had ever talked to anyone with a lower opinion of their own brother.

"You were in North Carolina on Monday night?"

"Yes, I went to a panel discussion on *Faust* and then home. Yesterday morning I was at an eight o'clock freshman English lit class. I don't blame you for the question. I had a lot of repressed anger toward my brother that took years to work through."

"But he left you everything?"

"I'm a little surprised at that myself. But then again, who else would he leave it to? He may not have cared for me, but the thought of the state getting everything would have really pissed him off. I'm sure that's the only reason he bothered to make a will at all."

"When was the last time you were in your parents' house?"

"Ten years ago, when my father first got sick. Not a fond memory. I tried to talk him out of letting Conrad move in, but Dad just accused me of being jealous and hateful. Told me to leave and not come back."

"And your mother?"

"My mother did whatever Dad and Conrad told her to do. I know she loved me, but she never believed that she had any power to oppose them. I tried to get her to stand up to them, but she wouldn't even try."

"When was the last time you talked to your brother?"

"When my mother died. She left me a few items in her will. Nothing valuable."

"You all didn't meet at the funeral?"

"He had her cremated. I didn't even know she had died until a week later. He said a funeral would have been a ridiculous expense." Earl's voice was a low growl and I saw anger burning in his eyes.

"What did he say when he called you?"

"He just asked me for my address and email. Told me he was shipping the items she'd left me and would email me the tracking number. Cold and calculating as always. I'll say this—he didn't cheat me out of those few items. He even packed them carefully."

"I'd appreciate you not going into your brother's house for a few days. We still might need to collect additional forensic evidence."

"Whatever. I won't own the house until the will is probated. Honestly, I might just sell it as-is. Contents included. All it is to me at this point is baggage."

I'd already sized him up for the clothes that were in the guestroom. He was too tall and the clothes were too new for them to have belonged to him when he was a kid.

"Would you allow me to take a DNA sample for comparison purposes?"

"I suppose," he said reluctantly. "Does anyone really have any privacy anymore?"

"I promise you that everything will be kept confidential," I said, getting up and retrieving gloves and a DNA kit from a cabinet. We kept them in every room where we might question a suspect or witness. If someone agreed to have their DNA taken, you didn't want to give them five minutes while you hunted up a kit to change their minds.

I took the swab from the inside of his mouth. If his DNA matched any fresh samples taken from the house, then we'd have a lot more to talk to him about.

"Your brother's body is undergoing an autopsy this morning and should be available to the funeral home in a day or two," I said, writing down the number for the coroner's office.

"He'll be cremated. I guess we'll see if I can resist the temptation to dump his ashes down the toilet," Earl said as I handed him the phone number.

After seeing him out, I saw an email on my phone from Beth Miller, letting me know that she had pulled all the records pertaining to Higgins. I ran down to pick them up, along with one of the most delicious blackberry muffins I'd ever had in my life.

At my desk, I started with the records of complaints against Higgins. A pattern soon emerged. Someone would call the sheriff's office requesting a deputy and reporting that a robbery had occurred. It would turn out that the "robbery" was actually the person feeling cheated by Higgins over some transaction involving a car, a family heirloom or even cash. The disappointed complainant would be told that the case was actually a civil matter and that they would need to sue Higgins in order to recoup their loss.

Occasionally, the case would come closer to the line of fraud and an investigator would follow up. Usually the investigator would decide that Higgins still hadn't committed a crime and the person filing the complaint would again be referred to the civil courts. But in three instances the investigator had taken the case to the State Attorney, who had filed charges. In each instance, Higgins's lawyer had eventually managed to get the charges dropped.

I made note of a couple of complainants that had seemed particularly angry over the lack of results, then started on the reports that Higgins had filed. The first one immediately grabbed my attention and I was deep into it when Pete came up behind me.

"Any luck?" he asked.

"Something *very* interesting. One of the reports filed by Higgins was against our best witness, Jason Harmon, who reported the body. The charge claimed that he pushed Higgins, who had him arrested for assault."

"Let me guess. He failed to mention this when you were talking to him?"

"Bingo."

"Got to hate it when your best witness turns into a suspect."

"It's early days. I still have three more reports filed by Higgins to review."

Pete was about to walk away when I remembered something. "Hey, I did want to ask you about the murder weapon." I pulled up some of the photos that Marcus had taken showing close-ups of the revolver. "Did Higgins have this gun at the historical society talk?"

"Or one just like it. He had several different revolvers, but that one's a Russian Nagant. They were made from 1898 through World War II. Very cheap. You can get one for about a hundred-and-fifty dollars now. Higgins passed it around. Which makes sense. If you're going to have a hands-on exhibit, you'd be sure that it wasn't something too valuable."

"A revolver doesn't take a particularly high IQ to use. Just point and pull the trigger."

"It depends. They made a double-action and a single-action version. Looking at it, I'm not sure which one this is. Was it fully loaded?"

"Yes."

"So it wasn't a quick jam-one-in-the-cylinder sort of thing. Your victim must have loaded it for some reason."

"And if we knew why, then that might give us a leg up. Just one of the things that could really help this investigation. Number one is finding his car."

After Pete left, I switched gears, deciding to make direct contact with as many local law enforcement agencies as I could and asking them to be on the lookout for Higgins's SUV. A general bulletin is one thing, but a little personal contact will often encourage other officers to use a bit of their free time looking for the missing vehicle.

After putting the word out over a two-hundred-mile radius, I put the phone down and retuned to the rest of the complaints that Higgins had filed.

The second assault turned out to be a man who had simply poked Higgins in the chest with his finger during a heated argument. The first vandalism involved someone writing some not-very-nice things all over Higgins's car with a sharp object. The second vandalism report detailed the destruction of Higgins's mailbox and that the word *thief* had been written on the sidewalk with an arrow pointing toward his house.

No charges were filed in any of the cases, though Higgins had provided a detailed list of possible suspects for both of the vandalisms. I made note of them, as all would need to be interviewed, though one already had been. Higgins had named Faith Osborne as his number one suspect in the mailbox incident.

"Careful or your butt will become attached to that chair," Darlene said, sitting down at her desk facing mine. "You want to hear all the gory details of the autopsy?" The fact that she said this with a toothpick hanging out of her mouth made it rather disturbing.

"Just the pertinent facts, thank you," I said.

"Short story is, he was shot in the head and killed by a 7.62 caliber bullet, which entered through his forehead and exited at a slight upward trajectory out of the back of his head. Before his head came in contact with the bullet, he was in pretty good health for a man his age."

"Time of death?"

"Still analyzing stomach contents, but with the body temperature taken by his techs at the scene, Darzi put the time of death in the ballpark we've been looking at, just before one in the morning."

"No other bruising or lacerations?"

"Just what you'd expect, a little at the back of his head when he fell. Everything is consistent with being shot and collapsing as a result."

"The toxicology will be done in due time, I suppose."

"I couldn't see any reason to ask for a rush job. No sense wearing out our welcome," Darlene said. "What about you? Got any hot leads?"

I filled her in on my day's work.

"This one isn't going to solve itself, that's for sure."

I showed her the list of names from the reports. "Lack of suspects certainly isn't the problem."

"Hey, maybe this is like that Agatha Christie book, *Murder on the Orient Express.* Everyone did it."

"Works for me. I'll write up the warrants and see if we can get them signed," I joked.

"Forget it. Arresting a dozen people for one murder would be a pain in the ass."

We made quick calls to the names on the new suspect list and arranged for most of them to come in the next day for an interview, then we both headed home.

Cara and I were spending a quiet evening with her Pug, Alvin, and my rescue tabby, Ivy, right up until my phone went off at eleven o'clock. I groaned. The ringtone was Pete's and, since he was working that night, I knew it wasn't a social call. Just as I answered my phone, Cara's also began to ring.

"You better get over to Faith Osborne's house. We just got a report of a possible homicide," Pete said, and I felt a chill go up my spine.

"I'm leaving now," I told him, and was surprised to hear Cara say the same thing to her caller.

"What is it?" I asked her.

"That was Dr. Barnhill. Cleo's just been brought into the clinic. She's all cut up and is going to need a transfusion." She stopped and looked conflicted. "I hate to ask, but we don't have any large dogs in the clinic right now. Do you think your dad would consider…?"

"I'll call him."

After I explained the situation, I heard him ask Mauser if he wanted to be a hero. I could only imagine the look of confused indifference he must have received from the big idiot.

"Tell Cara we'll meet her at the clinic," Dad said.

CHAPTER EIGHT

When I arrived at Faith's house, the night was filled with red and blue flashing lights. I saw at least two of our patrol cars, as well as one from the Calhoun Police Department and a Florida state trooper, plus two ambulances. Pete hurried over to my car.

"She's alive," he said breathlessly. "Barely, but alive."

I sprinted toward the ambulance. "What happened?" I asked.

"Someone broke in and tried to strangle her. Still a little cloudy on the rest of it. You can't talk to her," Pete said to my back as I out-distanced him.

I stopped when I saw two sets of paramedics huddled around a stretcher. I got the attention of one who didn't seem to be involved in the immediate efforts to help Faith.

"How is she?"

"Hey, Macklin," the EMT said. Her name was Tammy and, though she couldn't have weighed more than one-hundred-and-twenty pounds, I'd seen her move patients three times her size with ease. "Her throat and neck are badly damaged. Hondo had to do a tracheotomy and get a tube down her so she could breathe. She was completely out when we got here. I'm not sure how long she was without oxygen, but we've got her breathing and her heart is beating on its own. Another minute or two, she'll be stable enough to transport to Tallahassee."

"Pete said someone tried to strangle her."

"They didn't try. Whoever it was *killed* her. For all practical purposes, she was a corpse when we got to her. You can thank Hondo."

She looked over at the EMT who was checking Faith's vitals. Hondo, whose real name was Alejandro Valdez, was a large, good-humored man whose bedside manner was as good as his medical skills. His dark black hair always looked a little wild, the result of his habit of hanging half out of the driver's window and waving vigorously to anyone he recognized. I'd been on the receiving end of both his enthusiastic greetings *and* his triage expertise. Faith had been lucky to have him on the scene.

"What did they use?" I asked Tammy. "Rope, cord...?"

"Nothing like that. It was a soft, terrycloth belt, the sort that comes with a robe. Not the most efficient, but it got the job done."

"Did any of you see anything?"

"We were second on the scene. Sergei and Leo were first, but only 'cause they drive like lunatics." This last was said loud enough for the other EMTs to hear. One of them lifted a finger to her.

As they were placing Faith in the ambulance, I saw a piece of pink fabric hanging from the edge of the stretcher. "Hold it!" I said and stepped forward to grab the piece of cloth. "Where's the other half?" Leo handed me another piece of cloth as they slid the stretcher into the back of the ambulance.

Pete had caught up to me and handed me an evidence bag. The cloth belt had been pulled so tightly around Faith's neck that it had lacerated the skin. There were traces of blood on the two pieces that the EMTs had cut off of her.

"Have you set up a grid?" I asked Pete.

"Done and done. We've secured a four-block area and

also have a watch on the main roads out of town." When it came to the tactical side of police work, Pete was always on top of things, though to look at him you'd never guess it. He gave every appearance of being the typical donut-eating stereotype of a burnt-out cop, but that was far from the truth. He served as our firearms instructor and lead tactical team sniper; with the right rifle, Pete could hammer a nail at a thousand yards. "I've also asked Martel to follow the ambulance to the hospital and stay with Faith."

"Do we have a description of the suspect?"

"You don't honestly think you're that lucky, do you? The neighbors who came to the rescue saw a suspect running from the yard, but they only saw him from the back. It's a long story. You might as well hear it from the horse's mouth," Pete said just as his phone rang.

"No kidding? Stay with it and don't let anyone near it. We'll be there in a minute," Pete said into the phone and then hung up with a big smile on his face. "Am I being paid to solve your case? Pretty sure they just found Higgins's car. It's parked right through there." He pointed to the back of Faith's house. "First the witnesses."

He punched me on the arm lightly with one of his big, meaty paws and I followed him to his car, where a man about my age was sitting with his wife. They both had a lot of blood on their clothes, which puzzled me since Faith Osborne's neck hadn't bled that much.

"This is Joe and Lauren Childs. They live next door," Pete introduced us.

"I'm Deputy Macklin. Who got to the scene first?"

"We both did," the husband said.

"Start at the beginning. Why did you come over here?"

"We heard this huge crash. I knew it was glass breaking, and then there was this horrible howl. Honestly, we didn't know what the hell was going on," he said.

"Where were you when you heard the noise?"

"Sitting on our back porch. We'd heard that there was going to be a meteor shower tonight so we thought we'd watch for a while. Then we heard all the noise and came running over to see what had happened. I wish I'd called 911 on our way over, but we just didn't know what was going on," Joe said and looked at his wife.

"And that's when I saw Cleo and she saw me. She was running around the yard and, when she finally came over to me, she was covered in blood. I told Joe to stay with her and I went to find Faith." She looked to Joe to continue the narrative.

"Cleo would hardly let me hold her. She was going nuts. I grabbed her collar at one point and she turned and snapped at me. The light wasn't good, but I could see cuts all over her." Again, he passed the ball to Lauren.

"When I got near the front door, I saw someone running down the driveway. I don't know who it was. I think I shouted 'hey' or something, but they ignored me and I was really freaking out at this point. But I went inside and found Faith lying on the floor. It was so weird and surreal. Like a movie, only not. When I touched Faith, she was warm, but her face was a really scary color, blue or purple. Thank God I had my phone. I dialed 911 and the operator talked me through everything until the ambulance showed up." The woman was trembling.

"Do you know how Cleo got cut up?" I asked them.

"I'm pretty sure I can answer that," Pete said. "Apparently, the dog was shut up in the den. When she heard Faith and the intruder struggling, she must have become frantic. At some point, she busted through one of the windows to get out. Bottom line is, she saved Osborne's life. Julio and a trooper got her loaded into a state K9 unit and rushed her over to Dr. Barnhill's."

"Yeah, Cara got the call the same time I did." I hoped everything was going well for both Cleo and Faith.

"I'm going to look at the car," I told Pete. "If you have this under control?"

"I've locked down the house. As far as the perimeter goes, I'm having them keep an eye out for someone on foot in dark clothing, or anyone acting suspicious. When you get back from the car, I've got something odd to show you at the house. Ooh, look at this looky-loo!"

I turned to see Darlene walking up behind us, wearing jeans and a sparkly blouse. "Is it casual Friday?" I asked.

"I was coming back from Tallahassee when I caught all the excitement on the radio," she said.

"You know, some of us turn off our radios when we're off duty," I responded.

"And some day you'll be calling me captain," she shot back.

"I'm going that way," I said, pointing to Faith's backyard. "They found Higgins's car. If you want to walk with me, I'll fill you in."

"Rock on," she told me.

By the time we got to the car, we'd searched the footpath that led to the street behind Faith's house, and I'd filled Darlene in on the events of the night as I knew them.

"Damn! There it is, parked in plain sight," Darlene said as we approached the Honda CR-V. Deputy Randy Spears was parked across the street from it. He got out and walked over to us.

"Did you see anyone near the car?" I asked him.

"Nope. I was looking for the runner when I saw the car and remembered that a Honda CR-V was on the BOLO list at the briefing this afternoon." Deputy Spears was one of the department's go-getters who was always willing to go above and beyond.

"It's definitely the same car I helped Higgins load the other night," Darlene said, going over the car with a flashlight. "It doesn't look damaged."

I pulled out my phone and called Marcus. He was already on his way to the Osborne house. "We're going to have to call in reinforcements," he said, sounding resigned. "I've still got items from the murder to catalog and this is going to be another level of work. If Shantel was in town then we could probably handle it all in-house, but without her I got to get some help."

"I'll talk to Dad and get him to authorize FDLE to come in and help," I told him. "But you'll have to hold down the fort until they can come on the scene. Do the car first. Go over the exterior and then we can have it hauled to the impound lot. Then we'll all pitch in and help with the exterior of the house. We can lock the rest of it down and, if it takes a day or so to get to the interior, that's okay."

"Thanks," Marcus said. I knew he must've been at his breaking point to ask for outside help.

"You mind watching this until Marcus gets here?" I asked Spears.

"Easy peasy."

Darlene and I headed back to the house. "So what's the deal with the car?" I asked her.

"Our perp drives it here, attacks the woman and flees, but doesn't go back to the car," Darlene said as if it was obvious.

"The only person on scene when the attacker fled was a bystander. He could have easily headed back to the car."

"Knew the car was too hot so he ditched it?"

"Seems like he would have used it to get out of Dodge and *then* abandoned it," I said as we approached the house.

"Hopefully we'll find out if there was any purpose to his madness."

"Was it Higgins's car?" Pete asked, seeing us emerge from the footpath.

"Yep."

A call crackled over the radio for Pete. It was Deputy Matti Sanderson. She'd stopped someone walking a couple of blocks away wearing a black hoodie and acting suspicious. Darlene and I jumped in my car and headed over.

"What've we got, Sandy?" I asked as we walked up. I could see the suspect beyond her, sitting on the curb with his hands cuffed behind his back.

"I was sitting in the driveway over there, watching up and down the street. I saw him sneaking around like he didn't want to be seen, so I got out and headed in his direction. As soon as he spotted me, he started to run. Not as fast as you thought, are you?" she threw back at the young man.

"What's his name? Any priors?"

"Aaron Healy, twenty-five years old. A DUI two years ago and a disorderly conduct last month."

Darlene and I walked over to him.

"I didn't do nothin'," he said, showing a severe lack of originality.

"You can at least let us ask some questions before you start denying everything," I said.

"She broke my knee, man."

"I identified myself and ordered you to stop," Sanderson said evenly.

"Did he have any drugs or weapons?" Darlene asked.

"No. Just a cigarette lighter and his wallet."

"Did he strike you?" I asked Sanderson.

"No. Once he was on the ground, he didn't resist."

"If we're satisfied with his responses, do you have a problem with us letting him go on his way?" I asked. I knew that Healy would be all ears, listening to us.

"He's yours," she said. I nodded and indicated that she could wait by her car.

"Stand up," I told him.

He looked up for just a second, then back down at the pavement. Darlene went over and started to lift him, but then he got up on his own, limping a little and a bit awkward with his hands cuffed behind his back. I shined my flashlight over him. I couldn't see any blood or any other marks on his skin or clothing.

"If we can clear this up, we'll let you go," I said to him in my "good cop" voice.

"I bet," he grumbled.

"Where do you live?"

"Old Mill Road," he said, indicating a rural area with a mix of older middle-class folks and lots of poor people in rented mobile homes.

"Why are you here tonight?"

Silence.

"Come on, give us a hint," Darlene said with a little menace in her tone.

"Nothin'," he said, still looking at the asphalt.

"Not good enough. Try again," I said.

"I was just walking around." He shuffled his feet as though he felt the need to demonstrate the concept of walking.

"Up to a point, I don't care what you were doing. We're dealing with an assault that occurred a couple blocks over."

He finally looked up at me. "I didn't attack no one," he declared emphatically.

"Fine. Then tell me what you're doing in this neighborhood," I said.

"Whose window were you peeping in?" Darlene surprised me with the question, but from the look he gave her, I could tell she'd come close to the mark.

"I ain't no pervert. I…" He went silent again.

"I'll make it easy. If you didn't assault or rob someone, then I don't care. I just need to know what you were doing here this evening before I can let you go," I said.

"I was checking on my girlfriend," he said softly.

"Girlfriend or ex-girlfriend?" Darlene asked cynically.

"She's my girlfriend."

"But?"

"We've been having some problems. I thought… I just wanted to see if she was home like she said she was going to be," he blurted.

"How'd you get here?" I asked.

"I drove. I parked a couple blocks away from her house so she wouldn't see the car."

We got the girlfriend's name and address, then drove him over to his car and checked it out. His story seemed legit. It turned out that the disorderly conduct charge he'd received the month before was because of an argument he'd gotten into with a guy he'd thought was hitting on his girlfriend. I let Darlene give him a stern lecture on stalking and then we let him go.

We got back to the house and found Pete helping Marcus.

"Come look at this," Pete said, and we followed him to the back porch. "This is how the intruder got into the house." He shined his light on the porch door where there were pry marks around the lock. He opened the door and we stepped into the screened-in back porch. "There." He shined his light on a coil of sisal rope.

I moved in close and squatted down to make sure that I was seeing what I thought I was seeing. "A noose?"

"Why would you strangle a woman with a bathrobe belt when you'd brought a noose along to the party?" Darlene mused.

"Makes you wonder, doesn't it," Pete said.

Inside, we found the den where Cleo had been locked up. The door to the hallway had been gouged by her claws, while it looked like everything in the room had been knocked off or knocked over. Cleo had gone wild for a while before she'd broken through the window. There was blood and fur on the glass.

Faith had been found in the dining room, face up. The room showed signs of a struggle. The tablecloth had been pulled off of the table and several chairs had been knocked over.

"He came in the back door. Why didn't the dog confront him there?" Darlene asked.

"Great Danes aren't your average dogs. Individuals vary, of course, but Mauser sleeps through a *lot* more than most dogs. I wonder if our intruder even knew that Cleo was in the house."

"Hard to say. Maybe he just got lucky, saw the dog and closed the door fast. Then when Faith confronted him, he attacked her," Pete said.

"Is this the same person who killed Higgins?" Darlene asked.

"Seems likely. Another night attack. Different MO where the weapon is concerned, but fleeing on foot is the same," Pete said.

"Except for the car. If he was the one that fled on foot from the Higgins murder, then how does the car fit into the two scenarios?" I asked.

"The car's a wild card, all right," Pete said thoughtfully.

"Hopefully, once we get in the car, we'll find something that will help clear some of this up," I said.

We heard the patrol cars in front of the house throw on their sirens and take off. A couple minutes later, Pete received a call.

"Got to go. A domestic dispute turned into a knife fight. In a pleasant change of pace, the woman apparently won," Pete said.

"He dead?" Darlene asked.

"Nah. He's on the way to the hospital and she's being patched up by the EMTs."

Darlene and I walked through the rest of the house, but didn't find anything that raised any more red flags. Hopefully, Faith would be well enough to do a walk-through with us in the near future.

"Everyone's house is different. How the heck do you know what's out of place or missing? I've seen houses that looked like a tornado went through them and had everyone tell me that that's the way the house *always* looked," I said, opening and closing drawers.

"A friend who works for Metro Dade told me of a case where a woman was missing. They went into her house and the place was neat and spotless. When her mother showed up, she collapsed on the ground, crying and screaming. Said that the only way the house could be that neat was if her daughter had been killed and the murderer had cleaned up afterward. Turned out, she was right. They found the body in a dumpster two blocks from the house."

"They catch the guy?"

"Caught him on video buying cleaning supplies at the

Home Depot."

We decided to take a break. "I'm going to run up to the clinic," I told Darlene.

"Hope the dog is okay."

Dad's van was in the parking lot, along with Cara's and Dr. Barnhill's cars. The front door was open and I found Dad sitting on the floor with his back against the wall, literally holding Mauser's paw as the dog lay beside him. The Dane looked up with sad, confused eyes. Genie Anderson, Dad's girlfriend, was sitting on a bench seat next to them.

"They've just about got the poor thing stitched up," Dad said, sounding tired.

"You all okay?"

"Mauser isn't completely recovered from the anesthesia," he said, stroking the dog's enormous paw. I tried not to be offended that he seemed more concerned about the dog than he ever had about me... apart from one recent exception that he would probably try to deny.

Genie and I exchanged greetings as I walked over to Mauser. He tried to stand, but his legs still weren't willing to cooperate.

"You don't have to get up," I said, getting down on the ground with him and stroking his head. "I guess you *are* the hero of the night."

"He was very brave," Genie said. She had fallen under the spell of my furry adopted brother months ago.

"What exactly happened?" Dad asked.

I gave him the short version.

"I remember Faith. She and your mom were pretty good friends in high school, and they kept in touch a bit afterwards."

"What was she like?"

"I didn't hang out with them much back then, but the few times I did, she was actually a bit pig-headed," Dad said. "Everyone would be up for going to the springs to swim, then she'd start arguing for a movie. And once she got her teeth into it, you couldn't change her mind. Half the time, she wound up going off on her own."

"Doesn't sound like they were much alike." I'd never heard anyone describe Mom as stubborn.

"I think that's why they got along. Most people wouldn't have put up with Faith's antics. I think Faith liked your mom because she'd smooth things over. I don't think Faith wanted to get on the outs with people, but once she'd done it, she didn't know how to make things right. That's when Jo would step in and mollify whatever hard feelings Faith had caused."

"What did Mom get out of it?"

"I think she admired the way Faith always stuck to her guns," he said, and I had to wonder if that's what Mom had also liked about Dad.

"Faith told me that she'd seen Mom a couple of times after she'd moved away."

"That's right. She was more mature when she visited. It makes sense. We were all pretty crazy in high school." Dad's eyes had that faraway look of someone remembering the past.

Before I could ask anything else, the door from the examining rooms opened and Cara came out, looking worn out.

"How's our hero doing?" she asked, kneeling down to feel Mauser's pulse and look at his eyes and gums. He ate up his role as the sad puppy, rolling his big brown eyes and letting his huge tongue loll out.

"How's Cleo?" I asked.

"She lost a lot of blood, but she should be okay. Dr. Barnhill had to put in eighty-five stitches. We just need to keep her calm and on fluids for the rest of the night. I'm going to stay with her. How's Faith?"

"I haven't heard." I looked at my watch. It had been a couple of hours, so I called Deputy Martel.

"They're bringing her up to ICU now."

"Make sure they understand that she's to be kept under guard. Once you feel comfortable that hospital security understands the gravity of the situation and can handle it, you can leave."

"ICU is pretty heavily monitored anyway. But I'll make sure they know that there's the possibility of an outside threat."

Talking to Martel was one thing, but I really wanted to hear her prognosis from a doctor. It took me a couple tries to get in touch with a doctor I knew who might bend the rules a bit regarding patient confidentiality.

"Deputy Macklin, you know better than to ask," he said and then paused. "Give me a second." A minute later he came back and said, "She's out of the operating room and headed for ICU. She's stable. Sustained a substantial amount of damage to her neck. I can't give you the details, but the bottom line is she'll live. Right now, they're mostly worried about any brain damage that she might have sustained while she was deprived of oxygen."

I thanked him, then relayed the information to Dad. He was trying to steady Mauser, who was on his feet now but trembling as he tried to maintain his balance. I kissed Cara goodnight, then helped Dad escort Mauser outside. Genie held the door.

Dr. Barnhill was also leaving. Obviously exhausted, he took the time to come over and ruffle Mauser's ears and thank him for his help.

"Mauser doesn't need his ego stroked like that. He's going to be harder to live with than ever," I told Dad after Dr. Barnhill had left. Mauser was lying on the floor of the van with his feet spread out and still looking a bit unsure why the world was so wobbly.

"You're just jealous," Dad said.

"You're right!" I agreed as Dad chuckled and backed out of the parking spot. "Good luck with those two," I told Genie, who smiled and gave me a wave.

Back at Faith's house, Darlene and Marcus were doing a last walk-through before shutting down for the night. "I don't think I can take many more nights like this," Marcus groaned.

"You're just missing your buddy," Darlene said.

"You ain't kidding. I'll need a vacation by the time Shantel gets back from hers."

"When's she get back?" I asked.

"Monday."

"Remember, we aren't getting any more sleep than you are," Darlene said.

"I hear you."

CHAPTER NINE

On Thursday, I got to the office by ten, having snagged a few hours sleep. I didn't even stop at my desk, but walked straight back to the evidence room.

"Let me guess what you want to do," Marcus said as he sorted bags of evidence from the night before.

Feeling a little guilty, I asked, "When did you get in?"

"I was here by eight-thirty. And, believe me, there wasn't any worm to get. This early bird is tired and hungry." Marcus was usually all smiles when he and Shantel were working together. I felt bad realizing how stressed he was now.

"I need to get into that car. You know I wouldn't push if it wasn't important," I said, trying to smooth it over a little.

"I know. Twice, I've seen what that guy has done to people. I want to get him as bad as you do. The good news is, your Dad's already talked with FDLE and they're sending a team over today to do the house. Here, help me carry some of this stuff."

I helped him lug his equipment out to the impound lot. It was already hot and humid. We were still in the dog days of summer where the daytime temperatures started out at seventy-two and climbed toward a hundred, with the humidity the same.

"We processed the outside of the car last night. So what I'm going to do this morning is open the doors and take pictures and video of everything, then we can start picking through the contents," Marcus said.

"You're the boss." I looked through the windows. I could see some papers on the passenger seat, but not much else. Against my usual nature, I was already daring to hope that the identity of our murderer would be revealed by what this car offered up.

Marcus used a shimmy to open the passenger door.

"You smell that?" I asked.

"Cleaner. Something alcohol-based. Not a good sign." It probably meant that someone had cleaned the inside of the car recently.

Once everything was photographed, Marcus backed up and let me sort through the papers on the seat. Wearing gloves, I carefully picked up and examined each piece before handing it over to Marcus to be bagged and labeled.

"Of course, everything will need to be fingerprinted. Hopefully it won't come down to transfer DNA," I said. I wasn't a fan of trace or transfer DNA. It was fine for adding suspects, but too often it was used like regular DNA evidence. The two were vastly different.

I found receipts for various items from a hardware store that predated the murder. There was also a receipt from a restaurant in Tallahassee, dated just a few days before the murder. It was for two meals and the amounts had been circled. Someone had taken the time to divide the cost of the meal into two amounts and the area for the tip was marked through. The credit card information was in Conrad Higgins's name. *It would be interesting to know who he was having dinner with*, I thought as I put the receipt into a clear evidence bag.

"Anything?" I asked Marcus, who was dusting the dash for fingerprints.

"No. This has all been wiped. We can hope for hair and fiber," he said, not sounding optimistic.

I understood his pessimism. The floorboards and the seats were also clean. The smell of glass cleaner when we opened the door had prepared us for the disappointment, but you always had to hold out hope. And there was still hope. It's a lot harder to get all hair and fiber evidence out of a car than most people think.

The glovebox and other cubbyholes didn't provide anything else. The car looked like it was ready to sell or trade in. "I wonder how much of the lack of clutter is the result of the killer cleaning the car out and how much was Higgins's doing," I mused.

"You said he was a wheeler and dealer. Maybe he was already planning to sell the car."

I opened the door to the backseat, which did hold one surprise. There was a small duffle bag on the floorboard with various sets of clothes stuffed inside of it. There were a couple of dress shirts, including one still wrapped in plastic, a pair of dress slacks, dress shoes, cowboy boots, jeans, ties and various belts.

"What's all that?" Marcus asked.

"My guess is that it's a character bag. We need to check the sizes, but I'd bet that these are Higgins's clothes and that he used them whenever he was trying to con a stranger. Our victim was quite a rogue."

"No matter how bad they are, you can't go killin' people," Marcus said as he started to work on the back doors.

Sweat was dripping off my forehead by now. I was just getting ready to open the hatchback when Darlene came out of the building. I filled her in on what we had found so far.

"Charming gentleman," she said. "It's going to be a real competition to see who's worse—the victim or the killer."

"It often is," I agreed, thinking of the times I'd had to notify family members when one drug dealer had shot another. It was only after I had talked to a wailing grandmother or a grieving father I would realize everyone involved had been a victim.

We popped the hatchback and there was... nothing. Or almost nothing. Just a few plastic bottles and a portable printer.

"This is where we put the guns after the lecture. I'm pretty sure the printer was also there," Darlene said thoughtfully.

"I'm sure the printer was used for making business cards and whatever documents a conman might need. I can't believe he wasn't on our radar already."

"You read the reports," Darlene said.

"He was always just this side of the line. Hell, sometimes he was standing right on the line between legal and illegal. For everyone who bothered to make a report, there must have been dozens of cases where he swindled people who were too embarrassed to tell anyone."

"Nothing worse than a crook who preys on the weak."

"Crazy thing is, I almost wish we hadn't found the car. At least while the killer still had it, we had something to look for. Now we have the vaguest of descriptions and nothing else."

"I hear you, brother. And there don't appear to be any hidden prizes in this car," Darlene said, closing the hatchback.

"Why did he take the car to Faith's house and then abandon it? That's what's driving me crazy," I told Darlene as we headed back to our desks, grateful to be inside out of the heat.

"Maybe he planned on driving away after the attack, but got spooked," she suggested.

"That's the best I could come up with. But you walked the path behind her house. It wasn't that far to the car. And I can't see a frightened neighbor spooking our killer. I think he had a plan and that the car was part of it, but when everything went balls up, he just ran."

"Maybe his plan all along was to leave the car," Darlene said. "But why?"

"You got me. Our bad luck. It's pretty easy to escape on

foot around here. Lots of trees and bushes."

"And we didn't have the manpower to really cordon the place off and search door to door."

"I did talk to patrol. They're going to post flyers in the area asking for information from anyone that heard anything last night. It's a long shot at best. Even if someone saw a person sneaking through their yard, all we're going to get is a non-description like the one we already have."

"Dark figure, medium height, medium build, average age."

"That's the one." We'd reached our desks. "Flip a coin for who goes to Tallahassee?" I asked.

"Which one of us has the best luck? 'Cause with a little luck, maybe she's awake and knows who attacked her."

"Honestly, I think we're about even in the luck department."

"Coin it is."

She took a quarter out and flipped it. I called heads and won, so I was on my way to the hospital fifteen minutes later. Darlene agreed to search local CCTV footage for signs of the car arriving at Faith's. Even if we couldn't see who the driver was, we might get an idea of which direction he came from. Even that tidbit of information would be more than what we had now.

At the hospital, I found the right floor and was pleasantly surprised that Faith's doctors and nurses were anxious to move the investigation forward. Sometimes the hospital staff was so entrenched in its procedures that the bigger picture could get lost.

"The intent had to have been to kill her," Dr. Abramson told me. She seemed suitably angry about the brutal attack on her patient.

"Did you document the wounds?"

"Photos, video, plus I wrote up a vivid and accurate description. I asked the surgeon and Dr. Little, who was working ER last night, to do the same."

I took a better look at her. She was middle-aged, short,

and had a pugnacious expression on a face framed by brunette hair. "Thank you," I said, impressed.

"I actually studied to be a pathologist. My first job out of medical school was at a hospital in Cleveland. There was a stalker strangling women when I was there. I saw two of his six victims in our morgue. It is not a pretty way to die."

"Did they ever catch him?"

"No. They had hair and semen samples, but never came up with a match. The murders stopped after two years, but it always leaves you wondering. Did he move? Is he terrorizing some other community? I kept up with the case and there haven't been any other exact matches. It's one of the reasons I decided to work in another field."

"How is Faith this morning?"

"She's still under sedation. I want to give her throat some time to recover before we let her wake up. If she's suffered brain damage, which is a real possibility, I don't want her trying to scream or panic and do more damage to herself."

"How long?"

"I have her scheduled for brain scans this afternoon. We may start letting her come out of sedation tomorrow."

"I'd like to see her."

"If you could find me some family, I'd appreciate it," she said, leading me to ICU and allowing me to peek in on Faith, who was attached to half a dozen wires and tubes in her cubicle.

"So far we haven't had any luck finding anyone, but I'll let you know right away if we do."

Looking at Faith, I was surprised at the strength of my desire to find her attacker. Knowing that she had been a friend of my mother's had created an odd bond for me. Obviously, I knew lots of people who'd known Mom, but Faith seemed to represent a side of her that I'd never known.

I collected some of the photos and asked Dr. Abramson to forward the rest, along with the reports, down to Dr. Darzi. We were going to push this forward as an attempted murder case, and having Dr. Darzi assess the victim in the same way he would a corpse could help. Darzi was used to determining grip strength, weapons used, the size of the attacker and other elements of a crime.

"I'll work with him in any way I can," she said.

Half an hour later, I was sitting with Dr. Darzi in front of his computer.

"Your strangler was focused. See, only the one line." Darzi pointed to a picture of Faith's neck showing a deep red ring around it. The skin around the ring was swollen a dark, ugly purple. "Not many other marks. He wrapped it around her throat and pulled it tight, never hesitating.

"This bruise on her forehead? That's from her going down on her knees and then to the floor. He was behind her." He pulled up another photo. "See this bruise on her back? He probably held her down with his knee to get leverage. She is very lucky to be alive."

"She wouldn't be if it wasn't for a Great Dane."

"Not that creature your father owns?" Darzi said, sounding appalled. He'd met Mauser once or twice and had been horrified. He couldn't believe that anyone would let a monster like that live in their house.

"No, the victim owns one herself. It busted through a window and alerted the neighbors."

"Lucky woman."

"If you could put together a rough physical profile of our attacker, that'd be a big help."

"You are very fortunate that most of the cases you bring me are interesting. Did you know I wrote an article about the victim found in the hot tub?"

I wondered if he knew that the mere thought of that body caused my stomach to turn over. I didn't think anyone had walked away from that particular crime scene without puking their guts up in the flowerbed. Except maybe Pete… there wasn't much that could quell his legendary appetite.

"No, I didn't. And please don't send me a copy," I told Darzi.

He waved his hand dismissively. "Grow a backbone. But,

yes, I will see what I can do with the facts."

On my way out of the hospital, I called Earl Higgins. "Have you had a chance to meet with your brother's lawyer?"

"I have. When do you think I'll be able to gain access to the house?"

"I'd be glad to meet you there this afternoon and go through it with you."

We arranged to meet at two o'clock. That would give me just enough time to get back to Adams County and check in with Cara. I called her to make sure she had a few minutes to see me.

"I do, actually. Dr. Barnhill was still pretty wiped out from last night and cancelled all non-emergency appointments this afternoon. Actually, I'm glad you're coming by. There's something I need to ask you."

"What?"

"It'll wait 'til you get here."

I spent the rest of the drive with my mind racing, wondering what Cara wanted to talk about. It always made me nervous when she was evasive.

I found Cara sitting with Cleo in the clinic's recovery room. The poor dog had stiches running from her head all across her back and belly. She moved stiffly and had a puzzled expression in her big brown eyes.

I gave Cara a quick kiss before kneeling beside Cleo and hugging her gently. "You saved your momma's life, girl. We should make you an honorary deputy."

It was hard to pet her between all the stitches, but she gave me an affectionate nuzzle.

"This kind of leads to what I wanted to ask you," Cara said tentatively. "Can we bring Cleo home for the night? I need to make sure she doesn't lick her wounds too much and that none of them start to bleed. And she's miserable here in the clinic." Cara's eyes were pleading with me as if she was afraid I'd say no.

"You want me to get Dad's van?"

"You're wonderful," Cara said and leaned in to kiss me.

The only one who I thought might have a hard time with the planned sleepover was Ivy. It had taken her a couple of weeks before she'd accepted Alvin, and she wasn't going to enjoy having a giant patient getting all the attention and taking up room in her house.

I swung by the office, asked Dad if we could borrow Mauser's van, then picked up the keys to the Higgins house. A rental car was parked in the driveway when I arrived and Earl Higgins was standing in the shade of the front porch.

"Feels strange to be on this porch again," he said softly, his expression somewhere between resigned and angry. "This is how it always was. Conrad would do whatever he wanted, damn the consequences, and I'd come along behind and deal with all the crap."

"He probably wasn't very happy with the way this turned out," I said, stating the obvious.

"You think I should be more gracious seeing as he's dead and I'm alive?"

"I do think you're getting the last laugh with this one," I said dryly.

He raised his eyebrows. "You might have a point." He paused and pulled a piece of paper out of his pocket. "Mr. Beck told me about this guy. You might want to take a look at him. According to the lawyer, he and my brother did some business together. Beck wasn't real clear about what the business involved. Something about this guy being a silent investor. Anyway, big surprise, they had a falling out. The guy has been after my brother for a couple of months, demanding money. Beck said the guy called him up as soon as he learned that Conrad was dead and said he expected to be paid out of the estate."

"Sounds interesting." I looked at the note. The name, Horace McCune, was familiar. The sheriff's office had made a few calls out to his house. I'd never been on one, but from what I'd heard, they'd usually involved civil matters, not criminal. I tucked the paper into my pocket, pulled the crime scene tape from the front door, and went inside.

"If there is anything that looks odd, out of place or missing, let me know. Of course, we've taken a lot of items to be cataloged and checked for fingerprints or DNA."

"I told you, it's been years since I was in this house. I doubt I'd know if anything is missing." He looked around with wide eyes. "Actually, there's *more* stuff here than I remember. Some of the furniture I recognize, but most of it looks like the kind of stuff he was always flogging."

We passed the spot in the foyer where Conrad Higgins had been found. There was still a puddle of dried blood on the hardwood floor. He hadn't bled much, but on a hard surface a little blood goes a long way. Higgins stopped and stared at it.

"I expect the house was happy to get some of our blood. I always felt like it wanted it. Did you ever read a book by Anne Rivers Siddons called *The House Next Door*?"

"No," I admitted.

"The story involves a house that draws the worst out of people. That's how I always felt about this place." The darkness in his voice sent a small chill down my spine. "I'm going to sell this albatross the first chance I get."

We finished with the downstairs and headed to the second floor. I was particularly interested to get his thoughts on the clothes that were in the guest bedroom. As we walked inside it, I paid very close attention to his reaction. When he saw the clothes in the wardrobe, I saw his back stiffen.

"Do you have any idea whose clothes those are?" I asked. Higgins had reached out and touched the jeans.

"No," he said quickly. Too quickly.

"If there was someone else staying in the house, that would be valuable information. Even if the person didn't have anything to do with the murder, they could have knowledge of your brother's actions in the days leading up to it that could be helpful." I tried to sound as officious as I could. I'd sized Earl Higgins up as a rule-follower.

"I don't have any idea whose clothes these are."

Liar, I thought.

"Take a good look at them," I said, holding up the shirts.

His eyes shifted away from my hands.

"I told you, I don't know who they belong to," he said emphatically.

But I don't believe you, I thought.

"The jeans are in pretty good condition. And this shirt has a Slovenly Records patch sewn over the left breast. The label was founded in 2002 and handles punk and garage bands. We checked. They don't have shirts like this, but they do sell the patches. This would be pretty unique." I was picking through and talking about the clothes, just to see how uncomfortable I could make Earl.

"I really don't need to stand around here listening to you talk about fashion," he said, and I could tell that he was working very hard not to snap at me. The clothes upset him, but he clearly didn't want me to know why.

"You're right. I'm just taking up your time. We've got one more room to go through."

The last room was being used for storage. You couldn't even walk into it more than a couple of feet. "What a mess," Earl grumbled.

"We'll need to pull everything out and look through this room. That's why we're going to need to keep the house sealed for a few more days at least."

"Sure, whatever," he said, already heading for the stairs. I let him get ahead of me and pulled out my phone. From the top of the stairs, I watched him go out the front door before I called Darlene.

"Where are you?" I asked her.

"I'm running down some leads we got from the flyers patrol handed out this morning."

"I need you to jump on this. I'm at Higgins's house with his brother. I need you to follow him when he leaves here."

"What am I looking for?"

"Just keep track of where he goes. I'll explain later."

"I'll be there in ten," she said.

"Text me when you're in position."

I rushed down the stairs and out the door. I needed to stall him until Darlene got there.

"Mr. Higgins, I know this has been stressful for you," I said, flagging Earl down before he could get into his car. Luckily, I'd pulled in behind him so he couldn't leave.

"I had some bad times in this house," he said through clenched teeth.

"Our experiences as children can leave deep scars."

"I hear people talking nostalgically about their Christmases, all the trips they took with their families, and all I think is, 'Thank God that part of my life is over.' But you're right, it's never really over. I'd like to burn it all down," he said, eyeing the house. He sounded so sincere that I thought I'd better ask patrol to keep watch on the place until he headed back to North Carolina.

"You're better off facing it. Most monsters are just shutters banging in the wind or shadows in the closet. If you look them straight in the eye, you can see them for what they are."

"What happens when you stare them in the face and realize that they really *are* monsters?"

I saw the darkness in his eyes. Had his childhood really been that terrible?

The text alert went off on my phone. *I spy with my little eye...* was the message from Darlene.

"I've kept you long enough," I said. "I'll almost certainly have more questions for you. In the meantime, if you need anything or remember anything else that might be helpful, give me a call."

He gave me a cursory wave and got into his rental car.

CHAPTER TEN

Ten minutes later, I'd explained everything to Darlene.

"So far, he's just driving in circles. I'd say he's looking for someone."

"Exactly. He knows who's been staying at his brother's house. What kills me is that we don't have any leverage over him to make him talk. You get used to having suspects that you can dangle a carrot or wave a stick at. I'm going back to the office and see what I can dig up about this guy."

"I'll keep following him. If he picks up anyone or talks to anyone, I'll find out who they are," Darlene said, talking to herself as much as to me.

Back at the office, I covered some of the same social media ground on Earl Higgins as Julio already had. It was all pretty vanilla. He was divorced; had a son named Donald in his early twenties. I called Higgins's department at Appalachian State and identified myself as a law enforcement officer doing routine background checks. After they called me back for verification, I was given contact information for a couple of his fellow professors. I got lucky and reached one of them on my first try.

"Dr. Lawton? This is Larry Macklin. I'm an investigator with the Adams County Sheriff's Office down in Florida and

I'm doing a routine background check on Earl Higgins. I was hoping you could talk with me for a few minutes about your relationship with him," I said, intentionally trying to put the person on the defensive.

"I wouldn't call it a relationship," he said. "We just teach in the same department."

"Can you tell me what you know about him?"

"I guess. I don't know much. He was married. Divorced now. He's a good teacher. At least, that's what I hear. Nice enough guy. Our relationship is strictly professional. I've been to his house a few times over the years for a staff party or get-together. But the last time was about five years ago. Since the divorce, I don't think he's invited anyone over. I'm not even sure that he's living in the same house." Once he got started, Dr. Lawton spilled his guts pretty fast.

"What about the divorce? Were there any rumors of an affair?"

"Now that's kind of personal. I don't want to be spreading gossip."

"Is that a yes?"

"No. Maybe. If there was, it was discreet. I think the divorce was caused by the usual things—stress, boredom, kid problems, they grew apart, all of that. Honestly, Earl's a pretty boring guy. We've got guys and gals around here that get up to some wild times, but Earl is not one of them. Really, I'd say that's why he doesn't have a ton of friends around here. He just doesn't do much other than teach and write. Come to think about it, that might be why his wife left him."

With friends like this... I thought. "You mentioned kid problems?"

"Earl complained about his son for years. Was always asking other parents for advice. Kind of sad. Not the kid, but Earl asking for advice. I mean, geez, raise your own kid."

"What did the kid do?"

"Most of it just sounded like typical kid stuff. Withdrawn, sulky, never wanted to do anything with the family, blah,

blah, blah. I think Earl might have been over-thinking it. A couple of times when Earl was in his cups, he started talking about his family when he was growing up. Father and mother ignored him, doted on his older brother. It didn't really sound that bad. No beatings with a belt or locked in a dark closet for hours. Just that his parents seemed to favor his brother more. Which I can understand, if Earl was as boring as a kid as he is as an adult."

Dr. Lawton paused. "I guess that's a little harsh. Earl's a nice enough guy. Anyway, I think he had dreams of giving his kid the perfect upbringing. The Griswold syndrome. But not all kids want their parents hovering over them. This is just speculation, but Earl might have pushed the kid away by being too clingy. I don't know. I haven't seen the kid since he was maybe twelve years old."

That was about all I got from Dr. Lawton. He didn't have any suggestions of other friends or family I could talk to, other than Earl's ex-wife. But I wanted to wait a bit before contacting her.

I decided to do a full background on his son. It took me a couple of tries to find the right Donald Higgins, but when I did there was a nice police history that went with him. I couldn't get any juvenile stuff, but there were enough hints in the convictions from his late teens to suggest a rough few years. He'd been charged with burglary a couple of times and pled guilty once. A few charges for disorderly conduct and resisting arrest. I was surprised that there weren't any drug possession charges, but maybe Donnie was just a thief. Surprisingly, it had all come to an end about a year ago. Maybe he'd wised up. It wasn't impossible.

His DMV picture was a lot better than his booking photos, though none of them were particularly endearing. Donald Higgins had black, shaggy hair and hooded eyes under a very wide forehead. He didn't look stupid. Like a good book, he left me wanting to know more about him.

With that rabbit hole fully explored, I called to check in with Darlene.

"He's finally headed back to his motel in Tallahassee. We're almost there."

"You can let him go."

"You could have told me that before I drove all the way over here," she said good-naturedly.

"Why don't you swing by the hospital and check on Faith?"

"10-4."

I told her about Higgins's son.

"Sounds interesting. I can already hear the wheels turning in your head. You think he came down here to visit his uncle?"

"Too early to guess. But that would explain Earl's reaction to the clothes."

"That it would, sparky."

"I say we throw it at him tomorrow and see what he says," I suggested and she agreed before hanging up.

I looked at my watch and realized I needed to go to Dad's house to pick up the van. When I got there Jamie, Mauser's babysitter, was sitting by a plastic wading pool where the monster dog was wallowing in the cool water, looking like a particularly ugly sea lion.

"That's the life I want," I said to Mauser and Jamie.

"Poor guy's been limping since they took all that blood," Jamie said.

"That's my hero."

Mauser chose that moment to get out of the pool and come over to rub his wet self against me. Then he shook himself vigorously, seeming to enjoy seeing us duck the shower of water that flew off of him.

"Thanks for that," I told him. "I'm stealing your van to chauffer your damsel in distress."

I filled Jamie in on how Cleo was doing, then headed for the clinic. When I got there, Cara was waiting with Cleo and a big bag full of dog food and medical supplies. Cleo looked like a very tired Frankenstein as she walked gingerly to the van. We eased her into the back and Cara got in beside her.

Cleo was more alert and interested when she got out of the van at our place. The woods and all of the animal smells made her forget for a moment that she was aching all over. She followed a couple of smells around the yard, dragging Cara behind her at the other end of her leash.

"She got some hero treatment this afternoon. A photographer from the *Tallahassee Democrat* came by first, then a crew from WCTV stopped in and did a spot with her," Cara told me.

"The media can't resist a good canine-to-the-rescue story. She'll be trending on Facebook any minute now. Okay, time to go meet the others."

Alvin and Ivy reacted exactly as I figured they would. Alvin thought that a sleepover with the Bride of the Monster was the greatest idea ever, while Ivy got up on the back of the couch and tried to shoot lasers out of her eyes.

"It's just for a day or two," I told Ivy, who wasn't buying any of it. When I reached out to pet her, she ran off to the bedroom in a huff. "Probably not going to be your biggest fan," I told Cleo, who was looking after Ivy with an amazed expression on her face.

"I hope this doesn't upset Ivy too much," Cara said guiltily, trying to keep Alvin from jumping up on Cleo.

"She'll be fine."

"Do you need to go back to work?"

I looked at my watch. It was already six-thirty. "I don't think so, but let me check in with Darlene."

"How's Faith?" I asked once I'd reached her.

"They've already moved her from ICU, so it was good that I went by. I was able to remind the staff on her new floor that she's under a security watch. Security came and put a portable digital lock on her door. Pretty cool, actually. The doctor I lassoed said that he thought she should be awake tomorrow. As far as brain damage goes, he said all the scans looked good, but the real test will come when she tries to communicate."

"We've got Cleo with us tonight."

"Good for you. I'm sure Faith will appreciate that."

Cara and I spent the rest of the evening watching the animals interact. Alvin reached a point where he just laid down as close to Cleo as he could and fell asleep, snoring loudly. Cleo was too tired to care about him, but she couldn't get comfortable in any one position and kept shifting. Meanwhile, Ivy stalked her and acted offended at anything anyone did the entire evening.

"I'm going to sleep out here with Cleo," Cara said. "She's going to be restless all night, and I need to keep an eye on her."

"We can take shifts," I said, hoping she would refuse the offer.

"No. You've had a couple rough nights already. Get out of here and get some sleep," she said with a smile.

Our morning routine was made a bit chaotic by the addition of Cleo. Alvin hadn't left Cleo's side all night and refused to be separated from her for breakfast, while Ivy pouted on a bookcase and refused to come down.

With everyone finally fed, Cara and Cleo dropped me off at Dad's so I could pick up my car. Dad came out with Mauser while we were in the driveway. Cleo looked down at Mauser from the window of the van like a queen looking down at a particularly scruffy peasant. For his part, Mauser was fascinated with the fawn Frankenstein.

Steam was rising off the pavement as Darlene and I drove toward Tallahassee to question Earl Higgins. According to the external temperature gauge, it was already eighty degrees at nine in the morning.

"What's the plan, Stan?" Darlene asked. "Good cop, bad cop?" She was in a great mood since I'd stopped at the Donut Hole and bought apple fritters and coffee before meeting her at the office.

"Since he's already lied to me about it, why don't you show him the shirt and ask him if he knows who it belongs to? He'll know when we show up that we suspect he's been lying. He'll either go angry or stupid."

"I hate it when they get all worked up and ask why we think they're lying. We think they're lying 'cause they're really bad at it."

"That's the perfect attitude to go in with," I told her with a grin.

"Good, because that's my default attitude."

Fifteen minutes out from Tallahassee, I called Earl. "My partner and I need to ask you a couple more questions."

"I guess. I just had breakfast and I have a call with my lawyer at eleven. I can come over there this afternoon."

"Actually, we have some business in Tallahassee. We can be at your motel in ten, fifteen minutes," I said.

"Well…"

"You said *your* lawyer?"

"Yes. I thought I might need my own representation. I'm not going to trust a lawyer that worked for my brother. I plan on having everything gone over by my own lawyer."

"Smart. We'll see you in ten," I said and hung up before he could argue with me.

Earl opened the door of his motel room before we had a chance to knock, a suspicious look on his face. "What can I help you with?" he said, backing away from the door and letting us into the room.

Darlene was carrying the T-shirt in a bag. She pulled it out and held it up. "Is this your son's T-shirt?" she said bluntly.

The expression on his face was one of confusion and frustration. It took him too long to come up with an answer, but finally he said, "I don't know."

"But you think it could be," I said.

"Maybe."

"Why didn't you tell me that yesterday?" I pushed him.

"Like I just said, I don't know for sure that it's his."

"Do you know where your son is?"

"No."

"Could he be here in Florida?"

"Obviously, if I don't know where he is then he could be anywhere." Earl's temper was close to the surface.

"Did your son get along with his uncle?" Darlene asked.

"As far as I know, he only met him a couple of times when he was a kid."

"When was that?"

"We came down to see my parents several times when Donnie was a toddler. Not that they cared. My brother was there sometimes. Then he came and visited us once. I guess Donnie was ten or eleven. That's all that I know about."

"When was the last time you saw or talked with your son?" I asked.

"Wait. What the hell right do you have to come in here and start asking questions about my son? I can damn sure tell you that he didn't kill Conrad. My son has problems, sure, but he's not a killer."

"We aren't accusing him of anything. But if he was staying at the house, then there's a possibility that he saw something, or he might have even been hurt himself. He might still be in danger," I said. I could tell by the puzzled expression on Earl's face that he hadn't considered that possibility.

"I don't know. I need to think about all this. Yes, I thought those were Donnie's clothes when I saw them. But I've been worried about him. I might just be jumping to conclusions. I haven't heard from him in four months. We had a big fight and he stormed out. My ex-wife blames me for the fight, but…" He looked lost. "… He… Donnie's never been like other kids. There's something… I shouldn't be talking to you about this. I can't. I've got to talk to his mother and my lawyer."

"Did you hear what he said? Your son could be in danger. Every second you delay could make a difference. What information does your wife or lawyer have that you don't? You need to step up and make the decision that your son's life is the most important thing on the table right now," Darlene said firmly, staring him down. "We need information to move forward. Do you really want to make us wait?"

He withered under her hard eyes and attitude. "A week after Donnie ran out, we reported him missing. I should say we *tried* to report him missing. The police told us he was an adult. On top of that, Donnie and I had had an argument, there were no signs of violence, and we couldn't give them any reason why he might be in imminent danger. I was so angry at their lack of interest." He paused and took a deep breath. "Now, here I am with two law enforcement officers who *want* to find my son, and I'm hesitating. Pretty ironic." He sat down on the bed and put his head in his hands.

"Look, if it helps, the only two crimes that we are investigating are the murder of your brother and the attack on Faith Osborne, which we believe are connected. I give you my word, if your son is involved in any crime that does not involve bodily injury to another person, or some major criminal operation, then I won't pursue it. In fact, if your son needs help, I'll go out of my way to see that he gets what he needs," I tried to assure Earl.

"I don't have that much information to give you. It's mostly speculation or conjecture on my part. I've never understood what motivates him. His mother has a much closer connection to him, but even she'd admit that there's something... distant about him. I was scared for years that he might be some kind of psychopath. I know how that sounds, but he just... didn't relate to us, or maybe we didn't relate to him. I watched him. I made sure that he never mistreated animals. Obsessively checked to see that he wasn't playing with matches or fascinated with torture porn. It reached a point where I thought that I was the crazy one." He stopped and finally looked up at us.

"Some children just don't form strong bonds," Darlene said.

"Yes, and that's the conclusion I came to. When I thought about who his grandparents and uncle were, it made sense. Every time he did something wrong, I felt like it was my genes that made him the way he is."

"You're a smart man. You know it isn't that simple," Darlene said.

"Regardless, it's what goes through my mind every time."

"Do you have a cell phone number for him?" I asked.

"I do. But it hasn't been used since he took off. I was able to check the records since we pay for it." I took the number anyway.

"What about girlfriends, boyfriends, anyone that he might have contacted?" Darlene asked.

"Donnie had a good friend from high school, but they had a falling out. As for girlfriends, he went out a few times. He wasn't good at dating. I assumed that the girls saw the same thing I did. That detachment. But what the hell do I know? Looking back, I think I was way too judgmental."

"Do you know what caused the break with his friend?" I asked.

"He said his friend got into drugs and took money from him." Earl shrugged. "I don't know if that's true or not. Donnie certainly had his own issues with the law a few years ago, but he does hate drugs. He doesn't even drink. That's the other side of his personality. He wants to be in control. Anything that makes him feel out of control freaks him out. We went to a theme park when he was a kid and he couldn't stand being strapped into a roller coaster. He didn't mind the ride, but it was being restrained that drove him crazy."

We talked a little more, but Earl didn't have much to add.

"One more thing," I said, pulling a flash drive from my pocket and walking over to the TV. After a little fiddling, we figured out how to play the video. I wanted Earl to watch the bank surveillance video. I thought there was a good chance that the person with Conrad Higgins could be his nephew. Earl watched the video closely and had me replay the little bit of footage where it was possible to see the figure moving.

"I just don't know. If I could see a bit of his face, then I might be able to say… or if there was more footage of him walking. This little bit…" He sighed. "I can't say one way or the other."

We thanked him and told him we'd be in touch.

CHAPTER ELEVEN

Darlene and I went to the hospital next. Faith was awake and was able to communicate via a keyboard and screen.

"She doesn't seem to have suffered any brain damage. Not quite a miracle, but she was lucky. Real lucky," Dr. Abramson told us.

Faith opened her eyes and smiled when she saw us. She was lying in bed, connected to an IV and feeding tube. Her neck was a purplish yellow and swollen. The doctor had told us that their main priority now was to get the swelling down.

"Do you remember me?" I asked.

"*Yes,*" she typed.

"Did you see who attacked you?" I didn't see any reason to beat around the bush.

"*No,*" was her disappointing answer.

"Do you have any idea who might want to hurt you?"

She shook her head, then she typed, "*Is Cleo ok?*"

"She's fine. My girlfriend is Cara Laursen from the vet's office. We're taking care of her."

"*Thank you! Thank you,*" she typed.

"What can you remember from the night of the attack?"

"*I was in the den when I thought I heard something.*" She was a good typist, but pain and lying in a hospital bed made it hard for her. Darlene and I waited patiently as she composed her thoughts. "*Came into the hall and didn't see anyone when I turned to go back was shoved and something went around my neck. Whoever it was was able to close the den door while they had me down on the ground. Knee in my back and something around my neck. I could hear Cleo scratching against the door and barking while I tried to turn over. I blacked out. Don't remember anything else.*"

Not good news, but then I hadn't expected much. "Did you see a shoe or his hand, maybe?"

She shook her head again.

"Could it have been a woman?"

"*Don't think so,*" she typed.

I didn't think it likely either. Faith was a good-sized woman. It would have taken a woman with exceptional body strength to have attacked and subdued her. But I didn't want to rule anything out until I had concrete evidence.

I asked her to review her whole day leading up to the attack, just in case she had seen or noticed anything odd. She responded that the day had been normal and she hadn't noticed anyone out of the ordinary. I showed her a picture of Donnie Higgins and asked if she'd ever seen him. Her answer was no. After a few more questions, it was clear that she was getting tired and wouldn't be able to go on much longer. We thanked her, and I promised to text her some pictures of Cleo.

I turned to Darlene when we crossed the Adams County line.

"Let's go back and talk to the neighbors. Particularly Jason Harmon. I think it's time we ask him why he didn't mention that Higgins had him arrested for assault."

"Sounds like a plan… We can re-canvass some of the other neighbors and see if any of them recognize Donnie boy."

I called Harmon and he agreed to meet us at his house. He was waiting at the door when we got there.

"What can I do for you all?" he said with a smile, ushering us into the house. "I got the air conditioning fixed.

Had to. If the wife got home and it was still broken, I'd be in the old dog house for sure."

"We just have a few more questions for you," I said after introducing Darlene.

"Sure," he said, all open posture and smiles, though he didn't invite us to sit down.

"First, why didn't you tell me that Higgins had pressed charges against you for assault?"

Bam! He crossed his arms, closing up like a panicked clam. "Oh, that," he said in what I took to be a bid for time to think.

"Yes, that. You led me to believe that you all had had a minor misunderstanding. In reality, he had you handcuffed and taken to jail. That sounds like a big deal to me," I said, leaning into his personal space.

While I was confronting him, Darlene was slowly looking around his living room. Harmon was having a hard time focusing on my questions while watching Darlene. A classic way to make a suspect slip up and say something they don't intend to.

"Yes, I guess it was a big deal. I should have said something, but it didn't seem important at the time. I mean, I didn't kill Higgins." He was looking very nervous.

"But you didn't like him, did you?"

"No. You're right. He was an ass."

"So why were you concerned about his welfare?"

"I don't know… I just heard a noise and went to see… if…"

"To see what? To see if someone you hated was hurt? What were you going to do, finish him off if he wasn't dead?" Darlene said from across the room, causing Harmon to shift his focus from me to her.

"That's ridiculous! I wasn't even thinking about him. I just heard a noise and went to see what was going on. I was just curious," he finished lamely.

"Okay, let's pretend that makes sense. What did you really think when you saw Higgins lying on the floor with a hole in his head?" Darlene asked.

"I think I want to speak to my lawyer," Harmon said flatly.

"Wow. That sure sounds like a guy who doesn't like our questions. But I don't think the questions are the problem. I suspect that it's the answer that has you spooked," Darlene said, now staring straight at Harmon. The man looked like he was thinking about running.

"Get out," he managed to squeak. Then he continued more strongly, "Get out now. This is over."

He marched over to the door and held it open for us. Darlene and I took our time walking out.

"Let me know what your lawyer advises you to do," I said as I left.

Harmon didn't say a word as he locked the door.

"What do you think?" I asked Darlene as we stood on the sidewalk.

"Hard to say. He's shaken up, no doubt about that. But I'd guess that lawyering up comes pretty naturally to him."

"Agreed. He might just realize how bad his position looks. A man with a grudge finds his enemy dead. The weapon on the floor. Who's to say he *didn't* shoot Higgins?"

"No matter what we think of him, he has to go to the top of the list now. He's the only witness that places anyone else at the scene."

"We probably should have gotten a few more statements on record before we forced him into the corner," I said.

She shrugged. "You never know which is the best approach. We might have come on strong and had him break down completely."

"Since he was arrested, we'll have his fingerprints for comparison. Be interesting if we find his prints inside Higgins's house."

"He's got an excuse for any that were found between the door and the body," Darlene pointed out.

"Still gives us an opening. He never said he touched anything in the house. I'll have Marcus pull his prints for comparison."

We went ahead and knocked on doors in the neighborhood, trying to find someone who might have seen Donnie and Higgins together. But it was a no-go. Everyone was used to seeing strangers at Higgins's house buying and selling stuff, so they'd learned to ignore the comings and goings as best they could. Added to that was the fact that most of them didn't like Higgins, so they really didn't want to get into any conversations with him. The afternoon was a waste of time, good only for eliminating possibilities.

I got home at a decent hour to find Cleo and Cara in the kitchen.

"I couldn't leave her at the clinic all weekend," she explained.

"It's okay. You don't have to work tomorrow?"

"No. What about you?"

"Right now, we're at an impasse. We have a vague description of a person fleeing the scene from both crimes. That's not going to get us much. Next we have Donnie Higgins, who may or may not even be in the area. We don't have a single eyewitness who's seen him. As far as the rest of the investigation goes, we have about a million pieces of forensic evidence sitting in boxes at various labs. And finding the car didn't help at all." I felt deflated after saying it all out loud.

"Then what I'm hearing is that you need a break," Cara said, wrapping her arms around my waist.

"Yes… You could put it that way." There really was no point in dwelling on the case when there weren't any new leads to follow.

"Why don't we get up in the morning before it gets too hot and take the puppies for a decent walk in the woods?"

"Is the patient up to it?" I asked as Cleo tried to push herself between us. I'd noticed that she and Mauser had one thing in common—they both wanted to be the center of attention.

"She could use the exercise. We'll keep it slow and easy. Maybe afterward, we'll drive into town and get them ice cream," she said, massaging Cleo's ears. Alvin jumped up on Cara's shins. "And look who's having an attack of the little green monster," she chuckled, bending down to scratch the Pug.

We got up early Saturday morning and headed into the woods. My twenty acres backed up to a neighbor's eighty acres that we had permission to hike through. The woods were a mix of oak and longleaf pine habitat that my neighbor had been working to restore. At one time, the entire southeastern United States had been covered in longleaf pine forest. Similar to a rainforest, the tops of the pines formed a canopy that still allowed light to reach the ground, encouraging a rich undergrowth that provided habitat for hundreds of species.

As we left my property and entered the forest, we were careful to stay on the path and not wander into the wiregrass that was home to millions of chiggers this time of year. You only needed to suffer from their itchy bites once or twice before learning to avoid them.

"So if Higgins was such a conman, how come he was never arrested?" Cara asked as we watched the dogs sniffing the ground at the end of their leashes.

"Several reasons. First, he never did anything overtly illegal. He made deals that bordered on fraud, but could also be interpreted in other ways that bring to mind the phrase *caveat emptor*."

"Sounds like some of what he did crossed that line."

"I'm sure it did. But our State Attorneys have their hands full with so much violent crime. Higgins's crimes were strictly the white-collar variety. Even with a conviction, a prosecutor wouldn't have been able to put him behind bars for more than a year or two, tops. And with a good lawyer, he would have fought it every step of the way. There'd be any number of postponements and filings that would have the prosecutor wrapped up for months with a case that didn't involve any blood being spilled. And even if the case made it to court, the prosecutor would be stuck trying to explain financial details that would be tough for the average jury to wrap their heads around. Bottom line, it would be a lot of time and money spent pursuing a case that wouldn't have any political pay off."

"I guess if you can say you sent an ax-murderer to jail for the rest of his life, then you'll get more press than if you send some guy to jail for a year because he defrauded someone."

"Exactly. And in court, the folks who got defrauded are often made to look greedy or stupid by the defense."

"Doesn't seem right."

"The civil courts are better designed to deal with it. The problem there is that you've got to get the victims to spend good money after bad, without much hope of recouping any of it."

"So how do you put conmen in jail?"

"Hope they use the mail or cross state lines. If they do that, then it becomes a federal crime and the penalties go up considerably. Plus, you have the FBI helping with the prosecution."

"I guess Higgins was too smart for that?"

"Looks like it. He did most of his cons in person. And they mostly involved selling items that were worth less than he led the mark to believe. That's borderline in anyone's book. But when you look at exactly how he was doing it, there's not much doubt it was criminal. Of course, he also bought items for a lot less than they were worth."

"Like when he was trolling the nursing home."

"Yep. Unfortunately, that's not really illegal. If someone gives you a bargain on an antique, then that's your good fortune. Maybe if you use excessive influence or coercion…"

"But morally…"

"If you're taking advantage of someone who can't afford the loss, yes, it's morally reprehensible. But I don't think those nuances bothered Higgins," I said as Cleo pulled me over to an Adam's Needle plant, sniffing loudly. "You'll poke your nose," I told her, just as she jumped back with a small drop of blood on her nose. "I warned you." She looked from me to the plant, then left a wiser dog.

By the time we finished our walk, the heat was becoming oppressive. Cara and I were dripping sweat while Alvin and Cleo were panting steadily.

"Okay, kids, back to the air conditioning," Cara said, holding the door for them. Both were sound asleep on the floor by the time we fixed ourselves French toast for brunch.

"What now?" Cara asked, snuggling up to me on the couch after our meal.

"No agenda," I said, then heard a truck pull up outside. "Who could that be?" I said with narrowed eyes, though I had a pretty good idea. With the gate closed across the driveway, there were only a few people who would consider coming over without calling first.

Sure enough, it was Dad and Genie.

"I wanted to see the patient," Genie said. "I told your dad to call first," she added, rolling her eyes at him.

"Wow!" Dad said, leaning down and carefully petting Cleo, who'd gotten up to see who the guests were. "That window sure did a number on you."

"Be gentle with her, she isn't your moose," I told Dad, who glared at me for suggesting that he wouldn't be careful. Cleo was sniffing him up and down, no doubt smelling Mauser on his clothes.

"How's Faith doing?" he asked.

"Stable." I explained that she hadn't seen her attacker.

"Figures. It's curious that the person who killed Higgins would also go after her," he said.

"I know. The fact that there isn't an obvious link suggests to me that if we *find* a link, it'll tell us a lot about the killer."

Dad looked at me and nodded. "Do any of your suspects

link up with both of them?"

"Darlene and I are working on that. Though if there is, I'm not sure what it could be, other than the fact that they lived in the same neighborhood and had a contentious history. But that's true of most of Higgins's neighbors."

"Could Faith have seen something and not known it?" he suggested.

"Possibly. I'm going to have to wait until she's in better shape before I interview her again."

That evening, I got a call from Darlene. "I need a favor," she said.

"Sure," I said without thinking.

"Would you take my on-call shift tomorrow night?" she asked, surprising me.

"Are you okay?" I said, genuinely concerned. Darlene never took time off. When I'd been Pete's partner, he had constantly asked me to trade shifts so that he could spend time with his family. Darlene didn't have things just come up. Her life was a well-oiled machine.

"I'm great. I just... got something tomorrow evening."

"Is your family okay?" I knew her family lived down in Tampa. "If you need a few days off, I'm sure Dad—"

"It's nothing like that. I just need to switch shifts." She sounded a bit evasive, causing my curiosity gene to activate.

"So it's not an illness and it's not a family matter. But you don't want to tell me what you need the time off for. Interesting."

"Look, if you can't do it, I'll just call Pete."

"Oh, I can do it. I just want to know a little more about why you need the time off. And as for calling Pete, I wouldn't bother. You know he's probably already lined up his Sunday family funday. Beer, steaks and time with his girls."

"Have I ever asked you to take a weekend shift for me?"

"No, and that's why I'm curious why you're asking now."

Then an odd thought popped into my head.

"Just yes or no," she said, sounding mildly irritated.

"Ooohh, you have a date!" I said, voicing the idea that had just occurred. There was dead silence from the other end of the phone. "Don't you try and lie to me."

"I don't know what you're talking about," she finally said.

"Would you be willing to take a lie detector test?" I asked innocently and got more silence. "Come on, who is it?" I said, changing tactics.

"If you must know, it's Hondo."

"Hondo, the EMT?"

"How many Hondos do you know?"

"Wow, interesting match. Not sure how two workaholics are going to find time for each other."

"Slow down, cowboy. This is one date. And the way I'm finding time for it is by asking my partner to cover my shift."

"Point taken. I've got your six. Go off and have a night of romance."

"Cap it, cupcake," she said, but added, "Thanks."

On Sunday morning, I got a call from Bernadette Santos, the artistic director at the local theatre and Faith's friend, who I'd run into the morning after the Higgins murder.

"I went to see Faith. It's awful! I can't believe anyone would do something like that to her. Anyway, she said that you were looking after Cleo and asked me to check on her. I babysit Her Highness when Faith goes out of town."

I told her we'd be around until ten, and she showed up almost immediately.

"Ah, the poor baby," she said, giving Cleo a gentle hug. Cleo was excited to see a familiar face and leaned into the woman, soaking in all of her sympathy and soothing words.

"She's obviously happy to see you," Cara said.

"We're good friends. Aren't we, girl?" she said to Cleo, who looked up at her with happy eyes. "But I bet you miss your mommy. She's going to be fine," Bernadette reassured the dog, pulling a treat out of her bag and giving it to her. Cleo gently accepted the biscuit and calmly chewed it up without taking her eyes off of her old friend.

"You'd hardly think that Cleo and Mauser are the same breed," I said, thinking of the ravenous way Mauser gobbled down anything that remotely looked like food.

"Oh, that's right, you're the sheriff's son. I ran into your dad and that big fellow at the ice cream shop a couple of months ago. He's a big, gruff male," she said, and for a moment I wondered if she was talking about Dad or Mauser. "Not a refined lady like you," she said to Cleo, who stretched as though to show off her more elegant and sophisticated physique and manner.

After some more praise for the Queen of the Nile, Bernadette headed out the door, offering to watch Cleo until Faith was fully recovered. As she left, I caught a look from Cara that I didn't like.

"You aren't getting too attached to Cleo, are you?" I asked.

Cleo had backed up to sit on Cara's lap. "No," she said, stroking Cleo and not meeting my eyes. "I know she's Faith's dog," she said, sounding rather unhappy about that particular reality.

"Cara," I said gently. I couldn't really blame her. Even with all the stitches, Cleo was a beautiful dog and had a loving and attentive nature that was endearing.

"I know it's stupid. I'm fine," she said, gently dislodging Cleo and standing up. "Let's go."

We'd planned to spend the day at Blue Cave Springs, Adams County's favorite swimming hole. Blue Cave was smaller than a lot of Florida's freshwater springs, but it had all of the standard features, including a sandy beach and fifty-thousand gallons a day of cool spring water pouring up from a hole sixty feet deep. Every kid who grew up in Adams County spent much of the humid summer months plunging into the seventy-two-degree water that felt like ice.

We brought masks, snorkels and fins and enjoyed

dodging kids and free-diving twenty feet down to watch the bluegill, gar and bass swim through the grasses that lined the side of the spring. I couldn't help but feel a little chill that wasn't caused by the water when I looked into the cave entrance. Blue Cave wasn't as dangerous as some of the state's more infamous springs, but I knew that Dad had overseen the recovery of the bodies of at least three divers during his time as sheriff.

We took a break from swimming to sit on a blanket in the sun, warming ourselves and eating hot dogs and chips from the concession stand.

"Happy and carefree," I said, watching a group of kids run in and out of the water, laughing and shouting at each other. "I can vaguely remember those days."

"You don't fool me. You've been a worrier all your life," Cara joked, closing her eyes and lying back on the blanket.

"You got me," I said, turning toward her. Even with her hair hanging in damp red tangles and her fair skin covered in sunscreen, she was beautiful. I was still amazed that someone so smart and compassionate could love me. And as though to prove her point, a small voice in the dark corners of my mind asked what I would do if I ever lost her. I cursed the voice and reached for her hand, which closed around mine as if it was meant to fit there.

"I kind of love you," I said softly.

Cara opened one blue eye and a smile spread across her face. "Of course you do."

"Hey!" I said, pretending to be offended at her assumption.

"Okay, maybe I like you a little bit too. Though that guy over there is pretty good looking."

I followed her gaze to a young man who looked like he could have played football for any college in the country. "Right. You wouldn't last a day with a guy like that. He probably can't add two and two."

"I wasn't planning to ask him to tutor me in math," she said, trying to control her laughter.

"You're bad! For that, it's back in the water."

"Didn't you ever hear of waiting two hours after eating?"

"That's an old wives' tale," I said, pulling her up from the blanket.

Hand in hand, we waded back into the cool, clear water, feeling the icy tentacles crawl up our legs until we plunged into the spring and swam out to deeper water. For a while, I almost forgot that I had agreed to take Darlene's shift. As we drove home, I hoped that this would be a quiet night for Adams County's criminal element.

CHAPTER TWELVE

Cara and I had time to walk the dogs, clean up and have a light dinner before my phone rang. I sighed when I saw that it was Julio. I'd officially been on call for only forty-five minutes.

"I think you'll want to come in for this," Julio said. "A guy tried to steal a woman's purse at the Supersave."

"That's a little below my pay grade. Isn't one of the robbery guys on call too?"

"Yeah, yeah, but I think this might be your murder suspect," Julio said. We'd kept him up to date with the investigation. "I looked at some of the store video and I can't be sure. There's never a clear image of his face. But the victim said she'd be willing to look at a photo line-up."

"I'm on my way."

The sun was going down as I pulled into the Supersave lot and parked next to Julio's patrol car. He was typing a report.

"Last sentence," he said, holding up a finger, then finishing the report.

As we walked toward the store, he filled me in on the incident.

"The lady was shopping with her purse in the little spot

in the cart where kids sit. She was looking for some spices and, when she turned around, the man was reaching into her purse. He snatched her keys, but she was quick. She pushed the cart into him and started yelling. He ran away and tossed the keys at her."

"She get a good look at his face?"

"Quick, just a quick look. But she says she can remember it."

"Tapes first."

"I had the manager save it."

Inside, we watched the black-and-white security video. The image was clear enough, but the camera was mounted in the corner of the ceiling and the angle showed the tops of heads more than faces. The key-snatcher was wearing a hoodie. *Don't they all*, I thought. He looked young and about the right size to be Donnie Higgins, but he also could have been any one of a number of local drug addicts. Though if he'd been a drug addict or a common thief, I would have expected him to go for her wallet and not the keys to her car. Was Donnie trying to get a vehicle in order to get out of town?

"She's going to meet us at the office in ten minutes," Julio said as he finished a call with the victim.

Tania Lynch was a middle-aged woman who looked like she'd seen better years. She gave me a small smile as I introduced myself.

"I'm impressed with the attention you're giving this. I had a suitcase stolen in Orlando two years ago and never saw a police officer, let alone a detective. I guess that's the advantage of a small town," she said after we had sat down in our small conference room. The building was quiet on a Sunday night.

"I appreciate you coming in." Before I could say anything else, dispatch radioed for Julio and sent him out on another call. He muttered something in Spanish and excused himself.

"I'm going to show you six pictures. If one of them is the man who tried to take your keys, just tell me the number."

I'd turned on the cameras in the room so I'd have a record of the interview, just in case. I pulled up the photos on my laptop and turned it around so Tania could see it.

"They all look similar," she said thoughtfully.

We had a great program for photo line-ups. All we had to do was import a photo of the suspect and the program would pull five more photos from a database of over ten thousand images to create the line-up.

Tania mused over the photos for another minute before saying, "Five. I'm pretty sure that's him."

"Are you sure that's him?" I asked.

She had picked Donnie's North Carolina DMV photo.

"Yep. I mean, it would be better if it was a full-body picture, but yeah, that's his face," she said firmly.

"Did he say anything?"

"No."

"What was his expression?"

"You mean, like, was he angry or something?"

"Exactly."

"I guess he looked scared. I think that's why I had the nerve to roll the cart at him and yell. And he ran like a person who was scared, if that makes any sense."

"Had you seen him before? Maybe out in the parking lot?"

"I didn't see him, but that doesn't mean he wasn't there. I was pretty focused on getting in and out of the grocery. My boys—I've got four teenage sons— were home alone this morning and managed to eat everything in the house while they were playing video games. They eat like horses. Two gallons of milk were in the refrigerator before I went to church this morning. I come home at two and there's not a drop left." She was on a tear and it took me standing up and thanking her to stop the tirade.

It was dark, but the air was still hot and humid as I walked her to her car. After watching her drive off, I sat in my car and thought about this new information. If Donnie was still in the county and didn't have access to money or a car, then the odds were good that he'd find his way to the seedier areas of town.

I called Eddie. "Want to earn a little spending money?" I asked, already knowing the answer.

"What've I got to do?" he asked suspiciously.

"I need some eyes and ears in your old stomping grounds."

"Wow, I don't know. My sobriety…" he said and I felt a little guilty. He appeared to be genuinely conflicted.

"I'm headed your way. We can talk about it," I said and started the car.

I pulled in the driveway of Albert Griffin's house. I was planning to head around back to Eddie's garage apartment, but I saw Mr. Griffin looking out the window. I waved and headed for the front door. He was standing on the front porch when I got there.

"Eddie's in the kitchen," Mr. Griffin said without his usual good humor. "I want to talk to you first." His eyes were locked on mine.

"What's on your mind?" I asked, puzzled.

"He said that you want him to do some undercover work in some of his old haunts."

"That's right. We're looking for a young guy I think might be hanging out in some of the darker corners of the county." I was a little pissed off that Eddie had shared the reason for my visit, though I hadn't asked him to keep it on the down low.

"You know he could fall off the wagon hanging out with his old drug buddies." It was a statement and not a question. I'd never seen Albert Griffin so serious, almost angry.

"He could decide to get high sitting in his apartment," I said with more attitude than was warranted.

"Don't play ignorant. You know the chances of him taking something will be a lot higher if he goes back to his old friends."

"And I think that's a choice he can make. Eddie can tell me no if he wants to."

"Not likely. He wants to help you. Eddie appreciates what you've done for him in the past and feels like he owes you."

"We've both gotten something out of our partnership." The truth was, Eddie had saved my life on more than one occasion. "I'll tell him that he doesn't owe me anything," I said and tried to walk around Mr. Griffin, but he stepped between me and the door. "Really?"

"You don't want to do this," he told me.

"Mr. Griffin, I like you, and you've helped me out in the past, but this is between Eddie and me. Honestly, I don't see where it's any of your business," I said firmly.

"I'm an alcoholic," he said bluntly.

"I've never heard you talk about AA," I said rather stupidly, though I knew that not all alcoholics got sober using the twelve-step program.

"I was one of the lucky ones who managed to get myself clean. But it took years. Failed relationships. Other problems. Run my record sometime if you don't believe me. Your father even took me to jail one time in 1986 for drunk and disorderly. That was the one that almost cost me my job. I hit your father hard enough to raise a welt on his cheek. If he'd charged me for assault on an officer, I'd have been out of a job and come out the other side with a felony conviction on my record."

"I'm glad that you came through it okay. Look, Eddie's going to be fine. I just need him to talk to some of his old friends and let me know if the guy I'm looking for is lurking about."

"You don't know what it's like to try and be around the people from your drunk life when you're sober."

"I'll give you that. Okay, I'll promise you that I will monitor Eddie closely. If it looks like he's going to backslide, I'll make him drop it." Mr. Griffin didn't look convinced. "I swear," I added and saw him wavering. "People's lives are on the line. A man's been murdered and someone tried to kill Faith Osborne. This isn't just some whim of mine to get an arrest. More people might die if we don't stop this guy, and I don't have a better way to check out the seedier parts of town than using Eddie. If I go in there, I'll just spook everyone and the suspect will disappear."

Mr. Griffin finally stepped aside, but he kept his eyes on me as I reached for the doorknob.

I found Eddie in the kitchen, eating cereal and talking to Brutus, who was licking milk from a saucer.

"Hey, boss," Eddie said. He looked good. Better than I'd ever seen him. I had to push away the guilt that Mr. Griffin had dropped on me.

"Eddie, you know you don't have to do this if you don't want to," I told him.

"I can handle it. I've been feeling a little guilty for ignoring Ella. She's sunk pretty low. But I just haven't felt like I could deal with it. You know what I mean?" I thought of the last time I'd seen his old girlfriend and could understand Eddie's hesitation. She'd been a mess, high and looking to stay that way.

"I'm only a phone call away. You sure that your family isn't still gunning for you?"

"There are a couple I wouldn't want to meet in a dark alley, but I'm pretty sure they've done a runner. I'm good."

"You will have to keep away from whatever it is that addicts take these days, even though everyone else is doing it," Mr. Griffin said from behind us. He'd come into the kitchen as quietly as one of his cats.

"Everyone's going to be high or drunk. They won't have eyes for me. Rule one, the addict doesn't care about anyone but himself," Eddie said. "Besides, Seth told me a trick that he learned from another alcoholic. This guy got sober, but he had to continue being a bartender. What he did was put a little dab of Vick's VapoRub under his nose when he was working. He said if he couldn't smell the bar or the booze, then it didn't bother him. So I got to get some Vick's."

"I've got some in the car. We use it when the smells are really bad." Not just bodies either. I'd been in a house where a dog hoarder had kept two dozen dogs. The vapor rub had just managed to cut the smell enough that it was possible to stand being in the house.

"So I'm ready," Eddie said eagerly. I wondered if life with Mr. Griffin wasn't getting a little boring for him.

"Okay, here's who you're looking for," I said, pulling out my phone and sitting down across from Eddie. "His real name is Donnie Higgins, but who knows what he's going by. He sports the classic hoodie look." I texted the photo to Eddie.

"I guess I can get started. Can you drop me off on North Jefferson?" Eddie stood up and I could just see a little bit of a bra strap showing underneath his shirt. I shook my head, wondering if Mr. Griffin was right.

"Let's go," I said, suddenly less enthusiastic than when I'd thought up the plan.

Mr. Griffin gave Eddie a hug like he was sending him off to war. "I'm here if you need me," he said. Honestly, I thought he was being a bit melodramatic, but I was touched by the bond that had developed between the two odd ducks.

I dropped Eddie off about a mile from the low-rent district that I thought would be the most likely hidey-hole for Donnie. The area had large lots with mostly low-rent trailers and run-down houses that catered to people who couldn't afford anything better. New people were always moving in and out of the neighborhood, so no one took notice of a stranger. With pop-up drug dens and dealers hanging out, it was a great place to find stolen goods and illegal substances of all different flavors.

The area generated more calls for service from the sheriff's office than any other neighborhood in the county, but it had an effective informal alert system that still made it a great place to hide from law enforcement. If a patrol car, marked or unmarked, drove into the area, somehow every bad guy and gal knew to dive for the nearest cover and wasn't seen again until the LEO drove away. That was why I needed Eddie to scout out the community.

It would take him a while to mingle with the local wildlife, so I decided to head home for a snack. It might be a long night.

"I was about ready to give up on you," Cara said, looking painfully good in a long T-shirt and not much else.

"You shouldn't dress like that when I can't stay," I said sadly.

"Talk like that will get you a sandwich made with some homemade bread from Mom."

"Your parents are a bit... odd, but I've got to admit that getting the occasional care package from your mother has its benefits."

"It's a little freaky to watch her take raw ingredients and turn them into real food. I've seen her go out in the morning, collect whatever she could find growing within a mile of our house, come home, clean whatever Dad had hunted, and make a meal that was so good it would shame the best restaurants in the world. But you're right. They're a bit odd."

She spread mayonnaise and mustard on half-inch-thick pieces of brown bread before adding a couple slices of cheese that had also come in the care package from their little co-op down in Gainesville.

"From cows that the neighbors milked. Mom said that they still drop some of this off especially for you. No one's forgotten that you saved them from a murderer in their midst."

"All in a day's work," I said, not even trying to sound modest. Cara rolled her eyes. I felt a nudge at my elbow as Cleo let me know that she wouldn't mind a little bit of my sandwich.

"Down that road lies madness," I told the dog. "You don't want to become an unsophisticated lout like your cousin Mauser, do you?"

She softened her eyes, trying to entice a treat out of me.

"I've got her," Cara said, bringing over a dog treat. "He's right. You shouldn't get food from the table." Cleo looked from Cara to me before taking the treat and walking off.

As I chewed my sandwich, my phone pinged with a text from Eddie: *He's been in the area. Trying to find him now.*

Go, Eddie, go, I thought, finishing my snack.

Not a second later, dispatch called with a stabbing at the Fast Mart.

"Uggg! I have to go," I said and grabbed a quick kiss from Cara before I headed out the door.

CHAPTER THIRTEEN

An hour later, I'd finished interviewing the clerk who'd been stabbed. A drug addict had come into the store and tried to do a grab-and-go from the beer cooler. The clerk had tackled him, but the man had pulled out a knife and stabbed him. Luckily for the clerk, he'd turned to the side and the knife had skidded off one of his ribs; otherwise, he could have been seriously injured or even killed. The suspect had dropped the knife and run off.

"We got him!" Sergeant Will Toomey said, coming up behind me as I watched the ambulance leave for the hospital so the clerk could be stitched up. "Martel chased him down. That Martel doesn't talk much, but when he runs it looks like he's flying. That meth head didn't stand a chance. Martel's going to book him into jail for resisting."

"Perfect. We'll let the State Attorney decide on the rest of the charges tomorrow. If you all aren't too busy, I'm going to let Sanderson take over and run with this one."

"Except for this and some domestic crap, we're pretty quiet tonight. It'll be good for her to get a taste of the paperwork involved in a real case," Toomey said. He was a tough but fair supervisor who was always willing to help a hard-working deputy start moving up the ladder. Years ago he'd moved into CID for about a month before requesting to go back on the street. He didn't like riding a desk, but was always willing to let others give it a try.

As for Deputy Matti Sanderson, she was tough and good at her job, but you could see the gleam in her eye that said she wanted more. She'd caught this call so it was only fair that, if I was going to let a patrol officer take the lead, she should be the one.

"You want to do all the paperwork on this one?" I asked her.

"What, like an investigator?" She seemed surprised.

"Of course, Lt. Johnson will have the final say, but I don't think he'll mind you doing all the heavy lifting."

"Are the other deputies going to think I'm brown-nosing?" I could tell she was excited about doing a deep dive on the case.

"Nope, they're just going to think you're another poor sod who's been conned into doing higher pay-grade work without the higher pay," I joked.

"You're giving this to me 'cause it's idiot proof, right?"

"Trust me, there are plenty of idiots that could screw it up. But, admittedly, this is a training-wheels case. You got the perp. You got video. He's not going to be able to hire a real lawyer. The guy's going down. But having said that, it's a chance to show that you can put a solid packet of paperwork together for the State Attorney."

"I wouldn't mind giving CID a chance someday."

"We'll see what you think the fifth time someone from the prosecutor's office calls asking for the report you sent them the first time they asked for it."

I left her to supervise the rest of the forensic work and to follow up on interviewing potential witnesses while I headed to the office. I didn't want to take the chance of Eddie getting a lead on Donnie and me not being close at hand. Plus, I didn't want to disturb Cara and the animals, especially if I was just going to have to go back out again.

I caught a half hour nap on the couch in the reception

area before I got a text from Eddie.

Found him, it said.

I was heading for the door when I realized that I didn't know exactly where Eddie was. I stopped and texted him back. He responded that he'd meet me at a spot about two blocks outside the neighborhood.

I got there before he did. Five minutes later, Eddie walked up to my car.

"I got his picture." He showed me an image on his phone that was too small and too dark to be sure that it was Donnie.

"It's him. He was bumming cigarettes and drinks from the small group that was hanging at the fire pit. Everyone was calling him Tom." I wasn't surprised that he was using an alias.

"But there's something wrong with him," Eddie said, shaking his head.

"What do you mean?"

"He mumbles to himself a lot. Gives people these weird stares. If everyone hadn't been so high, they would have kicked him out."

"Was he out of his head from drugs?"

"No. He was just out of his head," Eddie said with conviction. The more I thought about it, the less surprised I was. Donnie was at the right age for symptoms of paranoid schizophrenia to start bubbling to the surface.

I got an old pair of cargo pants, a ball cap and a T-shirt out of the trunk and changed clothes.

"You better dirty yourself up a little," Eddie said with a critical eye for drug-addict chic. I rubbed some dirt on my hands and clothes until my personal cleanliness, or lack thereof, met with his approval. I also grabbed a couple of pairs of flex cuffs, some tape and my radio, which I was careful to turn off.

The walk was made easier by a full moon. Out here, there weren't any streetlights, and I didn't want to use the flashlight I'd brought along. My plan was to find Donnie and get him to a secluded area where I could subdue him before calling for backup.

Of course, he was no longer at the house where Eddie had left him, so we had to drift around until we found another house where a small party was going on. "Party" didn't seem like quite the right word. It mostly involved small groups of addicts huddled around each other, trying to figure out ways to con each other out of whatever the other person had. We crept around the inside of the house, trying to look for Donnie while remaining inconspicuous. The electricity was off and the house stank like a sewer. I worked hard at not touching anything.

"He's not here," I muttered to Eddie.

"Maybe out back," he said as we made our way through the kitchen, where someone was splayed out on the floor with a needle in his arm. I made a note to check with our vice squad whether we could do some targeted raids on the area, though the drug war is really nothing more than a giant game of Whac-A-Mole played out in human suffering.

There was a small group sitting around a fire in the backyard. It was almost a full acre, with an old singlewide trailer and a couple of rusting trucks lying around. I counted six people near the fire and wondered how many more were lurking in the shadows.

"Hang here by the door. If you see things going south, call for help," I told Eddie.

"Are you sure?"

"Success to the brave," I said, picking up a beer bottle from a stack by the back door.

I walked toward the group by the fire, trying not to look too focused. The fire was small, meant more for light and to keep the mosquitoes at bay than for heat. The closer I got, the less I liked the looks of the group. There were two females and four males. The guy on the end had his hoodie up over his head and was swaying a little on the stump he was sitting on. Every once in a while, one of the other people would toss something at him and they'd all laugh. All except for the girl sitting next to the biggest guy. She just stared into the fire and shook herself every couple of seconds. She was small, maybe five feet, and the man next to her kept pulling her against him possessively.

A couple of people looked up at me when I joined them. I had my hat pulled down and kept my eyes on the fire or the beer in my hand. Knowing they were watching, I raised the bottle to my lips and tried not to cringe as I pretended to drink from it. I'd shaken it out when I picked it up, but still something wet touched my clenched lips and I hoped that this wasn't a prelude to a trip to the doctor.

"You holding?" the big man asked me. He had an unkempt beard that covered most of his face, but I could still see the gaps where teeth should have been.

"Shit, no."

"Hell, son, this group is for sharing. You ain't got nothin' to share, you ain't got a ticket to get in," he said, and there was subdued laughter from the others. Except for Picked-on Boy and Zoned Girl. Those two didn't seem to be aware of their surroundings.

"Yeah, I get that," I said, moving nearer to the boy. When I was close enough, I pretended to stumble and dropped my bottle near his feet. He looked up. Just for a second, the face of Donnie Higgins was clear in the glow from the fire. He looked rough. It might have been the reflection of the fire in his eyes, but there was something about his face that made me feel like I was looking at a person who was irretrievably lost.

"You got any money?" the big guy asked. I knew that if I answered no, they'd be pissed that I had come without drugs or money, and if I answered yes, I'd be marked as a target.

"A little," I answered.

"Geek. You got anything to sell this dildo?" the big guy asked one of the other guys sitting around the fire. A lanky guy who appeared to be with the other girl looked up and pulled a bag out of his pocket.

"Got something for every budget," he said, and I realized

I'd backed myself into a corner. I wasn't going to get a seat at the fire. I'd just have to retreat and keep an eye on Donnie until he got up and moved.

I pretended to search my pockets. "Shit! Damn it, man! I… Someone took it," I mumbled, trying to sound drunk. Luckily, I was playing for a stoned audience. "I'll go look for it," I said and walked off. I headed toward the house until I figured they'd probably stopped watching me. Eddie was sitting near the door and I gave him a brief wave.

I changed course for the old trailer and sat on the rickety wooden steps that led up to the door. From there, I had a good view of the group by the fire. I didn't have to worry about them noticing me since the light from the fire blinded them to anything in the shadows.

People came and went. Drugs were passed from hand to hand, and occasionally money too. Donnie got pushed off his stump at one point and I thought that might cause him to leave the group, but instead he just sat cross-legged on the ground.

A little after two, the big guy got up and half lifted the young woman off the ground. He started toward the trailer, saying something I couldn't hear over his shoulder while the others laughed. The creep fondled the girl as he made his way toward me. I got up off the steps and moved away. That's when I noticed that one of the other guys had started to kick Donnie.

I moved around, trying to stay out of the big guy's way while edging closer to Donnie, who was now standing up. The guy who'd kicked him was giving him hell and Donnie started to walk away. I looked back at the big guy and the drugged-out young woman he was abusing. He was headed straight for the trailer. I didn't need to be Dick Tracy to know what was going to happen to the girl. I looked back at Donnie, who was walking toward the house.

I caught Eddie's eye and pointed toward Donnie. Eddie looked confused. Frustrated, I walked over to him as fast as I could without looking too suspicious. Donnie got to the house a minute before I did. He brushed past Eddie, who stared at me.

"Follow him!" I hissed.

"But you're going to take him in, right?"

"I need to deal with that," I said, pointing over my shoulder toward the trailer. Eddie still looked clueless. "That asshole is going to rape that girl. I can't let that happen." I couldn't live with myself if I walked away from a situation where a woman was going to be abused, no matter how important Donnie was to our case. I was just going to have to rely on Eddie to keep an eye on him.

"You can't arrest him," Eddie said, looking around. "Not here. Not by yourself."

"I'm going to subdue him and then call for backup. I don't have a choice," I said. "Go. Don't lose him."

Eddie didn't look convinced that this was the right course of action, but he turned and followed Donnie.

I made my way back to the trailer, looking around to see who might be watching, but by that time of night everyone was pretty far gone. The group by the fire seemed the most active, but they weren't aware of anything beyond the fire.

I stopped outside the trailer and listened. No noises came from the other side of the door, so I opened it slowly. Inside, the trailer smelled of stale beer, mold and other things too disgusting to think about. I heard grunts and furniture moving in the back room and saw a dim light coming from the hallway.

I made my way down the hall. The floor creaked, which forced me to go slow. I got to the doorway and, by the light of a candle burning on an old nightstand, I saw the big oaf pulling at the woman's clothes. She was unconscious and unable to put up any resistance.

I cursed myself for not picking up something to hit him with. I was afraid that pulling my gun on him would just cause him to bellow out for help, or to attack me. Drug-fueled idiots seldom make rational decisions. I looked around and saw a short piece of two-by-four on the floor a few feet inside the bedroom.

I looked at the man, who had taken the girl's shirt off and was going to work on her pants. He was focused on his lechery, which I hoped would give me the time I needed. I took a breath and ran forward, grabbing the piece of wood and swinging it with all of my strength at his head. Unfortunately, he heard me and moved his head, so all I managed was a glancing blow. I had no choice but to launch myself at him.

He was dazed, which gave me the chance I needed to get my arm around his thick neck and cut off the flow of blood to his brain. I felt like I was trying to choke off a manatee. Within a minute, he quit flailing and dropped down on the bed. I took out my flex cuffs and secured his hands behind his back. Looking around the room, I found a rag that I could stuff into his mouth and an old belt to bind his legs together. Once I'd done that, I checked the woman's pulse. It was slow, but steady.

I took a breath and relaxed. As I reached for my phone, I caught movement out of the corner of my eye. A man was standing in the closet. His pants were around his ankles and his mouth kept opening and closing like he was talking, but no sound came out. Even by the dim light of the single candle, I could tell that his eyes were dilated. I walked slowly toward him.

I reached to pull him out of the closet, but when I touched him, his eyes suddenly focused on me and his mouth flew open as he took a deep breath. I knew he was going to yell loud enough to wake everyone within a mile of the place, so I drove my fist into his gut. Air exploded out of his mouth and he collapsed to his knees, gasping.

I knocked him down onto his stomach and used another pair of flex cuffs to secure his arms. As soon as I was sure he'd caught his breath, I stuffed an old T-shirt into his mouth. Then I pulled out my phone and called in the cavalry.

An hour later, I was trying to explain it all to an irate Lt.

Johnson.

"So you just decided to go on some half-ass undercover mission?" Johnson yelled, giving me his best drill sergeant's glare.

"I didn't know if we'd even find Donnie Higgins. I was just scouting things out," I said lamely.

"You were just 'scouting things out,'" he said, mocking me. "You're on call tonight, but instead you decide to turn your radio off and go on a hunting expedition without backup. You can't possibly be that dumb. Do you see me? I'm awake at—," he looked at his watch, "four-seventeen in the morning. I am *not* supposed to be awake at this hour. But I'm here because you pissed off the watch commander. And I don't blame him one bit. You've stirred up this mess." He waved his arms at the deputies, crime scene techs and paramedics swarming the yard. "Now we have to clean it up!" He was madder than I'd ever seen him.

"Us having to walk through needles and broken crack pipes and Lord knows what else in the middle of the night. We *plan* raids on drug dens like this. And the reason we do that is so that when we go in, we have all the support and cooperation from other resources that we need. Fine, it's done." He took a deep breath. "Did you get your damn suspect?"

"No." Which was the worst part. I had called Eddie as soon as the other deputies had arrived and secured the rapist. Eddie said he'd been right behind him until Donnie had heard the sirens, then he took off running and Eddie couldn't keep up.

"Perfect, just perfect," Johnson muttered. "So this is what you're going to do. You're going to write up all the reports. The rapist, the numerous under-the-influences, the two resisting arrests and the two we've caught for dealing. *All* of them." He stopped and took another deep breath. "What I'm going to say next in no way mitigates anything I've already said, understand?"

He looked at me and I nodded, not knowing what was

coming next.

"Good job nailing that rat-bastard rapist." He looked around and lowered his voice. "I hope you kneed the son of a bitch in the balls." Then Johnson turned and stalked away, leaving me alone in the swirl of activity.

CHAPTER FOURTEEN

I grabbed a few hours' sleep and arrived at the office by eleven. Pete was headed to his car and met me at the door. He started shaking his head when he saw me. "Good luck," was all he said.

"You've been a busy boy," Darlene said cheerily as I walked to my desk. There was a huge pile of reports from the night before. "They left you a week's worth of work."

I grunted, still feeling the lack of sleep.

"Did you really see Donnie?" Darlene asked, offering me a cheese Danish.

"I did, but we lost him," I told her. "I hope your night went better."

"It was nice," she said, sounding mellower than usual. "I called the hospital this morning. Faith is going home today."

"I hope she's having someone stay with her. With Donnie still on the loose…"

"That's what I told her. She said she had a couple of folks who could watch over her. But she did ask if you would mind keeping Cleo for another day or two."

"Cleo is no problem. I'll check in on Faith later."

"Why do you think Donnie attacked her?"

"Maybe he heard his uncle ranting about her. Eddie said

Donnie sounded paranoid and a bit crazy. He might have gotten it into his head that she was part of some conspiracy."

"Of course, we could be getting ahead of ourselves. We've got to keep those open minds. Can't narrow the focus before the evidence is in," Darlene preached.

"Agreed. Though it's hard not to zero in when you have a runner. But you're right, we still have other suspects in the Higgins murder. Jason Harmon, for one. And the financial backer that he had a falling out with."

"Horace McCune. We need to interview him."

"See if you can set something up for tomorrow," I said, looking at the stack of reports on my desk. I knew I'd be getting even more from the crime scene techs. All of it would need to be organized, and I still needed to write my own report and coordinate everything with the State Attorney.

I spent the day cleaning up the mess I'd created the night before. Pete chipped in and gave me a hand with some of it. Darlene coordinated the search for Donnie. No one was dedicated to the search since all we could do was name him as a person of interest, but we wanted all of our patrol officers to be on the look out for him. We also put out a BOLO to all the surrounding counties.

Around midday, I called Earl Higgins. "I saw your son last night."

"You did?" he said, sounding less interested than I would have expected.

"I did. He also tried to steal a car yesterday."

Earl didn't answer.

"Do you know something about your son's whereabouts?" I prodded.

Still nothing but silence from the other end of the phone.

"Mr. Higgins, if you know something, you need to tell me. Your son is in an agitated state and could hurt himself or someone else."

I thought he was going to continue to stonewall, but he finally spoke. "He called me this morning."

"Do you know where he is?"

"No. He sounded... odd."

"I know you aren't going to like this, but I have to ask. Do you think your son might be schizophrenic?"

There was another long silence. "Maybe. He certainly sounded... off."

"Paranoid?"

"I'm going to talk to him."

"Does he have a phone?"

"This is my son. I'm not giving you any more information until I've talked to him again. And maybe my lawyer." His tone sounded desperate. I didn't like his response, but I understood it and would probably have done the same.

"Be careful. I can't stress that enough. If Donnie's having some sort of break from reality, he might lash out at anyone. Call me if you need help," I said sincerely.

I'd dealt with a few young people who, whether due to drugs or a medical issue, had become mentally unstable. I found it hard to blame someone who was hearing voices and unable to make rational decisions for the damage that they did. They were just like rogue animals, thrashing and tearing apart both property and lives. It was sad, but they still needed to be stopped before they hurt themselves or others.

"I will," Higgins answered and hung up.

Later that afternoon, I remembered to call Faith.

Her voice was still very hoarse. "Bernadette brought me home from the hospital. I want to thank you so much for taking care of Cleo. I miss her terribly."

"She's a very sweet dog. Alvin, Cara's Pug, is enjoying having a canine playmate. I can't say the same for my cat."

"I'll be able to bring her home in a couple of days."

"Is Bernadette staying with you tonight?"

"She said she'd come back after rehearsals. Don't worry, I've got all the doors locked tight. I'm not going to let someone sneak up on me again. On top of all of that, I've got my gun and I'm a good shot. My husband insisted that I learn to defend myself."

"If you're sure." Though having met her and hearing the alertness and determination in her voice, I believed her.

Darlene informed me that we had an appointment the next afternoon to meet with Mr. McCune at his home.

"Thanks for setting that up. I'm heading home," I told her.

"You sure you don't want to take my on-call shift tonight?" she joked.

"I think I did enough damage last night, thank you."

"Yeah, I wouldn't be surprised if Johnson doesn't ask your father to decree that all shift switching must receive prior approval from now on."

"Ha! That'd be the icing on the cake. Everyone knowing that I screwed up their happy-go-lucky shift trading."

I spent a quiet evening at home with Cara and the menagerie. Cleo and Alvin had become very chummy. I think Alvin would have been more jealous of the attention that Cara was paying to Cleo if he hadn't been so infatuated with the big girl.

On Tuesday, I woke up prepared to hunt for Donnie, interview McCune and review all other possible suspects to see if we'd overlooked anything. "It's a new day" was my motto. It lasted right up until I got to the office. I'd just sat down when my phone rang.

"Wherever you are, pick up donuts," I said. Caller ID had told me it was Darlene.

"Honey, I think you're the one who'll be grabbing the donuts. A body was called in about half an hour ago. It's Earl Higgins."

"Oh, hell! On my way."

Earl Higgins's body had been found on a power line right-of-way about two miles outside of town. Half a dozen emergency vehicles were parked at all angles, held back from the body by yellow crime scene tape.

"One of two things happened. First option is that he met someone out here and they shot him. The second option is, they shot him somewhere else and then dumped his body here," Darlene said, shaking her head. "Sure is looking like the kid. You said the dad had been in touch with him yesterday, right?"

"Damn it! I was so close to grabbing him Sunday night." I couldn't see what other options I'd had, but I was beginning to wish I'd tried something else. Letting Donnie go wasn't looking like my best decision.

"What could you have done? Let that poor girl get raped by the Neanderthal? That wasn't an option. You just gotta let that one go, Louie," Darlene said. "Now it's time to put your eye on the prize."

"You're right."

"I'm baaaaack," said a familiar voice. I turned to see Shantel Williams walking up, carrying her crime scene video equipment.

"Good to have you back. Where's your shadow?"

"Marcus has taken the day off. Said you all ran him into the ground while I was gone." Shantel looked refreshed from her vacation.

"How's Tonya doing?" Tonya was Shantel's niece. She'd been abducted back in February and we'd been lucky to get her back safe.

"She had a great time while we were up in Atlanta. She really wants to get accepted at Spelman. She said to give you a hug. Thinks you can do no wrong. I set her straight on that. Now, what you all got here?"

Darlene pointed out the highlights of the crime scene while standing outside the tape, then we both stood back to watch Shantel work. She had an intern with her, and twice Shantel had to grab his arm to keep him from getting ahead of her. They looked hot in their protective gear as they filmed and documented the ground, the body and any items that stood out.

"I had Julio go to the motel and secure Earl Higgins's

room. I told him to look for his car while he was there."

"If you've got this, I'll drive around and see if his car is nearby," I said. There were several rural residential roads within walking distance of the power lines. Earl could have parked on any of them if he'd come here of his own accord.

"Go ahead. They probably have another half hour of work before we can look at the body."

I called Julio, who reported that the car was not at the motel and that he'd gotten the room sealed. He was also able to give me some details about the car from the motel registration. I drove around for thirty minutes and felt comfortable saying that Earl Higgins's car wasn't within easy walking distance of the crime scene. Then I called Julio back and asked him to go by the car rental company and ask them to file a stolen car report. We'd put it out on the wire with an alert that the driver was wanted for questioning in a homicide investigation and should be considered armed and dangerous.

When I got back to the crime scene, Shantel gave us the all-clear to walk out to the body.

"I don't know. He could have been shot here, but there isn't much blood. More likely he was dumped," I said to Darlene as we looked down at Earl's body.

"Who's going to check his pockets?" Darlene asked.

"We could toss a coin," I suggested. There was something about putting my hand into the pockets of a dead person's clothes that creeped me out.

"I'll do it, cupcake," Darlene said, snapping on a pair of gloves and getting down on the ground next to the corpse. She patted him down and pulled out a wallet and his room key. "No car keys."

"And no cell phone. Earl said that Donnie had called him. I'd sure like to know what number he used."

I put on my own set of gloves and opened the wallet. Inside were credit cards, his driver's license and a couple hundred dollars in cash. "Whoever killed him didn't rob him."

"Which goes back to, if it was Donnie, he's probably not thinking straight."

"True. The Donnie I saw needed all the money he could get. If you're going to kill your father, you might as well take his money."

"Dumping the body doesn't seem to fit with a wigged-out killer either," Darlene said.

"No, it doesn't," I said, trying to see all the angles. We were certainly getting mixed messages from the case. "I'll be interested to see if any of the tire tracks could be from Higgins's rental car," I said, watching as Shantel and her assistant took photos and casts of one of the three distinct tire tracks we'd found. I was sure that one of them was from an ATV. Riding up and down power line rights-of-way was pretty standard entertainment in Adams County. The other two looked like car or truck tracks. "Even if one set of tracks *is* from his car, that doesn't mean that he didn't drive it out here."

"True. He and the killer might have been sitting in the car when he was shot and then the murderer just shoved him out of the car and drove off," Darlene said.

"What have you got for me now?" I heard a familiar voice call.

I turned to see Dr. Darzi walking toward us.

"What are you doing coming to a crime scene?" I asked, surprised. Usually he only came in person when there was something highly unusual to see.

"It's a lovely day. Ninety degrees and a hundred percent humidity. Why wouldn't I want to be out here with you and your latest victim?" he said, smiling broadly. "Actually, I was driving by and told my office I would take a look."

"Driving by?"

"Coming home from a conference in Pensacola," he said as he began to circle the body of Earl Higgins.

"Died of a bullet wound is my preliminary assessment," he said. "But since this is one of your cases, I'm sure there is something peculiar about his cause of death." He got down on the ground with his bag and started probing the body.

Darlene and I left him to his work. We walked around the area in larger and larger circles, looking for anything that we might have missed the first time. We found more trash, including condoms, condom wrappers and small plastic jewel bags that had no doubt been used for a drug transaction. On top of that was all the usual trash. We dropped markers by each piece so Shantel could bag and tag it, then returned to the body.

"Death occurred between nine last night and three this morning. Unless the autopsy or toxicology comes up with anything surprising, I stand by my first assessment. Death by gunshot wound to the heart. It was very quick. There would not be a lot of blood, but," he indicated the ground, "there would be more blood than what we see here."

"Thanks. We appreciate that personal touch," I told him.

"Too damn hot for this. What was I thinking?" he said with a smile as he wiped sweat from his forehead and waved his team over to collect the body.

I hated to do a notification over the phone and even more so over a cell phone, but I needed to let Higgins's ex-wife know about his death and find out if he had any other next of kin. I placed another call to Dr. Lawton in North Carolina.

"Is this a joke?" he asked, sounding more shocked than suspicious.

"No. I'm sorry to say that Earl Higgins was murdered last night."

"What the hell is going on down there?" Dr. Lawton asked.

"I just need contact information for his ex-wife," I told him.

He was quiet for a minute, then said, "I'll check with HR. They should have her information. I'll call you back."

He was as good as his word, calling back ten minutes later with a phone number and address for Julia Musgrove, Earl's ex-wife and Donnie's mother.

Julia answered on the second ring. I introduced myself and got straight to the heart of the matter. "I'm afraid that I have some bad news."

"Is it Donnie?"

"No. It's your ex-husband, Earl Higgins. He's been killed."

"Oh," she said. It was more a groan than a word. "What about Donnie?"

"We know your son has recently been in Adams County, but we don't know where he is now. We'd like to ask him some questions about his father's death."

I could hear her choking back tears. "I don't know where he is either. What happened to Earl?"

"We won't know for certain until the autopsy has been performed. But from what we know now, it appears that he was shot and killed last night. His body was found this morning."

"Dear God. No, no, no!" she cried. I suspected that she was thinking of Donnie as much as Earl.

"Have you been in contact with Donnie recently?" I asked, but the only answer was a drawn-out pause where all I could hear was her soft crying. "It's important that we find him. The sooner, the better. He could be a danger to himself or to others."

"No... I don't know."

"When did you talk to him last?" More hesitation. "You need to tell me."

"Yesterday. He called me yesterday."

"What did he say?"

"He was upset. Said that his uncle had been killed and that he thought someone might be after him next."

"How did he sound to you?"

"Upset. Really upset. Donnie was never emotional. He got sad or mad, but he didn't show it. This was different. I've never heard him so cra... I don't know."

"Were you going to say crazy?"

"Not crazy, but crazed. Manic. I... Oh, dear God... I

begged him to call his father. What have I done?"

"Don't beat yourself up. What you need to do is to help us find Donnie."

"I don't know." She sounded lost.

"Have you tried calling Donnie back?"

"I tried calling him a couple of times last night and again this morning. But his phone just goes to a recording that says his voicemail hasn't been set up."

"Could you give me that number?"

"He didn't kill his father. I don't believe that."

"We just want to find him. You said yourself that he sounded distressed. You can't reach him, but if you can give me the number, we'll be able to get a warrant for the cell phone company to give us all the information they have on where his phone has been used," I argued.

"What if he resists arrest?"

"First of all, we aren't going to arrest him until we know that he's done something wrong. Right now, we just want to question him." I didn't mention the incident in the grocery store, though I planned to use the attempted robbery as a reason to hold him. "Secondly, we don't want to hurt him. For everyone's safety, if he's having a mental break, then he needs to be questioned and detained. We'll Baker Act him if we feel it's necessary for him to be under the care of a doctor."

"I've just heard so many horror stories of people being shot by the police..."

"Our department has a very good record when it comes to officer-involved shootings," I assured her. "Also, I'll give you my personal guarantee that I will do everything in my power to see that Donnie is brought in safely." I didn't point out that the odds were he was on the run and that it would be another jurisdiction, one in which I had no control, that would attempt to detain him.

"Okay. But I'm coming down there," she told me.

"Maybe this isn't the best time. Let us find him and then you can come down," I cautioned.

"He has no one but me now."

"One more thing. Besides Donnie, who would be Earl's next of kin?"

"As you know, his parents are both dead. Now his brother. This is all… overwhelming. I think he has some cousins that live out in California. I'll see if I can get some information on them. Here's the number that Donnie used when he called me." She read off the number and I encouraged her once again to wait to hear from me before coming down to Florida.

"We need to step the search for Donnie up to ten," I told Darlene after getting off the phone with Julia.

"I'll call all the agencies north and east of us if you'll do the ones south and west," she said.

"Deal."

While Donnie was already listed as a person of interest and possibly endangered, we needed to make sure every agency understood that there was also the possibility he was dangerous himself. It was a fine line. If he was listed as possibly armed and dangerous, it upped the odds that he'd be shot reaching for his wallet or cell phone. I had promised his mother that I would try and protect him, but at the same time I didn't want to put law enforcement officers at a disadvantage. The only way to get the whole message across was to contact the different agencies personally.

We divided our time between making calls and helping Shantel with the crime scene. By two o'clock, we were finally finished.

"Oh, shit!" I said, stunned at my own stupidity.

"What?" Darlene asked. She'd been on her way to her car when I'd spit out the expletive.

"I forgot about Faith. She went home yesterday."

"Bloody hell, you're right," Darlene said, her own eyes growing wide. "If Donnie is our killer, then he might have headed over to Faith's to finish off what he'd started."

I tried to call Faith, but her phone went straight to voicemail.

"You can follow me if you want," I said, jumping into my car. I peeled out of the right-of-way, flipping on the blue lights hidden in my grill. I restrained myself from using the siren. It was only three miles from where Earl's body was found to Faith's house and, if Donnie was there, I didn't want to warn him.

CHAPTER FIFTEEN

I wasn't sure if I felt better or worse when I saw another car in Faith's driveway. *At least it's not Earl's rental*, I thought as I pulled in and parked behind the Honda minivan.

Darlene parked at the curb and hustled across the lawn to meet me at the door as I knocked hard and fast.

"Stop! Stop! I'm coming!" a voice shouted from inside, and I felt my adrenaline level start to return to normal. The door opened and Bernadette Santos stared out at us. "Oh, it's you," she said, looking surprised.

"Is Faith all right?" I asked, already pretty confident of the answer.

"She's fine. She'll be better if she can get some rest. I don't think she was able to sleep very well last night," Bernadette said.

"Earl Higgins was killed during the night, and we were worried that Faith might be in danger. No one answered her phone," I explained.

Bernadette appeared startled at the news of another murder, but recovered quickly. "I turned her phone off. The last thing she needs is to be talking to anyone. She can hardly talk as it is."

"Okay, we don't want to bother her. Just be aware that

Donnie Higgins is still on the loose. And also remember that we aren't positive that he's the killer, or even the person that attacked Faith. Basically, be suspicious of everyone."

Darlene and I both handed her our cards. "Call us if you see anything that doesn't look right or if you see someone hanging around," I said.

"Will do. How's Cleo?" she asked.

"She's doing well. The doc is happy with how she's healing."

"Good. Faith should be able to take her back soon. I miss her too. Oh, wait a minute, I've got something for you." She disappeared back into the house and reappeared a minute later with two tickets in her hand. She handed one to each of us. "This is for Saturday night's show. It's *Little Shop of Horrors*. The musical numbers are great. Wait until you see Audrey II! I'm hoping Faith will be well enough to go."

"At least Faith is fine," Darlene said as we walked back to our cars. "I can't blame you for being worried, though. I'm kicking myself for not thinking of her as soon as I saw that the victim was Earl."

"Here." I handed her my ticket to the show. "Take Hondo."

"Are you sure that Cara wouldn't want to go?" she asked, holding the tickets out to me.

"No, we're good."

"You're a spoilsport. Maybe I *will* take Hondo," she said and put the tickets in her pocket.

My phone rang. I waved Darlene on so she could head back to the office while I answered the call. It was Albert Griffin.

"I'm worried about Eddie," he said without preamble.

"Why?"

"He went out yesterday afternoon and hasn't come back."

"Eddie's a grown man. He could have a good reason for not coming home last night."

"You need to take this seriously," he insisted.

I sighed. "Okay. I'll swing by in a few minutes."

When I got to his house, Mr. Griffin was waiting for me on the porch. "What do you want me to do?" I asked.

"I expect you to look for him." He glowered at me.

"Why are you so worried about him?"

"Because… I suspect he's taking drugs again."

"If that's the case, looking for him isn't going to do much good. If I find him, he'd probably refuse to come with me. I don't know what you think I can do."

"You bear some responsibility for this. I warned you that he wasn't ready to go back and mix with his old party crowd, but you ignored me and pushed him to do it," Mr. Griffin said heatedly.

"Yes, I asked him, but he was happy to help. And I made sure he got home safe."

"You sent him back to the same world that fed his addiction, and then you dropped him off feeling like he had disappointed you by letting Donnie Higgins get out of his sight. Plus, you gave him money. You might as well have put the drugs in his hands."

"That's a little unfair—"

"No, it's not! I've been there, and I tried to tell you that Eddie needed to concentrate on his recovery and not on some case you're working. But you ignored me." I had never heard him so angry.

"Fine. It's all my fault. But I don't know what you think I can do about it now."

"Look for him! When you find him, then at least we'll know what's going on… And you can let him know that he's welcome to come back, even if he has done some backsliding."

"Did you see him leave?"

"Yes. He got up about noon on Monday and had breakfast. While he ate, he told me what had happened the night before. I told him it wasn't his fault that this Donnie character got away, but I could tell Eddie took it hard. Then, about three o'clock, I saw him walk down the driveway. I thought he was going to the Fast Mart, but he never came back."

"So he's been gone since three yesterday afternoon?" I had to admit that it was a little odd. Since Eddie didn't have a car, he'd have to make his own way to wherever he was going, or hitch a ride. There was no bus service in Calhoun.

"You tried calling him?"

"Of course."

I pulled out my phone and tried calling him anyway. No answer. I sent him a text that it was urgent he get in touch.

"Okay, I'll look for him," I said, irritated that Mr. Griffin had managed to make me feel guilty for asking for Eddie's help in the hunt for Donnie. I was equally irritated at Eddie for whatever the hell he'd gone and done. Finally, I was pissed at myself for involving Eddie and then letting Donnie slip away.

"That's all I'm asking," Mr. Griffin said, sounding mollified.

"No promises."

"Call me if you find out anything."

I took several deep breaths and let go of some of the anger as I waved to him and walked to my car. *He's just trying to do a good deed and help Eddie*, I thought. *And I do owe Eddie*, I reminded myself.

I decided to look for Ella Shaw, Eddie's ex-girlfriend. He'd mentioned her the other day, but I'd never asked him if he'd run into her Sunday night. There was always the chance that he had been drawn back to her. I'd last seen her in a run-down dump of a house north of town. I took a few side trips through the rougher parts of Calhoun on the way, keeping an eye out for Eddie. Nervous people dodged into houses and hopped into cars when they saw me.

The front door of Ella's last known address was plastered with a condemned sticker from the county. Not surprisingly, no one answered my knock, but looking through the dirty windows I could see that addicts were still using the place. There were numerous signs of recent fast-food meals and drug activity. What I didn't see were any signs of Eddie or Ella. I was just wasting my time. Eddie would come back whenever Eddie wanted to.

Darlene sent a text to remind me that we had a four o'clock interview with Horace McCune, Conrad Higgins's silent, and possibly angry, business partner. I was closer to McCune's house than the office, so I told her I'd meet her there.

McCune's property was hard to miss. There were two large wrought-iron gates across the driveway with a large letter "M" centered on each of them. Off to the side was a call box. As soon as I identified myself, the gates started to swing open.

While I had seen the gates a thousand times, I'd never been on the property or seen the house. It looked like it should have been in the French countryside—ten thousand square feet, at least. The drive leading up to the home was meant to impress, and it did. But there was a carelessness to the landscaping that detracted from the opulence of the house.

Darlene was standing at the large double doors of the grand entry into the monstrosity. "He said I could wait until you arrived." She didn't sound happy.

"I'm here. Press the button, princess."

"Don't get sassy with me." She pressed the doorbell and a loud gong sounded somewhere deep in the bowels of the house.

After a couple of minutes, the door opened and a scruffy looking older gentleman wearing a polo shirt, tan slacks and a nickel-plated Ruger Blackhawk revolver on his hip looked us both up and down.

"Get those badges out so I know you are who you say you are," he told us with a little growl in his voice. We showed him our IDs and he finally backed away from the door after reading them both from top to bottom. "Can't be too careful," he grumbled.

The inside of the house had the same mix of expensive

tastes combined with neglect.

"This is some place," I said, following him into an office that looked like something out of *Downton Abbey*.

"Damn third wife. Spent money like it was water from a faucet. Should have burned the place down after I kicked her ass to the curb. Costs a damn fortune to maintain. Are we done with the pleasantries?" he asked.

Not sure they'd ever started, I said, "The reason we're here—"

"Hell, I know why you're here. Question is, why weren't you here days ago? Conrad Higgins cheated me, then the darn fool went and got hisself murdered. I assumed I'd be a prime suspect. But here we are days later and you're just now getting around to questioning me. Hell's bells, I could have been on the other side of the world by now. Maybe your daddy ought to lose the election this fall if that's how his office handles a murder investigation." The speech was delivered at a rapid-fire pace that left his face red.

"We had other suspects," Darlene said as she walked around the room, clearly annoying the old man.

"I bet you did. He was a crook, a cheat."

"You didn't know that before you went into business with him?" I asked.

"Of course I did. Like buying a wild horse. You think, hot damn, I can tame that beast. I harness all that cleverness, we could make a lot of money."

"But the beast turned and bit the hand that was feeding him?" Darlene asked.

"Exactly right. I should have whipped him in the streets. When I was younger I would have," the old man said. I figured now wasn't the time to point out that he would have been arrested for assault if he'd beaten Higgins with a whip.

"How did you all meet?" I asked, trying to drag the interview down more productive avenues.

"Well, now that's a story in and of itself. We were both at a military antiquities auction where I was trying to acquire a rather nice Colt Walker. This one was owned by a Texas gentleman who fought in the Mexican war. He was given this particular gun after the war by Samuel Colt himself. Seemed the man had taken a bullet that was meant for General Scott at the battle of—"

"I don't think we need the full history of the Mexican War," I said.

"Yeah, yeah, okay. Point being, I was bidding on the gun, but Higgins out-bid me. He was good."

"Higgins had that kind of money?" Darlene asked from the other side of the desk where she was browsing McCune's wall of books.

"Hell, no! He was acting for some other guy he was fleecing. Gettin' beat made me curious about Higgins. We got to talkin' and he convinced me that we ought to work together."

"What kind of work were you two collaborating on?" As soon as I asked, I saw McCune's eyes get cagey.

"Now I'm not sure we need to get specific about my private business dealings."

"Don't make me dig for the information," I warned.

"The details really aren't important. In fact, I didn't know the details. I put up the money, and he was supposed to give me a… generous return on my investment." McCune was looking less self-assured.

"How much of a return?" I pressed him.

"We agreed on anywhere between twenty-five and fifty percent," he said flatly.

"Wow, that's great," Darlene said, her tone laced with sarcasm. She had moved over and was looking out a window, causing McCune to swivel his head to look from me to her. "That does seem a little more than I get on my IRA."

"Not that unusual in some areas of investment. Think of a pawnshop," he said, trying to climb back up to the high ground.

"You're claiming that you don't know what he did with the money?" she asked

"Exactly."

"That wouldn't seem very smart," I said, and anger flashed in his eyes.

"Now, see here! You don't have the right to come in here and insult me in my own house."

"I'm just saying that a man like yourself, who takes pride in his skills as a businessman, wouldn't normally be loaning his money to some guy without knowing what the money was being used for."

"Think of it as a signature loan," he said, staring daggers at me.

"How much money are we talking about?" Darlene asked.

McCune didn't take his eyes off of me. "Again, I don't think that is relevant to our discussion."

"Okay, how much are you claiming he took from you?" I asked, knowing that would be easy enough to find out from Higgins's lawyer. From the look on McCune's face, he knew there was no sense in hiding the amount.

"Somewhere around half a million dollars."

"That must have pissed you off," Darlene said.

"Damn right it did! I'm going to get it out of his estate too. I can promise you that." His eyes were blazing and he looked twenty years younger in his anger.

"So what were you doing on the night of August eighth and the early morning hours of August ninth?"

"Sadly, I wasn't out killing that egg-sucking dog. Truth is, I was right here."

"Can anyone confirm that?" Darlene asked.

"A gentleman never tells," he said with a wink.

I moved into his personal space. "You may find this all very amusing, but a man is dead. Murder is murder, whether the man was a… What did you call him? … an egg-sucking dog or not. And I don't care how much money you have, I'm going to press you until I get the answers we need."

I'd apparently crossed a line. He moved his face so close to mine that I felt the spittle fly when he spoke. "Sonny boy, you don't want to go down that road. I just told you I didn't kill him. I let you in my house and offered to answer your questions, but if you're going to show your ass, I'll chew you a new one. You better think long and hard about how you want to talk to me, 'cause not only do I have money, but I have friends who owe me some favors. So you push me a little harder and see how fast I smack you down."

The darkness in his eyes told me that, if push came to shove, he'd be willing to use that big iron on his hip. I didn't have any reason to test him. Yet.

"I got your six," Darlene said in a cool, hard voice from behind McCune. I think he'd forgotten about her. That would have been a big mistake in a fight. He visibly backed down.

"I got a right to be riled up, being accused of who knows what in my own house," he said defensively.

"We weren't accusing you of anything. I appreciate that you have information you want to…" I was going to say "hide," but in the interest of civility I said instead: "…keep close to your chest. But we're charged with finding Conrad Higgins's killer, and we'll turn over whatever stone is necessary to do it." I stared at him until he blinked.

"You do what you have to. I know I didn't have anything to do with his death. End of story."

"We'd like to eliminate you as a suspect. Easy enough to do if you tell us where you were and who you were with that night," Darlene said reasonably.

"Fine! I bought some companionship for the night."

"And the lady's name?"

"Mindy. I use a service."

"Tell you what, have Mindy give us a call and we'll take it from there," I said, pulling out one of my cards.

"Drop it on the desk," he told me.

"We'll look forward to hearing from Mindy. By the way, does anyone else live here?" I asked.

"No. I have a cook who comes in four days a week and a house-cleaning service."

"You just hire all your help, don't you?" Darlene said with a smirk.

McCune suggested we leave at that point.

When we got to our cars, I looked at my watch.

"I'm going home."

"I'll touch base with Julio and see how the search for Donnie is going. I asked him to stay on top of it."

"Good idea. Make him earn that move into CID. Between him and Sandy, we're going to lose our jobs."

"They can have 'em. There are days I wouldn't mind being back on patrol. Three twelve-hours shifts, then four days off. Most of the time you can leave your work at work. I didn't know I had it so good."

"You can go back to working for Maxwell and the Calhoun Police Department," I suggested with a grin.

"Now that I *don't* want to do. Maxwell treated me all right, but all they do is write tickets. That gets old."

"We'll take Shantel or Marcus over to Earl Higgins's motel room in the morning."

"Juilo said he looked in the room before sealing it. Everything appeared normal so, yeah, it can wait."

"Hey! Are you two ever going to get in your cars and get off my property?" McCune shouted from the door.

I waved cheerily, which caused him to slam the door.

"Guess we know where we're not wanted," I quipped.

I got home to find Cara looking sad and a little lost.

"Bernadette came to the vet this afternoon and got Cleo."

"I'm sorry, love, but you knew she'd have to go home eventually," I said, pulling her into a hug. I wasn't going to admit it, but I felt a pang of loss for the big girl too.

Alvin began to jump back and forth between us. I couldn't tell if he was trying to tell us that we still had him, or if he was asking us where Cleo was.

"Bernadette thought Cleo might help Faith get better

faster. And Bernadette's going to stay there for a while, so she can take care of Cleo."

Ivy jumped down from the back of the couch, rubbed against both our legs, then gave Alvin a whack on his butt as though to say: *I'm in charge again.* Alvin looked shocked, but accepting.

"Our happy family," I said, and gave Cara one more squeeze. "I'll fix dinner. I'm thinking omelets."

"You must have seen the box," Cara laughed. One of her co-workers had a chicken collection that had recently gotten a bit out of hand and the woman had taken to bringing eggs to everyone at the clinic.

"Eggs aren't just for breakfast anymore."

"I brought something else home too." Cara picked a couple of tickets up off the counter. "Bernadette left them. I thought we could go to the show. I love *Little Shop of Horrors*."

"Great," I said with Academy-Award-quality enthusiasm.

Later, as we were washing dishes, Cara asked me how things were going.

"The short answer is bad. Finding Donnie would make all the difference."

"With everyone looking for him, how long can he hide?"

"A long time. If he ditches the car and fades into the homeless population, we might never find him."

"You're kidding?" she said, handing me a wet plate to dry.

"People don't realize how big the homeless population is. And shelters respect their clients' privacy, so that can make it hard to search for someone."

"But if he's a fugitive…?"

"A number of homeless are fugitives. Admittedly, most of them have warrants for things like bad checks or failing to appear in court. But the shelters aren't going to rat him out, and his fellow travelers have a no-rat policy too, so it would just be luck if we find him. If he's falling down the rabbit hole of paranoid schizophrenia, then he might lose his awareness of his own identity."

"That's horrible."

"There's also the possibility that he'll just head off into the woods. If he disappears into a wildlife management area or the Apalachicola National Forest, he could be gone forever."

"He could get lost and die of exposure out there."

"Exactly," I said grimly.

"I see the problem."

"And whether he's the murderer or not, I think finding and questioning him is the whole key to moving forward with this investigation."

"Is there a chance that he's not the killer?"

"We talked to one asshole this afternoon who I'd *like* to pin the murder on. Unfortunately, he's probably not our guy. In reality, Donnie has to be number one on the charts right now."

"Can't you mount a big search for him?"

"Trouble is, he's just a person of interest. You can't call the cavalry in for someone who's just wanted for questioning. There's just so little evidence tying him to the crimes."

After the dishes were done, we settled in to watch monster movies on Netflix.

"I hate to say it, but the house does seem empty without Cleo," I finally admitted to Cara. Ivy's head butted my arm as though she was saying: *Speak for yourself.*

"I know." Cara sighed a little, then called Alvin up on the couch and the four of us watched Godzilla destroy Tokyo.

CHAPTER SIXTEEN

I'd just gotten out of bed when dispatch called a little after seven on Wednesday morning. "What?" was my less than joyful salutation.

"Wake up!" Marti said in an annoying singsong voice. "The devil's work is never done."

"It's too early for jokes. What's up?"

"You've got another dead body," he answered, jolting me awake.

"Who?"

"Hey, I just take the calls. Pops found it."

At that hour of the morning, it took me a minute to figure out who he was talking about. "Pops Davis, the lawn guy?"

"That's him. He's at a property just outside of town. We've already sent a patrol car and an ambulance, but since it's Pops, I believe what he's telling me."

"What makes this my body?"

"That rental car you've been looking for? It's parked on the property."

"Text me the address. I'll be there as soon as I can."

I threw on some clothes, clipped on my holster and badge, and grabbed a couple of pieces of bread and my keys before kissing Cara and running out the door.

I beat Darlene to the scene. Parked in front of the farm gate were two patrol cars and an ambulance. The EMTs were getting ready to leave. The driver was Hondo, but he seemed to be dragging his feet a little.

"Nothing for us to do," he said to me.

"I heard it was a body."

"Yeah, Spears wouldn't even let us in."

"I don't know why they bothered to send you," Deputy Spears said from his post by the gate. "Should have known that Pops knew what he was talking about."

"So why are you still hanging around?" I asked suspiciously. "You aren't waiting for anyone in particular, are you?"

Hondo's face flushed red. "We're just taking our time. What you want us to do, go hang out and wait for the next knifing at the Fast Mart?"

"It's rush hour. I'm sure there'll be some work for you soon. No sense hanging out here looking for love."

"You... Don't start with me," he said good-naturedly, just as Darlene drove up in her unmarked.

"Do what you want. I got work to do." I walked over to the gate, trying to hide the grin on my face.

"I had Pops and his guys stay where they were," Spears told me. "If they turned the truck around or walked out, they were going to disturb the ground worse than what it already is."

"Good job. Are Dr. Darzi's guys on the way?"

"Yep, and Shantel and Marcus will be here soon."

I looked over the gate and saw tire tracks clearly marked in the morning dew. "I guess we can walk to the scene if we follow in Pops's tracks."

The property was enclosed on all sides with well maintained field fencing. The front few acres were covered in white oak trees and second-growth scrub so thick that it was impossible to see more than a dozen feet through it. But on the other side of the tree line, the property opened up to reveal a clearing with a small cabin and a pond. It was the standard layout for hunting property in Adams County. Pops's truck and equipment trailer were parked near the cabin, with Earl Higgins's rental closer to the pond.

Pops Davis had grey hair, dark brown skin and eyes that always seemed to see the best in the world around him. Even today, though they showed a touch of fear and sadness, there was a little gleam in them when he saw me.

"Little Mac! Bet you don't remember me calling you that."

"You'd lose that money. How you doing, Pops?" I said, sticking out my hand. I remembered the warm summer days when he'd come to mow our lawn. He'd let me drive his riding mower, which had seemed like such a big adventure when I was seven.

"Not so good. I shouldn't have come up to the cabin when I saw that the lock was off the gate."

"That was the first thing you noticed that wasn't right?"

"Yep. I'd told Mr. Swain he needed to buy a lock as good as his chain. No sense having a dollar lock on a ten-dollar chain," Pops said, shaking his head.

I looked at the other two men in the crew cab truck. Neither of them looked like they had understood much of our conversation.

"We'll need to get everyone's name, phone number and address," I said, and Pops turned to the men, speaking to them in broken Spanish.

"Gil is all right," Pops said, turning back to me. "But his cousin Teeko might have some problems if you dig too deep into the paperwork. I had to reassure them that there wouldn't be any trouble. Teeko wanted to do a runner."

"No, it's okay. All I need are their real names and where I can get ahold of them for the next couple of weeks. Turning Teeko in to you-know-who," I didn't want to say "INS" and spook them, "would be counter-productive for me at this point. They might just take him and toss him out of the country. Then how would I find him if I need to question him? Reassure him that, as long as he cooperates, he's safe."

Pops went through a routine that was half English, half Spanish and a third-half sign language to convince them to relax.

"This is one of your regular jobs?" I asked Pops, once I'd gotten everything I needed from his help.

"Yep, I do this one personally. Mr. Swain's real particular about how the place is mowed." Pops managed at least three other lawn crews. "During the summer, we come in and mow and trim around the cabin twice a month. I also put out deer corn on the plots."

"What time did you get here today?"

"Sun was just about up. I guess it was close to seven. This time of year, you want to beat the heat," he said, but I knew he worked just about every day from sunup to sundown, regardless of the weather. There was some speculation about how rich he had to be. I'd never met a man in the county with a stronger work ethic. Pops had put one of his sons through medical school and the other was a mechanical engineer.

"So you saw the lock was off the gate and you drove on in. What happened next?"

"I saw the car. When I seen that I thought, oh Lord, something is going on. We parked here and I yelled out that I was here to cut the grass and didn't want no trouble. Then I called Mr. Swain and told him that there was a car here and what'd he want me to do. He said to go see if anyone's around. So I got my gun out. It's just a .22 for snakes, but I thought, who knows, could be drug dealers or whatnot."

"You went over to the car?"

"That's right. I looked in the windows real careful. Didn't look like nobody's car. I mean, there wasn't anything personal-like. Then I saw the Avis sticker and I knew it was a rental. I was going to call Mr. Swain back when I looked toward the pond. I'd been looking, but it wasn't until I was up next to the car that I could see it in the reeds."

"A body?"

"That's right, a man. I just walked a little closer. When I was sure what I was seeing, I hightailed it back to the truck and called 911."

"Did your helpers get out of the truck?"

"No, no, I told them to wait."

"Good job."

I heard voices behind me and turned to see Darlene, Shantel and Marcus carrying equipment and walking toward us in single file along the tire tracks. "As soon as we get casts of the tire tracks, you all can turn around and go on about your business," I told Pops.

"What about Mr. Swain's property? When do you think we can mow it?"

"Wait a couple of weeks and call me before you do. If Mr. Swain has any problems with that, have him give me a call. I'll need to talk to him anyway."

We all donned protective gear, then Darlene and I assisted the techs as they filmed, dropping markers next to anything that might be evidence. Luckily, unlike the power lines the day before, this property was secluded and clean.

"This is going to be one of the easiest scenes we've processed in a while," Marcus said with a smile. It was clear he was happy to have Shantel back.

"It would be a nice day if it wasn't a hundred degrees in the shade," Shantel said. She wasn't a fan of summer.

"You could take a swim in the pond," I said, pointing to the body.

"Someone who has three unsolved murders stacking up shouldn't be making jokes," she said, wagging her finger at me.

"My bad," I said with a rueful smile.

The body was on its stomach so we couldn't see the face, but it was clear that it was a young, white male. And I was pretty damn sure it would be Donnie Higgins.

We heard a shout and looked back to see Dr. Darzi's assistants standing by Pops's truck. I recognized Linda, but not the man with her. I waved them over. Half an hour later, we were looking at the water-logged face of Donnie Higgins.

"Gunshot wound to the chest," Linda observed.

"How long do you think he's been in the water?" I asked.

"At least twenty-four hours."

"And the marks on his face?"

"Turtles… maybe some other critters. I've seen a lot worse. I did my intern work down in Fort Lauderdale. You should have seen some of the bodies that came out of the water down there." She shook her head.

I turned to Darlene, who'd been helping Shantel and Marcus process the rental car. "Any sign of a gun?" I asked her.

"No. Not much in the car except some blood stains. Maybe Earl's blood?"

"Or Donnie's, if he was shot by someone else and dumped here along with the car."

"Why put him in the water?" Darlene asked with a thoughtful expression.

"Maybe as a forensic countermeasure?"

"We'll need to search the pond," she said.

After a brief discussion, we decided that a special team from the Florida Department of Law Enforcement would be needed to properly search the water. We made the call and FDLE was onsite by one o'clock. They deployed seines to drag the shallow areas and divers for the deeper parts of the pond. It covered about an acre and was only ten feet at its deepest point, but it still took a serious effort by fifteen people to examine the entire body of water.

In the first half hour, they came up with the gun. It was located in knee-deep water, buried several inches into the silt.

"An old Colt revolver. A .38 Special. Looks in good shape," Darlene said, holding up the bagged handgun.

"Think it was one of Conrad Higgins's guns?"

"Maybe. Though there were tens of thousands of these made."

"True. I think Dad's first service weapon was a Colt .38.

Serial number is still on this one. Maybe we'll get lucky." I pulled out my phone and called Dr. Darzi. I got his voicemail and left a message. "I'm wondering if he's pulled a bullet out of Earl Higgins."

"If this is the same gun, we could be looking at a murder-suicide," Darlene said thoughtfully.

"That would tie things up in a neat package," I said, turning the theory around in my mind. "Seems too… simple."

"Occam's razor, puddin' head," she said.

I was getting ready to make a snide comment when my phone rang.

"It's not bad enough that you're sending me bodies at all hours of the day and night, but now you have to interrupt my afternoon nap?" Dr. Darzi joked.

"We found a gun at this scene. It's a .38. We're wondering if you pulled a bullet out of Earl Higgins."

"Your lucky day. I found one .38 jacketed bullet behind Mr. Higgins's heart. Unfortunately for him, it had passed through his left ventricle on the way to its resting place. Your luck came in the form of the bone that stopped it from exiting through his back."

"Thank you. All of that sounds like good news. Linda and her assistant are packing up Donnie Higgins as we speak."

"Great, he can get in line," Darzi said and hung up.

I turned to Darlene. "Same caliber. The million-dollar question is going to be, did he wade into the pond and shoot himself?"

"Looks like this is going to come down to forensics and the autopsy."

We found Shantel and Marcus finishing up with the rental car. "We'll tow it up to the lot and tear it down there," Shantel said.

"The rental company will love that," I said.

"That's why they have insurance."

"What have you found so far?"

"There were some smudged prints on the steering column and on the dash. One or two might be good enough to get an ID."

"But it wasn't wiped?"

"Some parts of the car did look like they were wiped down. But it's a rental. They clean them every time they get turned in, so it's hard to say."

"Hair and fiber?"

"Some, but not much. Again, it's not like a personal car that would be coated in biological material. The car company would have vacuumed it each time it came in."

"Donnie's autopsy is looking more and more important."

"You thinking he killed himself?" Marcus asked.

"I think it's a possibility," I said, while a part of me didn't want to believe it.

Darlene and I headed back to the office and sat down in the small conference room to discuss strategy.

"We need a plan, Stan," Darlene said.

"It's just like Conrad Higgins's car. I thought that when we found the car, we'd find the killer. But the car only led to more questions. Then everything started to point toward Donnie and I thought that when we found him, we'd get some answers. Now we've found Donnie, and…"

"It does seem like we're trying to make lemonade out of lemons without any sugar." Darlene frowned.

"The way I see it, there are two possible conclusions to the autopsy. One, Donnie was killed by someone else. Two, Donnie killed himself. If we know that we still have a killer on the loose, then we can proceed full speed ahead with the investigation. Of course, Darzi could just tell us that the results are inconclusive."

"It would be nice if Darzi can give us evidence one way or the other. Donnie looks like such a good candidate for the murder of Conrad and his father."

"I can't disagree… Though I want to. And I don't even

know why I want to disagree."

"Maybe it's occupational bias. You're a homicide investigator and you want a killer to chase. Takes all the fun out of it if the killer kills himself," Darlene said.

"Maybe. One thing's for sure, I'm going to be at that autopsy."

"Not without me, sport. Not that Darzi isn't good at what he does. But I want to be there to ask questions on the spot."

"You're as bad as me. You don't think he killed himself either," I kidded her.

"What the hell do I know? The truth is, my Spidey senses aren't going off the way they did last month with Joel Weaver. So maybe, maybe not. I just want to be sure, if we close out this case, that it's really solved."

"Amen, sister. When we put this one to bed, I want it to stay in bed. On the other hand, I don't want us spending ten years beating a dead horse. If he did it, I'm fine with that. Also, I realize that I'm not going to get a hundred percent guarantee. But I do have an idea. If we don't get a definitive answer from Darzi, I suggest we bring Pete in here and sit him down at the table with all the reports and evidence."

"I see where you're going. Pete doesn't have a dog in the fight, so he can look at it with fresh eyes."

"Exactly."

"I'll go you one better. We should each take a side. One of us will argue that Donnie is the killer and the other will argue that he's a victim. That way, Pete can hear both sides laid out clearly."

"Debate Club! I like it. The first rule of Debate Club is you don't talk about Debate Club."

"Calm down, rooster."

I called Dr. Darzi, who promised he'd do Donnie's autopsy first thing the next day so he could be done with us.

"As a squeaky wheel, I appreciate that," I told him and assured him that he was going to have a captive audience kibitzing his every move during the procedure.

"Can't wait," he said.

"Should we tell Pete that he may be playing King Solomon?" Darlene asked when I got off the phone.

"Nah! If it comes to that, we'll spring it on him. He loves surprises."

CHAPTER SEVENTEEN

I was leaving the office when I got another call. It was Dill Kirby, the front desk sergeant.

"I've got someone on the line for you. Some lawyer, says he wants to talk to one of the detectives working the Higgins case." Dill was an old-school deputy and sometimes I thought he purposefully tried to sound like a cop from a vintage noir movie.

"Patch him through," I said, giving it right back.

"10-4."

I heard the line click, then said, "Hello?"

"I'm Ira Bowen. I've got a law practice in Tallahassee."

"Deputy Larry Macklin. How can I help you?"

"It's a delicate matter. I was contacted by your victim, Conrad Higgins, two months ago on June tenth," he said hesitantly.

"And…?"

"The delicate part is the lawyer-client privilege aspect. He told me in confidence about some concerns he was having. I'm loath to break that confidence, even when the client has… passed."

"I can assure you that we will treat anything you say as delicately as we can in a murder investigation," I said. "And I can't think of many murder victims who wouldn't want all possible leads explored."

"You are probably right. What concerns me is that there have been more victims. I hope that my caution hasn't caused a delay in the apprehension of a murderer." Bowen spoke slowly and deliberately.

"If the information you give me isn't of any value to the investigation, I promise you that I will bury it."

"My conscience demands I tell you what I know. I'm going to give you the brief version. If you need more information, I'd rather do it face to face. When Conrad Higgins came to me, he expressed concerns about his personal lawyer. He didn't tell me who his lawyer was. In fact, I asked him not to. I didn't want to get into any ethical situations, or a position where I was hearing gossip that could interfere with my judgment at some later date. Does that make sense so far?"

"It does. Did he specify what kind of problem he was having with his lawyer?"

"Well... He thought his lawyer might be cheating him. Working behind his back with his enemies, was how he put it. But after meeting with Mr. Higgins for a couple of months, I learned that he had a... suspicious, I might even say paranoid, outlook on life."

"I'd say that's a fair statement. And he had a somewhat spotty relationship with the law."

"Hmmm, yes, both criminal and civil."

"What did he want you to do?"

"He wanted my opinion on several of the lawsuits that his lawyer had filed. A second opinion, if you will."

"And?"

"They seemed to be in order. Not necessarily the way I would have gone, but competent enough."

"Was there anything else?"

"There was one more thing that seemed more... problematic. He thought his lawyer had been skimming money from Higgins's offshore funds."

"Was he?"

"That's part of the problem. I don't know. Mr. Higgins was so paranoid that he didn't want to give me any information on the funds. Without that information, I couldn't check them to see if anything shady was going on."

"When was the last time you met with him?"

"Two weeks ago. At the time, he said that he was going to talk with his lawyer again. Higgins said that if he wasn't satisfied with the answers he got, then he would turn everything over to me. I never heard back from him."

"These monies he had offshore, did he tell you what the amounts were?"

"Not exactly. I did get the feeling that they were substantial."

"How substantial?"

"Upper six to seven figures, but that is just a guess based on what he told me."

"Knowing Mr. Higgins, you were still willing to take him on as a client with large sums of cash offshore?" I asked, trying not to sound too accusatory.

"I made it clear to Mr. Higgins that I would not be a party to any illegal activities. I don't launder money."

"And what did he say to that?"

"He told me that by the time I saw anything, the money would be clean."

"Seems like you would have been walking a pretty narrow line."

"Mr. Higgins was just more honest than a lot of my clients. I work with people who have very large sums of money. Most are honest businessmen, but others have certainly dipped their toes in less savory practices. I am there to serve my clients, not to judge them. As long as I'm not participating in anything illegal, then I'm not crossing any ethical lines."

That's one way to look at it, I thought. I thanked him for the information and told him I'd get in touch if we needed to look further into the matter.

My phone rang again before I could start my car. It was Albert Griffin.

"Do you have any news?" he asked anxiously.

"No," I said, feeling guilty that I'd let Eddie slip my mind. "I'll drive around on my way home and look for him."

"You already did that and didn't have any luck."

"I'm going to talk with some people, see if anyone knows where he is."

"You didn't do that yesterday?" Mr. Griffin asked incredulously. He really knew how to serve up the guilt.

"I'll let you know what I find out," I said and hung up before he could say anything else.

Damn it! I thought as I drove through the seedier parts of Calhoun. I tore my shirt squeezing through a chain-link gate into an abandoned piece of property where Eddie had taken refuge the month before. I found his nest in an old cargo container, but there was no evidence of recent habitation. Next I swung through Rose Hill Cemetery, where we'd met on numerous occasions to exchange information about his drug-dealing family, but there was no sign of him there either. I even stopped at the Fast Mart, but the clerk, who knew Eddie well, hadn't seen him since Saturday.

I called Cara and told her I'd be late.

"Have you tried that cargo container he used last month?" she asked when I told her I was looking for Eddie.

I sighed. "Yes, and the cemetery *and* all his regular hangouts. I'm really starting to worry about him."

"You didn't force him to do anything."

"I kinda did. Mr. Griffin is right. Eddie wasn't ready to face his demons yet."

"I'm sure he's fine. What about that ex-girlfriend? What's her name?"

"Ella Shaw. That's why I'm going to be late. I've got to find her. I tried yesterday, but it looks like she's moved from the old house she was living in last month."

"Good luck. Stay safe!"

Since it was August, I still had a few hours of daylight left. I thought about my next move. Knowing what I did about Ella's drug use and party lifestyle, I called up one of our deputies who worked in vice.

"Benjy, buddy, I need your help."

Ben Morris hated to be called Benjy, which is why we all did it. Ben was everything I wasn't: an athletic adrenaline junky and a by-the-book deputy, the perfect type of officer to serve on a vice squad. He and his pals liked nothing better than hiding in the bushes to watch a drug dealer or raiding a meth lab.

"You're already getting off on the wrong foot, junior," Ben said, knowing I couldn't stand to be called that.

"Fair enough. I need some info, since I know you spend all your time in our county's proverbial gutter... and not just when you're off work."

"Har, har. Who are you looking for?"

"I'm looking for Eddie Thompson, which means I'm also looking for his ex-girlfriend, Ella Shaw."

"What's she look like? Distinguishing marks?"

"Substance-abuse-thin, she's got some tattoos, one is a strand of barbed wire around her left wrist. Hair changes colors, but it was dirty blonde with bilious green streaks the last time I saw her."

"I've got some thoughts, but let me look through my notes." Ben was also a meticulous note-taker. I used to wonder why he hadn't moved on to a bigger agency until I met his wife. She was from a large local family and wasn't going to move, come hell or high water. "You got any aliases?"

"No." I gave him her last known address.

"We busted a low-level dealer there a couple of weeks ago. Not in the house. He was standing in the front yard. Usually, any users who aren't tied down will scatter from a bust site for a couple of weeks. So we might have spooked her. Here it is. Yeah, got a girl matching her description hanging out next door to a known dealer. Same neighborhood, but the trailer she's staying in sits back off the road. The dealer is working out of the house on the left. If you're going out there, you'll want to proceed with caution. The dealer is a pretty bad hombre."

"Why haven't you closed him down?"

"Slow down, hoss. Do I tell you how to investigate violent crimes? We're trying to catch him when he's got enough in the house to put him away forever. I got your dad's approval to sit on it."

Dad hated it when cops allowed a dealer to operate just so they could run up their arrest stats by picking up the customers. There were communities all over the country that were being used as drug-bust generators for local law enforcement instead of them really trying to clean out the bad guys. But it made sense that Dad would be willing to wait awhile to land a knockout punch on a big-time dealer.

Ben gave me the address and I drove out to the house. There was an old gate across the dirt drive leading to the trailer in the back of the property, so I parked farther down the road and walked back. I climbed over the gate, hoping they didn't have a pack of junkyard dogs guarding the place. I snuck quietly past the dealer's house, not wanting to attract his attention.

The trailer was a run-down doublewide, probably twenty years old. I saw an orange tabby cat grooming itself on the porch steps, so I figured I didn't have to worry too much about vicious dogs. The yard wasn't as messy as I would have thought. Everything was overgrown, but unlike a lot of places in the area, there wasn't a lot of garbage or spare car parts spread around.

I stepped around the cat and knocked on the door. Nothing. I knocked a couple more times until I finally heard movement inside.

Sure enough, Ella opened the door. She dropped the f-bomb and turned, fleeing back into the house but leaving the door open.

"Hey, Ella, what the hell?" I called, truly puzzled by this response.

She came back carrying a baseball bat. "Get out of here!" she screamed at me.

"What is your problem?" I asked. "Do you know who I am?" I was trying to get a good look at her eyes. I assumed she was higher than a kite, the way she was acting.

"You can't come in here!" she screeched.

"I'm not coming in," I said, holding my hands out to my sides to show her that I wasn't making any move to enter the house. The orange tabby walked around me and moseyed through the door, letting me know that Ella's hysterics weren't anything out of the usual.

"Don't try anything or I'll video your ass." She fumbled with her phone, trying to turn on the video function while still holding the bat in a menacing way. "I'll YouTube your shit if you hurt him again." She looked so awkward with the phone and bat that it would have taken little effort on my part to waltz into the house and take both of them away from her.

"Calm down and tell me what you're talking about. I'm here looking for Eddie."

"Duh! We know you're after Eddie. You almost killed him!" she said, her panic returning in full force. I could see that she was confused and scared. Clearly, she couldn't decide if she should drop the phone and threaten me with the bat, or hold onto the phone so she could shame me to the world.

"Listen, you moron. Calm the hell down and tell me what you're talking about and where Eddie is." I'd just about had my fill of this nonsense.

"I'm not telling you anything."

I was done. I looked past Ella into the house. There was a huge bong on the table, a scale and a few plastic bags with small amounts of green material in them. I had probable cause to believe that drugs were being dealt on the premises. I pushed past Ella and dodged one feeble swing of the bat before I grabbed it and wrenched it free of her grasp. When I did, her phone fell to the floor. I barely restrained myself from smashing the phone with the bat.

Ella was now screaming an impressive number of obscenities. The cat had jumped up on the kitchen counter and was meowing at both of us. Apparently, he felt that our fight should be suspended long enough for someone to feed him.

"If you don't stop screaming, I swear I'll arrest you. Your choice." Now that I was in the house, I could see that the stupid woman was actually petrified.

She just stared at me.

"Is there anyone else in the house?" I asked her, speaking slowly and firmly.

The question reanimated her. "You aren't going to hurt him." Thankfully, this was delivered at a lower volume than most of the other irrational things she'd screamed at me.

"I don't know what you're so worked up about. I'm not going to hurt anyone."

"You almost killed him."

"Who? Who did I almost kill? Eddie? Is Eddie here?" Now I was getting concerned.

"Yeah, Eddie."

"Where is he?" I asked, already moving toward the hallway. I was careful to keep an eye on Ella and my hands on the bat, not knowing what to expect from her.

She didn't say a word, but followed me as I made my way through the trashed bedrooms. In the second, I saw Eddie lying on an old mattress. His breathing was ragged and there was a large lump and smears of blood on his head.

I ran over to him, taking my eye off of Ella just long enough for her to launch herself at my back. She weighed less then ninety pounds, so when I felt her land on my back I was able to grab her with one hand and toss her onto the floor. She let out a huge huff of air and sat on the grimy carpet, trying to catch her breath and glaring at me.

I didn't need medical training to see that Eddie, who now

resembled an extra from *The Walking Dead*, needed to get to the hospital. I pulled out my phone and asked dispatch to send an ambulance ASAP.

After doing what I could for Eddie, I looked over at Ella, who had curled up into a ball on the floor and was crying.

"Stop crying or I swear you'll spend some serious time in jail." This got her down to sniffling. "What happened to Eddie? And I want the truth the first time out of the box." A stern warning of bad things to come was in my voice.

"We found him. He was... like that when we found him."

"Why the hell didn't you take him to the hospital? Or call an ambulance?"

"He said you did it."

"That's ridiculous. What did he actually say?"

"I'm telling you, he said you did it to him."

"Back up. Where did you find him?"

"He was lying up against the side of the Fast Mart by the dumpster."

"Now, think back. What happened when you found him?"

"Rock went over to him, and Eddie said you beat him up."

I knew Rock. He was a big guy with no neck who used to play pretty good football in high school, but nowadays spent most of his time trying to chase down his next hit. I was beginning to see how this might have played out.

"Did Rock say anything when he went over to Eddie?"

"Yeah, he asked him who'd hurt him. And Eddie said you did."

"He said my name?"

"That's right."

"Just my name?"

"Yep," she said as though that proved her point.

"Did it ever occur to you or your fellow rocket scientist that he might have wanted you to call me?"

Ella looked gobsmacked at the concept. "No," she finally

squeaked.

I was shaking with anger. Luckily for Ella, at that moment I heard the first whines of an ambulance siren in the distance.

"Do you have the key to the gate?"

"What?"

"The gate across the driveway. Do you have the key?" I said through clenched teeth.

"Well, yeah, how else could I get out?"

"Go and open the gate for the ambulance, now!" I ordered her.

A few minutes later, I was relieved to see Hondo come tromping into the trailer. He asked a few questions and took Eddie's vitals.

"He's dehydrated. We need to get him to the hospital for X-rays and scans. I'm pretty sure he's got a severe concussion and that's why he's unconscious. But we need to make sure there's no internal bleeding. The good new is, from what I can tell, the head injury is the only damage that he's sustained."

"I'll follow you," I told Hondo.

On the way out of the trailer, I gave Ella a look and told her, "Don't say a word, don't even breathe, or I swear I'll arrest you and throw you into the secret subterranean prison underneath the sheriff's office where no one will ever find you." The look in her eyes told me that she believed me, which gave me some grim satisfaction.

Reluctantly, I called Mr. Griffin, telling him that Eddie had been found and that I'd let him know when there was news on his condition. He didn't lay too much guilt on me, which was fine because I was piling it on myself. If I'd found Ella the day before, it would have given Eddie a better chance. *Do I still think of Eddie as a junkie and that's why I didn't take his disappearance more seriously?* I wondered.

On the way to the hospital, I checked in with Cara and then called Darlene.

"Could this be related to the other attacks?" Darlene

asked the question that I'd already been asking myself.

"I don't know. There's a possibility that he got hit when he went looking for Donnie."

"I hope he's okay. I've got a fondness for the weirdos of the world," Darlene said kindly.

It was one o'clock in the morning before they had Eddie settled into a room for the night and a doctor came to talk to me.

"He'll be okay. He had a little bit of bleeding and swelling in his brain, but he was lucky. The bleeding stopped on its own. He should come around in a day or two. We'll monitor the swelling, but I can already detect signs that it's subsiding. With a little bit of luck, he won't suffer any ill effects."

I called Mr. Griffin with the good news and headed home.

CHAPTER EIGHTEEN

On Thursday morning, Darlene and I checked in with Shantel and Marcus in the evidence room before we headed to Tallahassee for Donnie's autopsy. They were still cataloging items from the two most recent crime scenes.

"This is going to take a while," Shantel said. "We did get two good prints from the rental car. We just need prints to compare them to."

"We can get Donnie's from law enforcement in North Carolina. That's going to be better than what Darzi can get off the waterlogged body," Darlene said.

"I talked to his mother after we found his body. She's going to be here on Saturday. Hopefully she'll provide additional information," I said.

"She might go all momma bear on you and try to defend his good name, dead or not," Shantel warned.

"I know. I've seen plenty of parents fight tooth and nail against a suicide verdict. How much harder would they have fought if their kid had been accused of a double homicide?"

We helped Shantel and Marcus prioritize a few items for the lab. The handgun was at the top of the list. Darzi had pulled one bullet out of Earl. If we could get one from Donnie and they both tied back to the gun, then that would give us some solid evidence to work with.

Darlene and I arrived at the hospital shortly after ten and went up to check on Eddie.

"He hasn't woken up yet. It's normal. Dr. Guzman was very optimistic when he checked him during rounds this morning," a nurse told me.

I gave her my card and asked her to call me as soon as Eddie woke up.

"Come in, come in," Dr. Darzi said with his usual good humor when we made it down to the morgue. "This time of year, what better place to be than a nice, cool autopsy room?"

As soon as I saw the woman lying on the table in front of him, I reflexively turned away from Dr. Darzi and tried to hold down my breakfast.

"Dear Lord, what happened to that poor woman?" Darlene asked. She was still facing the table, her eyes wide.

"She was hit by a car last night out on 90. They didn't stop and at least two other cars ran over her before someone called the cops. No chance of an open casket with this one. And I don't think I'm going to be of much help to the officers investigating the hit-and-run. With this much trauma occurring in such a short span of time, it's almost impossible to sort out what happened first. I'm having to make assumptions and that's never good. Not good at all. For instance, I assume she was standing up when she was struck. But is that true? I don't know. There are plenty of wounds that are consistent with a victim who was struck while standing, but… The bottom line is that there are injuries consistent with almost any scenario you could imagine. I'm done with her. Phillipe, you can tidy this up the best you can. Poor woman," he sighed.

"Never a dull moment around here," Darlene said.

I kept my mouth closed, my stomach still roiling.

"After I clean up, I'll go get your victim out of the vault," Dr. Darzi said. Between autopsies, he had to strip out of one set of protective wear, wash thoroughly and get into a new set before handling the next body to prevent cross-contamination.

Twenty minutes later, Dr. Darzi wheeled Donnie into the room. "We're short-handed today. Phillipe, come and help me when you have her back in the cooler."

"Yes, doctor," the man said with a slight accent. I couldn't decide if it was Canadian or Cajun.

"Let's see here." Dr. Darzi leaned over the very white body of Donnie Higgins. "Animal predation. Turtle, most likely. Some fish too. Soft tissues got the worst of it. Luckily, he was clothed." The coroner did a running commentary as he went. The sessions were videotaped and a separate audio recording was also made.

Dr. Darzi went over the front side of Donnie's body, probing and checking every orifice. When he got to the bullet wound in the chest, he looked at the area around the wound with a magnifying lens.

"There is some pitting from the powder. Of course, he was wearing a shirt so the cloth would have absorbed a little. And being in the water washed some of the powder off and damaged the skin, but… Yes… I would say that the gun was fired at a distance that would be consistent with a self-inflicted gunshot wound."

There was more probing and poking. Phillipe had joined us by this time, and he helped Dr. Darzi turn the body over.

"No bullet. I don't think you got lucky this time. Though the exit wound is a little unusual." Dr. Darzi indicated two holes in Donnie's back separated by half an inch.

"Why are there two exit wounds?" I asked.

"I can think of two possibilities," Dr. Darzi said in his best professorial voice. "One is that the bullet broke apart and two pieces exited out the back. Another possibility is that he fired two shots."

"Can you tell anything from the size and shape of the wounds?"

He leaned over and measured and poked at the holes. "Hard to say for sure, but there's a better chance that it was two rounds."

"Unusual for a suicide, but I've heard of it before," I said thoughtfully.

"Especially with a smaller caliber like the .38 used here. The second round could almost have been fired as a reflex action."

"Wouldn't they be farther apart? If you shoot yourself once, wouldn't you flinch and cause the second bullet to take a different path?"

"Strange things happen. I couldn't say one way or the other. Looking at what I've seen so far, I wouldn't say that there is conclusive evidence for suicide or for murder."

An hour later, Dr. Darzi had finished examining Donnie's lungs. "He had to have been dead before his face went into the lake. There's no water in his lungs."

"How long would it take for the bullet wound to kill him?" I asked.

"At least one of the bullets, if we're assuming there were two, did go through his heart. A minute, possibly two."

"Isn't it likely that, if he committed suicide standing in the lake, he would have face-planted into the water before he had a chance to stop breathing?" Darlene asked.

"Tell me how deep the water was where he was standing. If he could go down on all fours and still be out of the water, then the possibility exists that he shot himself, reflexively shot himself a second time, fell to his knees, died and then went face-down into the water."

"Is there anything else you could find that would sway you toward murder or suicide?" I asked.

"Drugs in his system. The labs will tell us that. Bruising might, but I don't see any. There are no marks from ropes or other abrasions that might suggest that he was restrained or manipulated. You aren't going to get me to come to a conclusion that is not supported by the evidence," he said, waving his hand dismissively.

"No, we want the truth. But don't expect us to be happy with it," I said.

We spent another hour watching him cut and weigh Donnie's various bits and pieces, then headed over to Earl Higgins's motel room.

"We really can't hold the room indefinitely," the manager told us. "Another day would be okay, but really, we can't do more than that." He was tall and well groomed with slick hair. When he talked, he had the habit of tilting his head back so that he was literally looking down his nose at us.

His attitude was pissing me off. I understood where he was coming from, but I thought he should have shown a little concern for the deceased.

"We need the security footage too," I told him. Julio had looked at the footage on Tuesday and had told the manager that we would need a copy.

"I've got it on a flash drive," he said. I just stared at him until he added, "I'll go get it."

Once I had the drive in hand, the manager escorted us to Earl's room. Inside, everything was neat and tidy, but there were used towels in the bathroom, so I assumed that Julio had managed to get it locked down before the maid had come in to clean. We put on gloves and started to poke around.

"Pretty basic," Darlene said, digging through his suitcase.

There was a laptop on the writing desk. I flipped it open and turned it on. The start screen came up, asking me for a password. I shut it down and bagged it.

"Do we need to have the crime scene techs process the room?" I said out loud, talking to myself as much as to Darlene.

"We can't assume anything," she said.

"You're right." I pulled out my phone and called Shantel. She said she'd send Marcus over as soon as she could.

"Sad thing is, we're probably doing the defense team's work," Darlene grumbled.

"That's the bitch of it. But it probably won't matter since Donnie's dead. If he was alive then you're right. In a motel room, we're bound to find fingerprints that we can't identify.

So during the trial, the defense could just harp on the fact that there were fingerprints from unknown suspects found in Earl's motel room."

"I can just hear them. 'Could this be the real killer or killers?'" she said in her best officious lawyer voice.

"But we don't have a choice."

"Agreed."

Though we both figured that the killer had never been in this room, we couldn't be sure, even though Julio had identified Earl on the surveillance footage leaving the motel for the last time on his own.

We stayed long enough for Marcus to get there.

"Just process for fingerprints," I told him. I wasn't going to make him vacuum the place for every little fiber. "Tell the manager that he'll be hearing from Higgins's ex-wife. He's not to do anything with the items in the room until he's spoken to her."

It was after six when we got back to the office. I called Pete before I headed home.

"Pete, my man, have I got a deal for you," I said cheerily.

"I don't like your tone. What are you getting me into now?" he asked suspiciously.

"Nothing, I promise. Darlene and I just want to run our murder investigation past you tomorrow and get your opinion."

"What's the catch?"

"It's actually two, possibly three, murders. With us presenting our cases for the two different scenarios, it will probably take you a couple of hours to review all the evidence," I said, still in the same cheery voice.

"You know, I have my own cases to work. I can't be solving yours and Darlene's too. If the brass wanted me to solve all the murders, they'd probably go ahead and fire you two deadbeats," he said with a chuckle.

"We just need your superior intellect to tell us which direction we should go in."

Darlene was listening and she rolled her eyes.

"Now you're just kissing ass. It doesn't become you."

"Please."

"The magic word. That's better. You know you'll owe me?"

"Anything for you, big guy."

He told me he'd be free first thing in the morning, so I told him to meet us in the conference room at nine. "We'll lay out all the evidence for you."

"No need to go to all that trouble. I'll just use a dousing rod."

"Yeah, we're going to expect a little more work from you than that. We're going to want to see you break a sweat."

"In August, I can pick up the phone and break a sweat. I went out to the range yesterday and, by the time I got done, I looked like I'd stepped out of a shower."

"I bet you didn't *smell* like you'd just stepped out of a shower."

"Touché. Hey, I gotta go. The girls are calling me to dinner."

By nine the next morning, we had covered the conference room table with interviews and evidence reports. I had also set up a laptop with a good sampling of crime scene photos.

"Okay, lay it on me," Pete said, busting through the door carrying a bag of bagels. "Sarah has me on a diet. I promised her no donuts for breakfast," he said as he laid out the bagels and containers of butter and cream cheese. I wasn't sure this was the sort of diet Sarah had in mind.

As best we could, Darlene and I had set everything out on the table in chronological order.

"First, we're going to let you look through the reports and evidence without any input from us," I said. "You can start here with the Conrad Higgins murder. Next is the attack on Faith, and finally the murders of Earl and Donnie."

"Was Donnie murdered?" Pete asked.

"You see, that's why we asked for your help. You know

how to get right to the heart of the matter. Was he murdered or did he kill himself? That's what we want you to tell us."

"We don't trust ourselves," Darlene said. "We're afraid that our preconceived ideas, or maybe our own biases, might influence how we see Donnie's death."

"Makes sense. I've got a death from the first year I was in CID that I still can't let go. A ten-year-old boy, found dead in a creek. Accident, murder or even suicide? We never could tell for sure. It still bugs the hell out of me. Okay. Go make phone calls or whatever you do when you're pretending to work. I don't need you all staring over my shoulder," he said and waved us out of the room.

"We've got time to do a few phone interviews," I said when we got back to our desks. "I'd be curious to know what Jason Harmon has been doing the last couple of days."

I got ahold of him on my third try.

"Are you serious?" he said when I asked him for his whereabouts during the two most recent deaths.

"Mr. Harmon, we have a job to do, and we have to treat everyone equally when it comes to means, motive and opportunity."

"I know I had a motive. A poor motive for... not liking Conrad. But do you seriously think I'd attack Faith Osborne and murder two more people because Conrad Higgins accused me of assault? That's nonsense." He was so angry that I could hear his teeth grinding together over the phone.

"I can come up with cascading reasons for you to kill or attack the others. But forget that. Give me a good enough alibi for the last few days and you're off the table," I said reasonably and honestly.

The silence from the other end of the phone went on long enough that I thought the call had been dropped.

"Mr. Harmon?"

"I'm here. I'd like to tell you to take it up with my lawyer, but I want it to end with this phone call. My wife got back from her trip and I've been with her since Sunday. We haven't been home."

I could tell that he didn't want to say where he was, but I asked anyway. "Where are you?"

"Camping." His voice sounded odd. Was he telling the truth?

"Just tell me where you are, I'll confirm it and you're done," I said, raising my eyebrows at Darlene, who was listening in. Most people with a good alibi couldn't wait to tell us.

"It's… We… This is something that we like to do. Not everyone understands. And let me say that it is not a sex thing," he said adamantly. Now Darlene and I were both listening intently. "We're at a nudist resort over near Destin," he finally said.

I rolled my eyes. "*That's* what you didn't want to tell us? Seriously?" I said before realizing I was being a little harsh. "We've heard a lot more embarrassing stories, trust me."

I managed to pry the name of the resort out of him and called their office. The resort manager confirmed that the Harmons had checked in on Sunday and she didn't think that either of them had left since arriving.

"We keep track of everyone's comings and goings. We work hard to protect our campers' privacy and security. You can imagine that, with everyone being nude, it's important that we don't have walk-ins that might take photos without permission or pilfer items from the campers' trailers."

"You have someone on the gate 24/7?"

"At midnight the gate is closed and you have to use a passkey to open it."

"Does the passkey record who comes and goes?"

"It does."

"Would you check to see if anyone left Monday or Tuesday night?"

"I did that while we were talking. No one opened the gates after-hours on those nights."

I thanked her, then turned to Darlene. "Barring something unusual, I think we can cross Jason Harmon off our suspect list."

"Which means we can assume that he was telling the truth about what he saw the night Conrad Higgins was murdered."

"If he isn't covering up for someone else," I couldn't resist suggesting.

"Are we back to a *Murder on the Orient Express* situation? Everyone is in on it?" she joked.

"Lots of people didn't like him," I said, "but that's probably far-fetched."

"If we go any further with this, we're going to want some better suspects. There's still McCune."

"I'd love to pin it on that guy. And don't forget the tip I got on Wednesday from Mr. Bowen about Conrad's lawyer. We need to follow up on the money trail. We've killed off three people in the same family. Where does the inheritance buck stop?"

Darlene picked up her phone, found Conrad's lawyer's number and dialed Franklin Beck's office.

"Hey, this is Darlene Marks with the sheriff's office. My partner and I just have a few questions to ask Mr. Beck about Conrad Higgins's estate. I was wondering if he could squeeze us in this afternoon. Maybe four?" Honey dripped from Darlene's voice.

"Three is the latest he makes appointments on Friday," I could hear the receptionist respond.

"Great, we'll be there at three," Darlene said and disconnected the call before the woman could say anything else.

I looked at my watch. "Our guru should have had enough time to look at everything."

"Are we going to do what we talked about yesterday?"

"Sure. I'll argue for Donnie being the killer and committing suicide," I said.

Darlene looked surprised. "I wouldn't have guessed you'd take that side."

"I'm hoping I can convince myself," I said truthfully.

CHAPTER NINETEEN

When we entered the conference room, Pete was shuffling through reports and frowning. "I don't have an autopsy report on Earl or Donnie," he said, not looking up.

"We're still waiting on the final ones, but I wrote up my summary of what Dr. Darzi has told us so far." I pointed to a couple of pages I'd typed up last night.

"I read those. So short of a revelation from various lab tests yet to be performed, he can't give you a definitive answer as to suicide or homicide for Donnie?" Pete was being very professorial.

"Exactly."

"Okay, I'm done reviewing what's here."

"We thought we'd start with you giving us your impression of the case before we enter Debate Club mode," I said.

"If this was my case…" He thought for moment. "I'd follow the obvious leads to their conclusion, but let them go if I couldn't find anything strong enough to hold onto. That said, the way it looks to me, Donnie killed his uncle for some reason and attacked Faith because he thought she'd seen him, or because he bought into his uncle's animosity toward her. Confronted by his father, he killed him too, then, in a fit of grief or guilt or insanity or possibly all three, he shot himself. Case closed."

"And why would you end it like that?" I asked.

"Because, without clear evidence pointing another direction, the State Attorney could never bring a successful case against anyone else. Too much evidence points to Donnie. A defense attorney for any other suspect would simply turn the trial into a referendum on Donnie's guilt or innocence."

"Logical, Mr. Spock," Darlene said, and Pete tented his fingers in front of his face and tilted his head in a slight bow. "But I've been chosen to argue against the case you've presented. I'll start with the fact that Donnie appeared to like his uncle. In fact, Donnie is one of the few people who didn't seem to have a problem with Conrad Higgins."

"Donnie has been reported as being paranoid. He's at the age that paranoid schizophrenia often strikes. So the motive might not be one that would be obvious, or even understandable, to a normal person," I countered.

"Second, Donnie appears to have taken Conrad's car, but Jason Harmon saw someone running away from the house that night," Darlene stated.

"Harmon is not the most reliable of witnesses, and he did say that he didn't get a clear look at the individual. He said he couldn't even be sure if it was a man or a woman. It's possible that Donnie took the car earlier, then parked it on a back street and walked back to Conrad's home and killed him. Which I would add is the very method that he used in his attack on Faith," I said triumphantly.

"Aha! That brings me to my third point. Why would Donnie attack Faith? By all accounts, they had never even met."

"I'll fall back on my paranoid schizophrenia answer from earlier. The voices in his head took his uncle's feud with Faith and turned it into his own feud."

"Another motive question: why kill his father? Why even contact his father?"

"Again, crazy is as crazy does," I tossed back.

"I'm not sure it's fair to use crazy as the answer to every question of motive."

"Crazy *can* be the answer. But to give Donnie his due, I think that he had moments of clarity and that's why he stepped into the pond and shot himself."

"So you're saying Donnie's motive in killing Conrad is that he was crazy. The reason for his attack on Faith is that he was crazy. The motive for murdering his father is that he was crazy, but it was suicide because he was momentarily sane," Darlene said, making it sound ludicrous. "Why get in the pond, then? Let me guess, because he was crazy."

"Suicides do strange things. But I'll throw it back at you. If it's not Donnie, what suspects have you got?" I challenged her.

Pete was sitting back in his chair, watching us lob our arguments back and forth like a spectator at a tennis match.

"Apparently, nudist neighbor is out. But that still leaves us with two prime suspects. First, his lawyer, Franklin Beck, who might have been stealing money from Conrad. We have testimony that Conrad thought Beck was stealing from him. If he was, and Conrad found out, then Beck had a solid motive for killing Conrad."

"Fine, I buy that. But what about the attack on Faith?"

"I think, for both my suspects, I have to go with the fact that they thought Faith saw something. She did take her dog out for a walk that night. A walk that went past Higgins's house."

"Maybe. But why was that rope left on her porch? And did they leave the car? Did they take the car in the first place? Why would they?"

"They brought the rope because they were planning to hang her and make it look like a suicide. They *did* leave the car, or maybe Donnie left the it there. It's not too far from Conrad's house. Maybe Donnie got spooked by the killing and just abandoned the car there. Making it just a fluke that it was near the house where Faith was attacked."

"Hmmm… a bit of a coincidence," I said, looking over at Pete, who was doing his best to look like a noble sage, his face giving nothing away. "We'll move on. Why kill Earl and Donnie?"

"If it's Beck, he has a good motive for both. Earl was going to inherit and he would have discovered the stolen money. Donnie was a loose end. Or maybe he just happened to kill Earl when Donnie was present, so he had to eliminate Donnie as a witness."

"Okay, I like the motive for Earl, and we know Earl was going to meet up with Donnie, so I'll buy the accidental witness motive for Donnie. Give me your next suspect."

"Horace McCune. That hateful man killed Conrad because of a money dispute."

"Absolutely accept that. And you've already given your reasoning for Faith. So why did McCune kill Earl?"

"Same as Beck. For financial reasons, he needed to eliminate Earl and Donnie."

"But who inherits now? With Beck, I kinda buy it because it gives him more fudge time to play with the books and maybe even manipulate who inherits. But with McCune, as much as I want him to be the bad guy, his motive isn't as strong for Earl and Donnie. If he already had money he'd stolen from Higgins, then he wouldn't be suing him. But the evidence points toward Higgins stealing from McCune."

"He did it for revenge. He killed the whole male line of Higginses because he was so pissed at Conrad." Darlene threw her hands up in the air, acknowledging how ridiculous her idea sounded.

"Having met McCune, I can almost believe he'd do that."

"Or he's trying to find something that Conrad had that he couldn't get from Conrad himself. Maybe he figured Conrad might have passed it off to his brother or nephew."

"You just came up with that one, didn't you?" I asked with a grin.

"I did. But it's not bad."

"It would be more believable if Conrad, Earl or Donnie

had been tortured."

"Maybe he found what he wanted. They had the money or whatever it was and then McCune just killed them because they knew too much."

"Maybe, maybe, maybe. That's what's so frustrating. Other suspects?"

"Not really. Lots of other people victimized by Conrad, but nothing to point to anyone else being involved."

"Okay, King Solomon, bestow upon us your great wisdom," I said to Pete, who sat in his chair with his hands folded over his ample waistline, looking more like Buddha than Solomon.

"I stick to my first assessment. Donnie is the simplest explanation. And as Mr. Occam tells us, the simplest solution is usually the right solution. Beck and McCune are both stretches. Beck is the best of the two because he could easily be manipulating money, which would provide him with a decent motive. Plus, you have a witness who says that Conrad thought Beck was stealing from him."

"We agree on that," I said, looking at Darlene, who nodded.

"There are three areas that, in my humble opinion, need more investigation. One is obvious: *was* Beck stealing money? Two: does he have an alibi for any of the murders? Three: is there a third possible suspect? Who inherits now?"

I thought about that. "Probably Donnie's mother, since it looks like the order of death was Conrad, Earl and then Donnie. She would be Donnie's closest relative, therefore she'd inherit everything. The only exceptions to that would be if Earl left everything to someone other than Donnie, or if Donnie left a will. We'll check that out."

"If she inherits, then you have to ask yourself, does she need money? Where was she when they were all killed? Could she have hired someone to do the killing?"

"Seems unlikely, but it does need to be looked into. She'll be here tomorrow, so we can question her then."

"Finally, the odd event out in all of this is the attack on

Faith. So you need to ask, was that attack really part of the sequence of killings or something unrelated? Assuming that it was related, why was she attacked? Did she really see something that might have made the killer or killers feel the need to eliminate her? And if the killer isn't Donnie, then is Faith still in danger?"

"Working up a victimology on Faith is going to the top of my priority list, because you're right. Her attack doesn't seem to fit with the other killings. The rest were killed with a gun while the person who attacked Faith tried to strangle her. Now that I think about it, strangling is more personal. You'd think that, if she was just a witness that needed to be eliminated, it would have been done as quickly and efficiently as possible," I said.

"Maybe they tried to strangle Faith because she's a woman, and they thought that would be quieter. And possibly appear unrelated to Conrad," Darlene said. "Of course, they underestimated both her and her dog."

"You got that right. Faith is in good shape. Teaches aerobics at the health center on the square. Doctors made it a point to say that the muscles in her neck probably saved her life. And it was Cleo that the bad guy really underestimated," I said.

As payment for his services, we took Pete to the Palmetto for lunch. Afterward, Darlene headed out to dig up more information on Horace McCune while I decided to interview Faith again.

No one answered her door. I went around to the side of the house and saw that her car was in the driveway. Concerned, I called Bernadette Santos.

"She's here at the theatre," Bernadette told me. "Faith always helps with the choreography for our shows."

The Grove had been a movie theatre until the '80s when folks in Adams County decided they didn't mind driving to Tallahassee, where they could select from ten different films and spend the day shopping at the mall. When the Grove closed down in 1989, a group of theatre aficionados got together and turned it into a music theatre. Built in the '40s, it had all the elements of a classic movie theatre, including plaster frescos and a balcony. The non-profit board that ran the Grove had worked hard to raise the money to restore the two-story neon sign out front. Whenever I saw it, I thought of big finned cars, girls in poodle skirts and boys with their jeans rolled up.

As soon as I entered the building, I could hear the ruckus in the theatre. The stage was full of half-costumed actors. Bernadette was up on stage, fussing with the actors. I saw Faith sitting four rows back in the audience, looking tired. Actually, I saw Cleo first. She was stretched out in the aisle, watching the scene on stage.

Cleo heard me coming and jumped up so she could lean against me. "How are you feeling?" I asked Faith.

"I'm doing better," she said hoarsely. "I see you've made a new friend. Thank you so much for taking care of her. Dr. Barnhill is such a wonderful vet and I've always adored Cara. It's so nice that you two are together. You are one lucky guy." Faith took a drink from a bottle of water.

"I need to ask you a few questions," I said, trying to speak loud enough to be heard over the chaos onstage, but not wanting to disturb the actors. A large green plant had just shuffled its way onto the stage and Bernadette was trying to show it where to stand.

Faith shook her head and stood up. "Hard to believe we open tonight. Of course, it's always like this. Pure craziness until opening night, and then, like a miracle, it comes together... mostly. Come on, we can talk up in the lobby."

Cleo couldn't decide whether she wanted to walk next to me or Faith. She kept shifting back and forth between us. Her injuries looked much better, and she didn't show any signs that the stitches bothered her.

"She's such a sweet dog. I'm so used to Mauser, who's kind of a lunkhead."

"Aren't all men?" Faith said with a smile.

"You may have a point."

We sat down on a Victorian-style sofa in the lobby, with Cleo lying across our feet.

"On the night that Conrad Higgins was killed, you said that you took Cleo for a walk, right?"

"Yes, it was about eleven that evening. I thought you wanted to ask questions about the attack on me."

"We're trying to get it all sorted. Right now, we're assuming that all the attacks are connected."

"I guess that makes sense."

"What time did you get back to your house?"

"About eleven-thirty."

"Okay, I want you to think hard about this. Did you see anything unusual on your walk?"

"I can't think of anything."

"Did you see anything around Conrad's house?"

"Like I said, I did look at it. But… Now that you mention it, I might have seen someone hanging around." She looked off into the distance. Finally, she shook her head. "I can't be sure. However, there might have been a shadow on the porch. Some movement."

"What did you do when you got home?"

"Got ready for bed. I read for a while, but that's all. I had to get up early the next morning to lead an aerobics class at the health center. That morning class is mostly for the folks who work there."

I tried to think what I was missing. "What did you do earlier on the day that Conrad was killed? Let's go through your whole day."

"The whole day? I'm not sure…"

"Please, just humor me."

"I got up and went for a walk with Cleo. After that, I came here and met with Bernadette. We were having trouble with our chorus and she wanted to go over some of their marks. After that, we went to the Palmetto for lunch."

"Did anything unusual happen during any of that? Anyone odd stick out?"

"No, it was just an ordinary day."

"What did you do after lunch?"

"I dropped Bernadette back here. Sometimes we walk up to the restaurant and back, but it was so hot that day. I came home and took Cleo for a short walk and fed her lunch. After that, I went to the nursing home to lead a stretching class. It's so rewarding to help out down there. Then back home. Wait, no, I did do some shopping at the Supersave. Then I came home and had dinner with Cleo. That was it until we went for our walk." Her voice was noticeably raspy as she finished talking. I felt bad, but I needed as much information from her as I could get.

Next we went over the night of the attack. She wasn't able to add much to what she'd told us at the time. Finally, having asked every question I could think of, I got up and said goodbye to her and Cleo.

I picked Darlene up at the office for our meeting with Franklin Beck. On the way, she told me what she'd learned about McCune.

"He's mean as a snake and rich as Croesus. He's been married three times. Made it his mission not to give any of his wives a dime when they got divorced, no matter how much money he had in the bank."

"Charming. Where's he from originally?"

"He grew up in Texas. His dad worked on oil rigs and was killed when McCune was ten. Oh, I should say that I found some of the info in magazines where he was giving interviews, so take it with a grain of salt."

"Made a lot of money in oil, I suppose."

"Nope, made a lot of money selling equipment to oil companies. I found a few down-and-dirty articles that said he was a master at getting guys to buy equipment on credit at outrageous interest rates. When they defaulted, he'd have his goons come and repossess the equipment. One account said he had a bigger team of repo agents than he did salesmen. He got in trouble about fifteen years ago when his guys killed three people in the same year."

"They went to repo a derrick and the owner came at

them when a gun, forcing them to shoot him," I guessed.

"Pretty close. There was one where the guy was chasing McCune's team down the road as they took back a water pump. They ran his truck off the road into a telephone pole. Another guy was crushed when they were tearing down a rig he'd bought on credit. And the third involved a fight where the guy died from being hit on the head with a pipe. The authorities put a lot of heat on McCune's operation after that. The long and short is, he packed up and left Texas. He was already a bit long in the tooth and had a pot full of money, so I guess it made sense to sell the company for another fortune and move on."

"How'd he end up here?" I'd known that the Pine Top Planation had been sold and that the buyer had built a house on the land, but I hadn't known who it was.

"Turned out that his last wife had some ties here. Also, McCune had come to the panhandle to buy oil leases out in the Gulf. Everyone speculated that he was really planning to set up an equipment company to cater to drilling off the coast of Florida."

"Which, thanks to a tourist industry that thinks tar balls and spring break don't mix, has never happened."

"You got it. And now I think he's just become so ornery and cantankerous that the only people who will put up with him are ones he's paying. I did follow up on his hired playmate. She said that they did the dirty and were done by ten-thirty. After that, he sent her off to another room for the night."

"So she can't swear that he was home all night."

"Exactly. With the size of that house, how would she know unless she went looking? When I asked her if that was normal procedure, she said it was. This was her tenth time visiting McCune, and she says it's always wham-bam, I'm done, go to another room. Which she says works out for her, because it gives her the rest of the night to work on video reviews of fashion products that she posts on YouTube. I have her YouTube identity if you want to check those out."

"I'm good."

"They aren't bad. She's got a lot better vocabulary than you might think considering her day… I mean, night job."

"Okay, so McCune is still in the running. I like that. Of course, after what you found out, it doesn't matter if he has an alibi or not. If McCune has used goons in the past, then he probably has the contacts to hire someone to take out Conrad."

"What'd you learn from Faith?" Darlene asked.

I gave her the details of my interview as we parked at the lawyer's office.

"It's a shame she didn't get a look at her attacker," was Darlene's only comment.

Beck kept us waiting for twenty minutes in the reception area before ushering us into his office. "What can I do for you?" he asked with a tight smile.

"We'd like to ask you some questions about Conrad Higgins," I said.

"Some new information has come out," Darlene said. We had decided that we'd do the old tennis match interview technique with him. We'd alternate questions and comments in the hopes that it would throw him off his game a little.

"What new information?"

"You know that Earl and Donnie have both been found dead?" I asked. Not answering questions is another way to keep control of the interview.

"Yes. That is disturbing." He did look unhappy about it.

"Do you have any idea who could be responsible?" Darlene asked.

"Like I told Earl, Horace McCune has been making threats for months."

"Why would he kill Earl and Donnie?" I asked.

"The man has a very volatile temper," Beck said and, from the look in his eyes, it was fairly obvious that he was afraid of McCune.

"What kind of threats?" said Darlene.

"Crazy stuff about cutting off Conrad's body parts and

sticking them… You can guess where. All pretty unhinged, if you ask me. He's even made threats against me. Told me once on the phone that I should be roasted alive along with every other lawyer in the world. Made some crack about barbeque sauce. I've quit taking calls from him and, in light of the murders, I'm considering a restraining order." He sounded serious.

"Where were you that Monday night?" I asked.

"Are you serious?"

"Did you know that Conrad suspected you of stealing from his offshore accounts?" Darlene chimed in.

"I don't…" He saw our faces and dropped the denial. "No, I didn't. But I'm not that surprised. He was a very paranoid man. I was the fourth lawyer he's had in the last ten years."

"So where were you Monday night?" I asked again.

"I was at home. I watched TV and worked on some files. My wife was home. She will probably confirm where I was."

"Probably?" Darlene said with raised eyebrows.

"We get along most of the time. But she has a nasty streak that comes out at the worst of times."

"Who inherits Conrad's money?" I asked.

"Earl inherited, so the question is who inherits from Earl and that is not my department. You'll have to talk to Earl's lawyer," he said testily.

"Conrad was in a dispute with Faith Osborne. Did you ever meet her?" Darlene said.

"I met her once early on when we attempted to arbitrate the matter."

"What did you think of her?" I asked.

"The people I met who were in a disagreement with Conrad were always the same. They were angry and uninterested in anything but confronting him." He paused and seemed to think about his answer. "I will say this, Ms. Osborne seemed more in control of her emotions than most of the people that sat across the table from him."

After a few more questions, we headed back to the office.

"Another hot date tonight?" I teased her.

"Sort of. Hondo is working, so I told him I'd meet him when he takes his dinner break."

"Ambulance chaser," I said.

"I am tonight, buttercup. What about you?"

"Cara and I are going to go see Eddie at the hospital and try out a new restaurant, a place called Backwoods Crossing out east of Tallahassee."

"You two lovebirds have fun."

CHAPTER TWENTY

Cara and I drove to Tallahassee with classic rock playing in our ears and the breeze of a late summer evening on our cheeks. An afternoon thunderstorm had rolled through for the first time in a week, cooling the temperature and leaving a freshly washed smell in the air.

At the hospital, I tracked down a nurse who had worked with Eddie.

"He was awake for a little while this afternoon, but he's still pretty confused. He's having trouble coming up with the right words for things, but he did pretty well on the memory and concentration questions. Remember, he suffered a grade-three concussion. It's going to take him a while to fully recover. There could be some permanent memory loss," the nurse told us.

"Can we see him?" I asked.

"Of course. But don't try to wake him up. He needs his rest."

She showed us to his room and stood in the doorway while we went up to the bed. Eddie looked thin and fragile. There was a box of chocolates by the bed, along with a cell phone and a note. The note read: *I got this phone for you. My number and Seth's are in the contacts. Call when you can. Your friend,*

Albert.

After a minute, the nurse shooed us out of the room and down the hall.

The restaurant was filling up fast on a Friday night, but we managed to get a table. Luckily, it was still summer. College students were just starting to dribble back into Tallahassee and many residents were off enjoying their last summer flings before sending the kids back to school.

"Isn't your steak good?" Cara asked, watching me pick at my dinner.

"It's great. I'm just feeling guilty about Eddie."

"And you should," she said, causing me to look up to see if she was joking. She wasn't. "I don't mean you should sulk about it, but you should learn something from what happened."

I felt a little stung by her response. I'd been looking for a little tenderness and not so much honesty.

"I didn't ask him to do anything Monday night. He did that on his own," I said defensively.

"Exactly, now eat your steak," Cara said smartly.

"You tricked me."

"You deserved it," she said, digging into her crab cakes. "On the one hand, Eddie *did* make his own decision to go out on Monday. But on the other hand, you know Eddie's background. You also know that he's imprinted on you like a baby duck. Mr. Griffin is right. Eddie probably *does* need a little time away from being your cloak-and-dagger man."

"I surrender. I will swear off using Eddie until he has had a chance to solidify his sobriety, at least as much as that's possible for anyone who's been an addict."

"I think they advise people in AA to refrain from getting into a new relationship for the first year."

"You inhaled those crab cakes," I said, watching as she forked the last bite into her mouth.

"Don't try to change the subject. We were talking about you giving Eddie a long-term break from being a foot soldier in the Larry Macklin Army."

"Yes, sir!" I gave her a mock salute, then reached out and took her hand. "It's very sweet that you care about Eddie."

"You don't fool me. You care about him too."

"Yeah, I do," I admitted with a sigh. "I just hope he'll be able to remember what happened to him."

"If he doesn't remember, then don't badger him or try to shame him into remembering. If he can't, he can't."

"Yes, dear," I said, earning a napkin thrown at me. "Just kidding."

I woke up Saturday with a full agenda. I needed to go over to Dad's that morning, Donnie's mother would be getting into town in the afternoon and we had the musical at the Grove that night.

I pulled up at Dad's just before ten. Steam was rising from the ground as the heat climbed and the sun burned off the last of the heavy morning dew. A very damp Mauser came bounding across the yard with Dad at his heels. The dog leaned against me and rubbed himself vigorously.

"Stop that, you moose!" I yelled at him. He just looked at me with his mouth hanging open in a goofy grin. "You know, I've met another Great Dane who is gentle and sweet and, on occasion, even obedient. In a word, nothing like you," I said, giving him a good body massage. My hands came away covered in fur, making me look like a werewolf.

I could still see the areas on Mauser's legs that had been shaved to take blood. "You all healed up?" I asked him as I wiped my hands off on my jeans.

"Don't remind him. He *just* stopped limping, the big malingerer," Dad said. He was wearing shorts and a T-shirt and looked surprisingly relaxed.

"You aren't out campaigning today?"

"I put out more signs last week. And I have a church picnic tomorrow. But I'm feeling pretty good. I've heard more rumors that Maxwell doesn't like his odds right now and that he's hesitating to dig into his own pockets for campaign funds." The chief of police had started this campaign with high hopes, but Dad had gotten some good publicity over the last few months.

"I remember when you ran for sheriff the first time. Even though you weren't running against an incumbent, you spent the whole time wondering if you were just throwing money down the drain."

"If I were in Maxwell's position, it would be hard to get people to pony up cash. I hate it, but I've spent a lot of time courting the big-money folks in the county."

"That's the game you have to play. The hard reality is that, in this day and age, you have to spend money to get elected to office. You can't unilaterally disarm, and you can't afford to finance your own campaign."

"I might if I could spend all my time going door-to-door talking to voters, but I don't have time to do that *and* the job I was elected to do. There's a catch-twenty-two wrapped up somewhere in all of that." He shrugged. "Enough talk of the election. Your text said you wanted to look through some of your mom's stuff?" He sounded a bit puzzled.

"I want to see if there is anything related to Faith Osborne. I'm doing a full victimology on her."

"Johnson said that Donnie's suicide would probably wrap up the case."

"And it might. But there are some loose ends that Darlene and I want to tie up before we call it solved."

"Just scanning the reports, it looks like the attack on Faith was all Donnie's doing," Dad said as Mauser left us to stand in the shade of the house.

"Monster Mutt has the right idea. Let's get out of the heat," I said, and we headed into the garage. "Faith couldn't give us any sort of ID of her attacker, so that's all speculation."

Dad stopped and turned to me. "One thing you need to be careful of is beating a dead horse. Every murder case has loose ends. I've seldom seen an investigation where *all* the questions get answered. An investigator can drive himself crazy with cases that should have been closed." He grabbed a towel from the top of the dryer and dried Mauser briskly.

"I know." I went on to explain how we had brought Pete in to review all the evidence. "We're just going to give it a couple more days. If we don't find anything else, we'll wait for the lab and forensic reports to come back and then close it down."

Dad nodded and led me back to the guestroom closet where he'd stored various things of Mom's that he couldn't bear to part with. "I'll leave you to it," he said, obviously not in the mood to take any trips down memory lane.

Mauser had followed us into the room. He looked from me to Dad as Dad turned to leave. I could see the wheels in Mauser's head turning as he tried to decide whether to follow Dad or to stay with me. The fact that the guestroom was closest to the central air conditioner, and therefore the coolest room in the house, made up his mind. He hopped up on the bed, turned in circles a dozen times and then flopped down to watch me sort through the closet.

There were a few boxes of clothes. I took them out and set them aside, recognizing the blouse on the top of one of the boxes. It was bright yellow with a flower pattern and only slightly faded. My mind was immediately filled with a host of idyllic childhood memories with only the dark cloud of Mom's sudden death hanging over them. It had taken years for Dad and me to process the loss.

I shook off my thoughts and got down to business, pulling out a box full of photo albums and school yearbooks.

"Move over," I told Mauser as I climbed onto the bed with the box. I leaned back against the headboard and started going through the books and albums. I found a number of pictures of Mom and Faith together. In many of them, they were clinging to each other and smiling at the camera as though they were about to burst into laughter. Faith had been very attractive, with high cheekbones and piercing eyes, while Mom was all girl-next-door. Looking at the photos, I thought about Cara and the old saying that a man will marry a girl like his mother. Cara and Mom didn't look much alike except in one way. They had the same smile—broad and happy, holding nothing back. I had no doubt that the two women would have liked each other.

In one of the albums, I found a photo of Mom and Faith walking a Great Dane. Their names were written on the back of the picture along with the Dane's name, Rodney Dangerfield. My grandfather had named the dog and it was quite the joke, as Dangerfield had been very protective and had demanded respect from everyone who met him. Mom had enjoyed telling a story about a boy she had dated briefly. After their final, unpleasant date, the boy had yelled at her as he dropped her off at her house. Before anyone could stop him, Dangerfield had cleared the backyard fence and lunged for the boy, who only just managed to escape up the nearest tree. Mom and my grandparents had sat in the front yard for twenty minutes watching Dangerfield stalk the bottom of the tree while the boy begged Mom to forgive him. Finally, she had put a leash on the dog and the boy was able to escape in his car. It had been three days before he'd had the nerve to show his face at school.

Flipping through the yearbook, I saw that Mom and Faith had been in many of the same clubs together. They had both avoided the stereotypical girls' clubs like future homemakers and had opted instead for science clubs where they were almost always the only girls in the group.

An hour later, I closed the last yearbook and sighed. Did I understand Faith any better after all that? The answer was, not really.

When I got up to put the boxes back in the closet, Mauser jumped off the bed and started dragging clothes out of one of the boxes.

"Quit it, you mongrel!" I yelled, but before I could pull him away, he'd used his paw to knock the box over, spilling everything onto the floor. The lid came off of a shoebox and I saw that the box was full of letters. From the postmarks, I could see that they were from Mom's high school and college days.

Flipping through the envelopes, they all appeared to be from friends and family. No letters from Dad. He must have taken out any of his love letters, or maybe she had kept them someplace more important than a shoebox. There were four letters from Faith and an official-looking envelope that caused my mouth to fall open.

The return address indicated that it was from the CIA's human resources department. Numbly, I took out the sheets of paper that were inside. There was a form and a cover letter. The cover letter was addressed to Mom using her maiden name. It had been sent during her second year in college.

The cover letter thanked her for her interest in joining the Central Intelligence Agency and said that if she filled out and returned the enclosed application, they would be glad to review it and get back with her. *Wow!* was all I could think. I knew the CIA did some recruiting on college campuses, so at some point Mom must have expressed an interest in applying. No big deal. But it was to me. This letter was a glimpse at a side of my mother that I'd never imagined. We had gone camping when I was growing up and Mom was always up for an adventure, but who would have guessed? The fact that she had kept the letter added weight to it. Some part of her must have dreamed of a life of excitement. And the CIA. I had always seen my mom as more of a Peace Corps kind of person. *Fascinating*, I thought.

Next, I opened the letters from Faith and read them in chronological order. The first two were the standard I'm-having-fun-at-school-how-about-you letters, but the third said that she was going to send in the application they had talked about. I had no doubt what she was referring to. So Faith and Mom had talked about joining the CIA together... Was this some sort of triple-dog-dare thing? I was looking forward to talking to Faith about the whole crazy scheme.

The fourth letter clenched it. It was a goodbye-for-now note. At the end Faith said that, if all went well, she might spend a lot of time out of the country, but that they would always be friends.

Apparently, she'd gotten into the CIA. Had she gone on missions? Or maybe she'd ended up sitting at a desk. I knew that most of the people who worked for the CIA were analysts who spent their days going over recordings or spreadsheets or both. No matter what, I had a lot to ask her about. *Will she be* able *to talk about it?* I wondered.

I put everything neatly back in the closet, then chased Mauser out of the room. In the kitchen, there was a note from Dad saying he'd gone into town to buy horse feed. Jamie was out in the barn and I was to let him know when I left so that he could keep an eye on the dog.

"Thanks for the help, you big oaf. I'll give your best to Cleo and let Jamie know it's your lunchtime." Mauser gave me one of his rare kisses on the cheek. I wiped the drool off with my sleeve and closed the door behind me.

I headed for the office, where it was nice and quiet. I could do a bit of research without the usual friendly banter interrupting me.

I searched online for information about Faith. She taught language classes part-time at Tallahassee Community College. According to the short bio on their faculty page, she was fluent in seven languages, including French, Spanish, German, Russian and Turkish. Aerobics and foreign languages. No wonder the CIA had been interested in her.

But what could any of this have to do with the Higgins murders? I doubted that they had died as part of some bizarre international intrigue, but something about all this new information was nagging at me.

CHAPTER TWENTY-ONE

My phone rang shortly after two o'clock. "Deputy Macklin, you asked me to give you a call when I got to town." Donnie's mother sounded like she was on the edge of tears. She probably was.

"Where would you like to meet?"

"I've got a car. I can meet you at your office."

I called Darlene and we were both waiting in the foyer when Julia Musgrove arrived. I opened the door for her.

"We're very sorry for your loss," I said. "Let's go back to the conference room where we can sit down and talk."

Once we were seated, I took a good look at Julia. She was well dressed, but there were deep wrinkles around her eyes and across her forehead that had developed over years, and not days.

"Mrs. Musgrove, I know my questions are going to be difficult for you and may cause you some pain, but my only reason for asking them is to solve the untimely deaths of three people, including your son and ex-husband. We want to know the truth. That's our only objective," I told her.

She stared down at the table, nodding her head slightly.

"If Donnie committed any of these crimes, then we don't see any reason to make a big production of that fact. There are no other relatives that we're aware of who would want to publicize who killed Conrad and Earl," Darlene said gently.

"My son didn't kill his father. They had differences, but he wouldn't do that." Now she was shaking her head adamantly.

"When was the last time you spoke to your son?"

"Monday. Before that, it must have been about two weeks ago, I guess, right before he came down here. Why didn't Conrad call us?"

"Donnie might have asked him not to," I suggested, and she nodded, wiping at her eyes. "Tell me about that last phone conversation."

"Like I told you before, he wasn't making much sense. He said that his uncle was dead and that he was scared for his own life. When I asked him why, he said because of what he'd seen. There was something else too." She paused, clearly dealing with some sort of internal conflict.

"Please, if there's anything that could help..." Darlene encouraged.

"He said that he'd done something... Something bad..."

"And?" I asked.

"He wanted to do more bad stuff. I'd never heard him talk like that. I begged him to call his father. I knew Earl was down here. Before he hung up, he agreed." She was sobbing quietly now. I moved a box of Kleenex over to her and gave her some time to compose herself.

"What about the call he made before he left? Why did he leave North Carolina?"

"Donnie was pissed at his father. It seems like he'd been angry ever since he turned sixteen. During the phone call, he just kept saying that he couldn't take his father bitching at him anymore. That was his word. I told him he could come stay with us, but he had problems with my husband too, so honestly, even when I was offering I knew he'd never agree to that. The call was short. At the end, he just said he had to get away."

"Do you think it is possible that your son killed himself?"

I asked.

"I don't know. The last couple of years, that's been my biggest fear. We got him to go see a counselor a couple times in high school, but after he turned eighteen, he wouldn't do anything we suggested."

"Did he ever exhibit any signs of aggression toward any family member?"

"That's not a fair question. Most teenagers are angry at their parents at some point or another. I smashed my mother's dishes when I was fourteen."

"You have a point. Did he ever talk about his uncle?"

"Conrad? He asked about him a couple of times growing up. He probably heard us talking about him and was curious about this guy that we all despised. He didn't hear us talk about many people that way. Looking back, I guess that might have made Conrad stick out. Donnie must have decided that anyone we disliked that much must be all right." Her expression had become empty and hollow.

"Now I'm going to ask you some questions that will seem offensive to you. But we have to ask. Remember that it's all part of getting down to the truth," I said and took a deep breath before continuing. "Who inherits your ex-husband's estate?"

"Now? I don't know. He has some cousins…"

"Donnie died after your husband. Was he your husband's heir?"

"Yes. In fact, I know that Donnie was also the beneficiary of Earl's life insurance policy."

"How much would that be worth?"

"The insurance was for half a million dollars, and his estate is probably worth close to that."

"You realize that, unless one of these cousins can prove that Donnie killed Earl, then all that money will go to you, including whatever Earl was to inherit from Conrad."

She stared at me blankly. Was she a good actress or had this really never occurred to her?

"Me? Why… I don't want that money." She sounded

sincere.

"We'd like you to give us a statement detailing your movements over the past week."

She just stared at me for a minute before she spoke. "You can't think I had anything to…"

"We need to eliminate everyone we can. All we need is to feel comfortable that you didn't have the opportunity and we'll drop that line of inquiry," I assured her.

"Someone killed my son," she said in a voice as hard as granite.

"If that's the case, then we will pursue them to the limits of our abilities."

"If that's the case? What does that mean?"

"We have to consider that your son may have committed suicide. You said yourself that you thought it was a possibility."

"I just don't know. I don't know anything anymore." She started crying again, her emotions all over the map. One minute she was angry and defensive and the next she was breaking down in tears. "When can I get my son's body?" she said through her tears.

"I'll check as soon as we're done," Darlene said, taking Julia's hand.

"I'll do your statement or whatever it is you want from me, but not now… Please. I was in North Carolina all week. I swear. I just can't think right now."

"I'm sorry," was all I could say.

We calmed her down and offered to drive her back to her hotel in Tallahassee, but she said she'd rather drive herself.

"I don't think she was acting," I said as I watched her drive away.

"No. But she'll probably inherit more than a million dollars. She has a motive. I wonder if anyone else, say her current husband, needs money."

"That thought occurred to me, but this was not the time to go down that road."

"As hardcore as I can be, I have to agree with you. At

this point, even *I* couldn't have browbeat her," Darlene said, trying to make a joke that just seemed flat confronted by that much grief. "I'm going to call Darzi's office and check on the status of Donnie's body. They're probably still holding onto Earl's too. Who's going to deal with getting him buried?"

"That will fall to his lawyer or that poor woman. You'll have to ask her when you're giving her the details on Donnie," I said, grateful that Darlene had volunteered to help Julia Musgrove.

It was only mid-afternoon and I was already feeling tired. The last thing I wanted to do was attend the play that evening, but I wasn't going to disappoint Cara.

On the way home, I made a last-minute decision to stop at the nursing home where Faith had worked the day she was attacked. I wondered if anyone had seen someone following her, or even someone unusual just hanging about.

Magnolia Ridge had beds for a hundred residents. When I opened the door, I was hit with the odor of industrial cleansers mixed with a hint of urine. Even so, the place was well kept and, the few times I'd been there, the residents seemed alert and mostly content.

"I'm Deputy Macklin. I'd like to speak with a manager or head nurse," I said, showing my ID to the receptionist.

"Is there something wrong?" the woman asked. Her name tag read "Caroline Foster" and her dark brow was furrowed in concern.

"No, I'm just doing some background on an investigation that doesn't involve you all."

I couldn't blame her for asking. With abuse hotline numbers posted all around the facility, they were used to having investigators show up on a monthly basis. For every serious report of abuse in a nursing home, there are dozens made as the result of perceived slights or neglect as a way for patients or their families to vent their frustration.

"Let me call." After a brief conversation, she told me that the manger would be right out. I moved aside to let a family sign-in.

Stepping back to the desk, I asked, "Do you know Faith Osborne?"

"Oh, yes, she's wonderful. Comes in a couple times a week," Caroline said, her face lighting up and then suddenly going dark. "Is this about the attack? What is the world coming to? Shameful!" She shook her head vigorously.

"On the day that Conrad Higgins was killed, Monday the eighth, Faith said she visited here. Did you notice anything odd that day?"

"Let me think, now. No... Wait, yes, Ms. Faith was upset. That's right. Mr. Kendell died that morning. He and Faith were good buddies. They got to know each other because of that business with Faith's mother." She lowered her voice before going on. "You know, that conman stealing from them. Ohhh, that man. I saw him in here a couple times. Sweet-talking like nobody's business. I'd just started back then and didn't know any better. Thought he was a nice guy. No such thing." She shook her head angrily.

"How upset was Faith that day?"

"She was crying. But she's the real deal and she still managed to teach the stretching class. Normally, she'd have stayed and visited with folks, but she left right away that day."

"The next day, did anyone ask about her? Maybe a stranger or a member of the staff?"

"No, not that I remember. We get a bunch of visitors. Some of them are family that only come once or twice a year. But I don't recall anyone in particular asking about Faith."

"Were there any workmen around here during the couple of days around the time of the attack?"

"No, just our regular guys, Tyrone and Kenny."

A tall, lanky man wearing a suit jacket and a ready-made smile came up to us.

"I'm the manager, Trey Arlen. How can I help you?"

I explained that I was doing follow-up on the assault on

227

Faith and went through the same set of questions that I had with Caroline. Arlen knew less about what had happened that day than the receptionist did. He took me around to talk to a couple more employees. Everyone gave me the same story. Faith was wonderful, but she was very upset that day at the death of Mr. Kendell. Everyone was hoping that Faith got well and would come back soon.

I thanked then all and headed home.

As I drove, I thought about what I had learned. Had Faith been so upset that she hadn't noticed someone following her? Why hadn't she mentioned Mr. Kendell's death when I asked about her activities on the day that Conrad was killed? Had she thought it wasn't important? And did any of this matter a hill of beans to the investigation?

When I got home, Cara was pressure-washing the front of the house.

"Wow, I'm impressed!" I said.

"I thought it would be a good chore for the end of summer. At least there's lots of water involved."

"I can't say I mind seeing you all wet," I said, making leering gestures with my eyebrows and receiving a quick squirt of water in return. "Okay. I give up."

She'd already done more than half the house.

"I'll help you finish up," I said.

I stripped down to my boxer shorts and slipped on an old pair of tennis shoes from the front porch.

"Who looks sexy now?" Cara asked, giving me a solid dousing of water.

"Okay, now. Do you want help or not?"

"I do. You spray. I'll move the ladder."

An hour later, all the equipment was put away and we were sitting on lounge chairs in the front yard, sopping wet and drinking cold beers.

"Thanks, I needed this," I said, enjoying the feel of the water, the summer breeze and the sun as it moved across the sky behind the live oak trees that shaded the yard.

"What, the beer?" Cara said, her eyes closed and her head resting on the back of her chair.

"No, the water, the sun, the silliness. There's been too much of this case whirling around in my head the last couple of days."

"Give your mind the evening off. Maybe if you can relax, the answers will come easier," Cara said.

"Good plan. I'll give it a try."

The Grove's production of *Little Shop of Horrors* was scheduled to start at seven-thirty. Cara and I arrived a little before seven.

There was lots of excited chatter in the lobby as cast members came and went, greeting family and friends that had come to the show. I saw Faith surrounded by well-wishers.

"I want to ask her about the CIA," I said. Cara had been surprised and impressed when I told her about the letter addressed to Mom.

"Tonight might not be the right time," she counseled.

"Maybe." I knew that my curiosity was getting the better of me, but I couldn't help myself. But before I could approach Faith, I caught a glimpse of movement behind me and turned, my eyes going wide. "Whoa! Is that Darlene and Hondo?" I exclaimed a little louder than I'd intended.

Hondo was wearing dress slacks and a silk shirt, while this was the first time I had ever seen Darlene in a dress and heels.

"They're cute together," Cara said softly.

"Big night on the town," I kidded them after we'd walked over and I'd introduced Cara to Hondo.

"I'll tell you a little secret. I love musicals," Hondo said conspiratorially with a broad smile on his face.

"We'll see if you love this musical," I whispered. "I saw some of the rehearsals."

"I don't worry. I'll tell you another secret: I'm an actor at heart. Did it in high school and college. I'd be doing local theatre now if the job would let me. So I know rehearsal don't mean nothin'," he said confidently. He turned to a young college-aged girl and said, "It's going to be a great show, right?"

"Def! My friend is one of the girls in the chorus. Awesome voice," she answered, smiling back at Hondo's cheery face.

Darlene was unusually quiet. She had a big smile and a goofy expression on her face, but I knew she was feeling awkward about being on a public date so early in a relationship when you don't quite know how everything is going to turn out. I gave her a reassuring smile and received a look of gratitude in return.

I saw Bernadette Santos over by the ticket booth, helping a volunteer with an issue on the computer. "I'll be right back," I told Cara, Hondo and Darlene.

By the time I'd worked my way through the crowd to the ticket booth, Bernadette was done and had started to walk away. "Oh, hello!" she exclaimed when she saw me. "I'm so glad you all decided to come to our show. It's going to be fabulous."

"Can I get a second of your time?"

"Sure."

"Did you see Faith on the day she was attacked?"

"No, I didn't. We were going to meet at her place that afternoon, but she called and said she couldn't make it."

"Have you seen anyone odd hanging about the theatre? Maybe someone asking about Faith?"

"What's this all about?" Bernadette asked.

"We're just exploring the possibility that the attack on Faith wasn't related to the murder of Conrad Higgins," I said.

Her eyes got wide. "I never asked... She wasn't... assaulted, was she?"

"No. But since Cleo interrupted the attack, we don't know what might have happened."

"Oh my. I never even considered that. I'm so glad that I'm staying there with her now. Before I go back home, I'll make sure that she has a better security system. Can't rely solely on Cleo. That poor girl has already gone through enough."

"But you haven't seen anyone suspicious around here or over at Faith's house?"

"No. Thank goodness, no."

I thought about the night that Earl and Donnie had died. Could Donnie have thought about attacking Faith? Was he only deterred by Bernadette staying at Faith's house? I was circling back to the attacks being connected.

"What about the night that Faith came home?"

"What about it?"

"Did you see or hear anything strange around Faith's house that night?"

"I wouldn't know. She wouldn't let me stay with her that night. Said she just wanted to rest. I begged her to let me stay, but she insisted. And she did seem in pretty good shape. Actually, a lot better than when I went by the next day. I think she knew it too, because she didn't argue with me then when I told her I was going to stay with her until she got all better."

So Faith had been alone that night. That was news to me. If someone had wanted to kill her, that would have been the perfect opportunity. With my head whirling, I thanked Bernadette for her time and the tickets.

"You know, you'd make a great actor. You should try out for one of our shows."

The mere thought of being on stage made me want to puke. "No, I don't think acting's for me."

"You're no fun," she said with a smile and a wink. "Be sure and stay after the show. The cast will come out and talk to everyone."

She bustled off and I started to turn back to where Cara was still talking to Hondo and Darlene. But then I changed my mind and headed into the theatre. There were still fifteen minutes before the show was scheduled to start, but I'd seen Faith go into the theatre and I wanted to see if I could corner her about the CIA thing.

I saw her making her way down to the front of theatre, stopping at the third row from the stage. I looked at my tickets and realized we were in the same aisle. Faith sat four seats in. My tickets were for the aisle seats. A couple passed me, also headed for row three. I peered at their tickets and saw that they were for the seats next to Faith.

"Excuse me. I've got a friend sitting over there. Would you like to exchange your seats for the two on the aisle?"

The couple readily agreed and I hurried out into the lobby to get Cara. Now I could sit next to Faith and talk to her about Mom and the CIA without making a special effort.

"Let's go ahead and get our seats," I told Cara, taking her hand and rushing her past the ushers who handed us programs. As soon as she caught sight of Faith and saw where our seats were, she gave me a dirty look.

"It's a coincidence," I said brightly.

I went in first and sat down next to Faith, who turned and smiled when she saw me.

"Larry! I'm so glad you all made it. I thought I saw you out in the lobby. Cara, it's wonderful to see you. And thanks again for taking care of Cleo while I was in the hospital. We've got an appointment to come in next week so the doc can look at her stitches." Faith's voice still sounded rough, but she was definitely healing.

"Dr. Barnhill feels really good about how well Cleo's doing," Cara said, talking across me.

When Cara opened her program, I turned to Faith. "I wanted to talk to you about some letters that I found in my mother's things," I said.

"Of course." Faith's expression was open and genuine.

"This is a little odd, but I found a recruitment letter from the CIA with Mom's stuff, along with some letters from you."

"Wow, it would be interesting to see those letters. I can

only imagine what my twenty-something self was prattling on about."

"I'm fascinated that Mom thought about joining the CIA," I said.

"Sounds exciting, doesn't it?"

"Did you work for the CIA?" I'd decided to be blunt.

Faith was still smiling. "When you say you work for the CIA, people think that you're James Bond or something. Yes, I did, but I just worked at a desk. Only for a few years until I met my husband."

She said this in such a casual way that I almost let it go. But I'd seen a lot of people lie. Some were better at it than others. Something about the way Faith turned her head, or maybe how her eyes looked up when she spoke, told me that she was shading the truth. I think that normally she would have been able to pull off the lie without a hitch, but maybe it was the talk about my mother that had made her stumble.

"What aren't you telling me?" I asked as the lights flicked off and on

"The show's starting. We can talk later."

Cara elbowed me in the ribs, so I let it go and turned my attention to the stage.

CHAPTER TWENTY-TWO

"Turn off your phone," Cara whispered as the lights went down and the band, made up of Adams County High School alumni, tuned up.

"I'll turn the sound off, but I'm leaving the phone on," I whispered back and got a frown and a shrug.

I saw Darlene and Hondo sitting to our left. He had put his arm around her shoulders. I took Cara's hand in mine. She squeezed it gently as the chorus began the first song.

I watched as Seymour became friends with the alien plant Audrey II and slowly began doing horrible things. Of course, no one suspected Seymour because he was such a nice guy. Meek and mild.

Just as the growing plant began to ask Seymour to feed him in song, my phone buzzed. I tried to take it out of my pocket as discreetly as possible, though I cursed myself for not dimming the light. The glow of the screen attracted some attention.

It was a text from Albert Griffin. It read: *Eddie wanted me to tell you that he followed Donnie to the home of the woman who was attacked. Can't remember anything else.*

My head started spinning. I forgot about the phone and ignored the jab in the ribs from Cara. The pieces of the puzzle were falling into a horrible pattern. A flashing sign in my head was asking: *Why had Faith not wanted Bernadette at her house the night she came home from the hospital?* The question changed to: *Why had she seemed better the day she came home from the hospital than the day after?*

Suddenly, I knew who had committed the murders. Like Seymour, it had been the person who seemed to be the good guy. My head whipped around as I felt movement on my right. I saw Faith get up and move down the row away from me. I looked down and realized that she must have been able to read the text.

I stood up and followed her, whispering loudly over my shoulder for Darlene. She turned and saw us shuffling for the aisle and quickly got the message, heading for the doors to cut Faith off from the lobby. I made it to the opposite aisle a second later and ran after Faith. But she didn't turn toward the lobby, exiting instead through a door on the left.

I saw Darlene as I opened the door behind Faith. "Go the other way!" I shouted.

I could hear some muttering from the theatre behind me, but I ignored it and entered a hallway that turned quickly to the left. I knew that we were headed backstage. Luckily, the theatre was full of all kinds of old props and furniture that Faith had to dodge, but she was still moving fast, quickly banging through another door ahead of me.

It only took me a couple of seconds to reach the door. When I flung it open, I found Darlene clutching her head and hanging onto an emergency exit.

"I'm fine. Go, go!" Darlene yelled.

I turned and could see Faith making her way through the ropes and clutter behind the stage. I heard Hondo yell, "Stop!" and saw Faith hesitate. The figure of Hondo blocking the opposite exit had flummoxed her for a moment, giving me time to get within three paces of her. I was prepared make a lunge for her when she made another left turn through the curtains. I followed her.

Bright lights hit my eyes. We were on stage, with a giant

plant and all the other actors staring at us and each other, trying to decide what to do. Faith paused, looking out at the audience. I reached out and grabbed her arm. She whirled around and shoved a Ladysmith semi-automatic in my face.

"Don't touch me!" she said.

At that moment, everyone in the theatre turned to stone. No one dared to move or breathe.

I don't think a single soul in the place, including Faith and me, knew what to do or where this was going to go. Finally, I heard a strange shuffling sound and shifted my eyes enough to see that Audrey II was slowly moving away from the crazy woman with the gun and the strange guy chasing her. It was enough to bring me out of my shock.

"We're good," I told Faith. "No one needs to get hurt."

"You don't understand," she said in a firm voice.

"I think I do," I said. "I know that the woman who was my mother's friend doesn't want to hurt any more people."

"I don't want to, but you better believe I will." Faith pointed the gun at my forehead with an unnervingly steady hand.

"I believe you. Did you learn your shooting skills at Langley?"

"Among other things."

"You killed Conrad because of what he'd done to your mother."

"Partly. That day, I was at Magnolia Ridge and found out that Mr. Kendell had died. Conrad had stolen from him too. Hurt him so bad. Just a poor old man who worked hard, served his time in Vietnam, just to have that snake come in and rob him. No different than if he'd ripped it out of his hands. But your lot wouldn't do anything and the lawyers were worse. I was so angry."

"You saw Conrad Higgins that night when you walked Cleo."

"I saw them, Conrad *and* his nephew. Not that I knew who Donnie was then."

"But you didn't kill him that time."

"No. But I did confront him. I told him he'd killed Mr. Kendell and that he'd helped put my mother in her grave. He laughed at me. Told Donnie that I was a fool and he handed Donnie that old Nagant pistol. Said the best thing to do with a crazy bitch was to shoot her. He ordered me off his property and threatened to hurt Cleo if I didn't. I left, but all the way home I was falling deeper and deeper into my anger. I'd heard about the red mist, and at that moment I felt it enveloping me. I barely remember what I did after I got home. Later, I found myself walking back to Higgins's place. I think I knew what I was planning to do, because I was staying in the shadows, trying to avoid being seen." She stopped talking.

I could see it in her eyes, that in her mind Faith had drifted back to the night of Conrad's murder. I pondered my chances of jumping her and taking the gun away. The trouble was that she was too close to the edge of the stage. Any attempt I made to grab her would probably result in both of us going off the stage and into the audience. If the gun went off, then someone in the audience could be hurt. It was difficult to see through the glare from the lights, but from what I could tell, most of them were still in their seats, too scared and enthralled by the unexpected drama playing out on stage to leave the theatre.

"What did you do when you got to his house?"

"I saw Donnie leaving in the car. Later he said that he'd seen me in the bushes as he drove off. He thought his uncle would probably shoot me, since he'd shown Donnie how to load the gun after I left. The door to the house was open. I just turned the knob and walked in. Higgins called out. He thought Donnie had forgotten something. That Nagant revolver was lying on the hall table. If I hadn't planned on killing him beforehand, I knew when I saw that gun what I was going to do. I picked up the revolver and there he was. When he saw me standing there, gun in hand, he just looked at me. I lifted the revolver, pulled the hammer back and fired. Higgins never moved until the bullet pierced his skull.

It was so odd. When he hit the floor, I felt all of that anger I'd been holding leave my body. In seconds, I felt like my old self. I remembered all of my training and just dropped the gun. When I did, I saw that I was wearing gloves. I turned and walked out. Calmly. I saw the neighbor, but I knew he didn't get a very good look at me. I used an old trick I'd practiced of walking like a man. Fifteen minutes later and I was home and in the shower."

"Donnie attacked you the next night."

"Yes. I hadn't really counted on that. I thought I could just act normal and no one would suspect me. I didn't know that Donnie had figured out that I'd killed Conrad. But I don't think Donnie was quite right in the head. He talked a lot of gibberish about people being after him. Of course, he was doing this while trying to strangle me. If it hadn't been for Cleo..."

"Did Donnie bring the rope to your house?"

"Later, when the tables were turned, I asked him what his plan had been. He still wasn't talking very coherently, but from what I could understand, he was going to make it look like I'd hung myself out of guilt. He figured if he left his uncle's car at my house and I was hanging from the rafters, then everyone would know that I had killed Conrad and committed suicide. Kind of funny that I turned it around and had you almost convinced that *he'd* killed Conrad and then committed suicide."

"You went home from the hospital hoping that Donnie would try again, didn't you?"

"I knew he'd come back for me. He was both unbalanced and obsessed with avenging his uncle. Sadly, I think his uncle was his only friend at the end. Apparently, Conrad had decided to groom him as his accomplice in crime. Choose your friends wisely." She seemed in a daze.

"Why kill Earl?" I asked, causing her to look directly at me for the first time since she had aimed that Ladysmith at my face.

"I wasn't given a choice. That's where things just got out

of hand. I'd set the trap for Donnie. Cleo wasn't in the house, I'd insisted that Bernadette go home, I was completely alone. Only this time, I knew he was coming. When he eased my back door open, I let him come in. I stood in the dark and shot him before he even knew I was there." I heard the audience gasp.

"You said you talked to him."

"He didn't die right away. I knew before he'd even entered the house that I was going to have to shoot him a second time if I wanted everyone to believe it was suicide. You see, the first shot was from about six feet away. Not enough powder residue on Donnie to point to suicide, so the plan was to shoot him again at close range, leaving clear signs that he was shot up-close."

"About Earl?" I prompted. It was clear she didn't want to talk about him.

"I guess he had been following his son. I heard him come in right after I shot Donnie. I didn't even think. As soon as I saw him standing there, I knew he had to die too, so I shot him. It wasn't until later that I figured out who he was. What choice did I have?" There were ominous mutterings from the audience at this revelation.

"And then you disposed of their bodies?"

"I dumped the father's body on the power lines and thought I would hide the car and Donnie somewhere where they wouldn't be discovered for a while. My father used to hunt on that property when he was a kid. He took me out there to fish a couple of times. When I was in high school, I went there a few times with boys. But there really wasn't anything linking me to the land. Just bad luck that he was found so soon."

She was done. I could see it in her posture.

"Give me the gun," I said.

"No." She pointed the pistol at her own head. There was an audible intake of air from the spectators.

"Faith, don't. My mother's friend would never do that to these people. Turn around and look. There are children in

239

the audience," I pleaded with her.

"Your mother was a wonderful woman. I remember us playing and laughing in the warm sunlight. I wish I'd made more effort to spend time with her. I miss her."

"I do too," I said.

"I don't know how I got here."

"You just started down the wrong path and kept taking one step after another, never stopping or turning back. Now's your chance. Hand me the gun and you can start to retrace your steps."

Faith hesitated. For a moment I thought she was going to shoot herself anyway and I wondered if I should just take the chance and jump her. But then I saw her muscles relax. She stretched out the hand holding the gun. There wasn't a sound in the theatre as I reached out to her and took the pistol from her hand. No sooner did I have control of the gun, than applause broke out.

I took Faith by the arm and led her backstage. Darlene, a nasty knot on her head, met us behind the curtain. Hondo was right behind her.

We walked in silence out to the front of the theatre where there were half a dozen patrol cars, their blue and red lights flashing. Cara was waiting for me.

"I'm going to ride with her to the jail," I told Cara.

"Of course," she said, reaching out to stroke my arm. "That was scary for a few minutes. But you were a hit."

"Thanks for the glowing review. I don't feel very good about this one. It's a lot more fun when the bad guys are really bad."

"Do what you can for her."

Darlene and I rode with Faith in Julio's car.

"That was crazy!" was Julio's commentary on the night's activities.

Three days later, I was sitting in Albert Griffin's parlor with him and Eddie.

"I'm giving you a reprieve from CI duty," I told Eddie.

He was still very pale and was acting quite subdued. "That might be a good idea. There are still things I can't remember."

"Doctor said you'd probably never remember everything that happened that night," Mr. Griffin said paternally.

"I saw Donnie, and I remember following him. I didn't want him to get away like that last time. I figured the best thing would be to find out where he was hiding out. But he was just lurking outside that house. At some point, I figured out whose house it was... and that's about the point everything goes blank."

"Donnie's father Earl was somewhere nearby. He might have thought you were stalking his son and hit you. Or maybe you confronted Donnie and he clubbed you upside the head. None of that matters. What does matter is that I'm cutting back on the CI work until you're cleared by Seth, your official sponsor, and Albert, your unofficial sponsor."

"I'm not going to complain."

The following Friday night, Cara and I were back at the Grove. Bernadette had insisted on us returning to see the full show. At the end of the performance, she embarrassed the life out of me by inviting me up onstage and giving me a certificate that made me an official member of the Grove Ensemble Players.

Before we left, Bernadette said, "Despite what she did, I still feel horrible for Faith."

"I think we all do," I agreed.

Bernadette nodded. "I'll do everything I can for her. That man was bound to drive someone into killing him. It's just a shame it was Faith." She shook herself and smiled again. "The good news is that Cleo is adjusting well to life at my house. She's used to the theatre and to me, so I don't think it's been too awful for her." Her smile widened. "Be sure to mark your calendar. Next quarter we're doing *Annie* and guess who's going to play Sandy?"

Larry Macklin returns in:

September's Fury
A Larry Macklin Mystery–Book 10
Coming Fall 2018

But if that seems too long to wait for Larry's next adventure, consider checking out my new paranormal mystery series, the Baron Blasko Mysteries, available this summer. Here's a special preview just for my readers:

Prologue

"I told you, Miss Josephine! I told you!" Grace Dunn shouted as she barged her way through the back door.

The solidly built, middle-aged woman was breathing hard as she came charging into the hallway, still yelling. "That monster has killed him, as sure as I'm breathin'! You got to do something, Miss Josephine. He's Satan's puppet." She rounded the bannister and started up the stairs. "I don't care what Mr. Roosevelt says, fear ain't the only thing we got to fear. We got to be afraid of that killer you got living in the basement."

Josephine Nicolson came out of her bedroom where she'd been dressing for dinner, pulling her robe tight around her shoulders. "What are you screaming about?" she said, watching Grace pound up the stairs toward her.

"I have warned you and warned you! What'd I say?" Grace yelled now, huffing as she mounted the last steps to the second floor.

"Please keep your voice down," Josephine said, "and tell me what you're talking about."

Grace took a moment to catch her breath now that she'd conquered the stairs. Her dark skin was slick with sweat as she visibly pulled herself together.

"Mr. Erickson, dead in his bed. Found just now by Myra. Killed. Murdered! And we all know who did it." Grace's chin was up and her jaw clenched.

The two women were now standing face to face at the top of the stairs. Grace was short and full bodied while Josephine was taller and a few years younger, but both of them had stubborn eyes that were locked on each other.

"We don't know anything. You say that Mr. Erickson is dead. Who told you this?"

"I heard it directly from Myra. She saw him lying there in his own blood," Grace answered, her voice laced with a certain flair for the dramatic.

Josephine wasn't surprised that Grace had heard it directly from Myra. The two maids were close friends who often spent their days off together. However, Josephine also knew Myra's tendency to exaggerate. She turned away from Grace and walked to the window that looked out from the second floor hallway onto the front lawn and across the street to the Ericksons' house. Sure enough, the last light of the day revealed a number of cars, horses and wagons parked or tied up across the street in front their house.

Josephine walked back to where Grace was standing with an *I told you so* smirk on her face. "Until I know more, you're to keep quiet about our guest in the basement," Josephine told her, watching the smirk evolve into a deep frown.

"You got to get him out of the house, Miss Josephine. He's going to murder us in our beds," Grace insisted, her eyes locked on Josephine's.

The two women stood inches away from each other with feet planted, Grace's hands on her hips and Josephine's arms crossed in front of her. They both held strong opinions about their current house guest, but Josephine wasn't so sure that Grace was wrong.

Chapter One
Six months earlier...

"I'm sorry, Miss Nicolson, but I can't do anything more for your father other than make him comfortable. His body is failing him," Dr. McGuire said, packing up his black bag.

Josephine thanked the doctor and walked him out the front door. The large Victorian house already felt as though it was in mourning. Nothing Josephine or Grace did seemed able to bring in more light or fresh air.

With a sigh, Josephine entered her father's room. Originally the front parlor, the space had been turned into a makeshift hospital room for Andre Nicolson. The man looked old and frail beyond his sixty-seven years, lying underneath the feather comforter on his large four-poster bed. It had taken five men and a master woodworker to disassemble it and carry it downstairs four months earlier.

"Josey, come here," he called to her. His eyes brightened just a little at the sight of his daughter, her honey-brown hair illuminated by the afternoon light coming in through the lace curtains.

"Papa." She sat down beside the bed and clasped his hand in both of hers.

"Ol' Doc McGuire told me the truth for a change. Of course, he didn't need to. I know I'm not going to get better."

"Don't listen to him. That old fool doesn't know anything."

"Ha, you are the worst liar I've ever met. I should have taught you better."

"We shouldn't have let them operate on you," Josephine said regretfully.

"Hush that kind of talk. We did what we thought was best. Who knows. I might already be looking up at six feet of dirt if it wasn't for the surgeons. And they never promised nothin'." His breath became raspy. Josephine picked up the glass of water beside the bed and put it up to his mouth. He took a small sip, knowing better than to argue with her.

Their black cat, Poe, chose that moment to jump up on the bed, curling into a ball on Andre's chest. He stroked the animal, his mind in turmoil as he tried to decide if he should burden Josephine with his guilt. *Keep it to yourself, Andre*, his conscience told him. *Take it to the grave with you.* But another voice, one fueled by regret, told him to talk, to unburden himself to his daughter. He wanted to settle his accounts as best he could. Deep down, he feared the grave and the unknown beyond the veil. Though he'd been born in this country, his parents were from Romania and his childhood had been swaddled in the superstitions of the old country.

"Josey," he said softly.

"Yes, Papa?" she said, leaning down to hear him.

"I have something to tell you." He stopped, still struggling with his decision.

"What is it?"

"Your grandfather... My father was an odd man."

"I remember that," Josephine said, smiling at the memory of the curmudgeon who'd shaken his finger at her, telling her that tomboys would always meet a bad end. But then he would show her how to make her own wooden sword so that they could have mock pirate battles around the front porch.

She had always enjoyed the time she spent with her grandfather, Grigore, but even as a child she had been aware of a darker side to him. It was a part of himself that he reserved for dark nights when he and the other men would retire to another room for bourbon and cigars. And there was no doubt that he could be a hard man. She'd heard him berate her father for imagined indiscretions more than once.

"When he was dying, he asked me to do something for him. Made me promise." Her father's eyes seemed to be focused on that spot in time ten years earlier when he had sat beside his father's death bed as Josephine now sat beside his.

"What?" Josephine prompted.

"There." Her father pointed to a vase on the large marble mantel above the fireplace. "In that vase are some of your grandfather's ashes. He asked me… Made me swear that I would take his ashes back to the old country and scatter them in the graveyard of his village in the Carpathian Mountains." He paused, breathing heavily as he tried to catch his breath. "I thought I had more time. No, no, that's a lie. I thought it was a foolish request from a querulous old man."

Josephine could see the tears welling up in his eyes. "You and your father didn't always see eye to eye. I know that."

"That's true. We *were* different. He was always the stern man of business. He never forgave a debt. Never."

"And you feel like you owe him something now?"

"I do." He grasped her hand tightly. "I should have done what I promised. Now… I don't want to think that I…"

"I'll do it," Josephine said without hesitation. She would have promised anything to make him better.

Andre squeezed her hand harder, pulling himself up from the bed a few inches. "Don't say you'll take it to the old country unless you mean it." He was looking her square in the eye as though trying to read her thoughts.

"I swear. I will take Grandfather's ashes to Romania."

Andre sighed. "What have I done? Forgive me for burdening you with this task."

"Papa, I'll do it. I've always wanted to see a bit of the world." Josephine wiped the tears from her eyes. "Don't think about it anymore. Just rest. I promise you, it'll be done."

He lay back in the bed and closed his eyes. Josephine gently removed her hand from his and stood up, looking more carefully at the vase on the mantel. It was a large blue vase that dated back to the last century. She hadn't even realized that her grandfather's ashes were in the house, though she vividly remembered the local furor the day her father took the body to Montgomery. The fact that her grandfather was being cremated was big news in the small town of Sumter, Alabama. Most folks had never heard of such a thing. But ten years ago, before the stock market crash and the onset of the Great Depression, every day had seemed to bring about new and different ways for people to spend their money.

Looking at the vase, Josephine wondered what she'd gotten herself into by promising her father that she'd carry the ashes all the way to Romania.

The next morning, Andre Nicholson passed away. Jerry Connelly and some men from Connelly's Funeral Home came and took the body away so that it could be prepared for the viewing.

"Don't you worry, Miss Josephine, I'll look after him like he was my own," the mortician told her as they placed the body into the hearse.

"We're going to have the viewing on Friday," Josephine told him.

The funeral would be huge. Andre Nicolson had owned the only bank left in town after almost four years of the Great Depression. New York and Chicago had been hit hard and early, but in southern Alabama the effects had grown over time. After four years, two of the town's banks had collapsed, leaving only Nicolson's Bank of Sumter still open and solvent.

"We'll have him back by tomorrow afternoon. Your father made all the preparations a couple months ago. There's nothing for you to trouble yourself over," Connelly said with just a hint of Ireland in his accent. He'd been born in Semmes County, but his father and mother had immigrated just before the War Between the States. His father had carried a piece of Yankee steel in his leg until the day he died and, when Jerry had prepared his father for burial, he'd removed that reminder of the cruel war with the words, "Aye, there, that won't be bothering you anymore." Connelly had put the piece of shrapnel inside the same box that held his father's old Colt Army revolver.

After Connelly left, Josephine walked through the house,

feeling like a stranger.

"You knew this day was going to come," Grace told her.

Grace had worked with Anna, the cook, and Jerome, the yard man, to get the house in proper order for the viewing and the gathering after the funeral. Even though neighbors and friends had brought enough food to feed a large army, under Anna's scrutiny much of it had gone to the farms to feed the dogs. Anna inspected every dish that came in the door, declaring only a few good enough to be laid out for the mourners.

"He went downhill so fast," Josephine said.

"The cancer will do that. I've seen 'em working one day and in the grave the next month. The good Lord does what he knows is best. Now you just rest. We'll have everything ready for the visitors," Grace said, easing Josephine over to the sofa.

The maid couldn't imagine not having any family. Her extended clan stretched out far and wide into all corners of Semmes County. When they got together for a marriage or a funeral, there wasn't room for anyone else. But here was Josephine, with her mother laid in the grave years ago of the fever and her father now ready to be placed in the churchyard beside her. Other than a few cousins scattered across the country, Josephine had no one. Grace just shook her head.

The viewing and the funeral went smoothly, with most of the town showing up to pay their respects to a man whose careful handling of the bank's and his customers' finances had left the community with more than most in these hard times of the boll weevil and economic uncertainty.

On Monday, Josephine tapped on the door of the bank well before opening time. She was let in by Martin, the head clerk. Her father had insisted that neither he nor Josephine should have a key to the bank. Due to Prohibition and the Depression, banks had become the prime targets of a new style of gangster. There had been quite a few bank owners who had been accosted at night and forced to open their banks by desperate men.

Andre Nicolson had thought that, if it was widely known he and Josephine didn't actually have a key to the bank or the safe, then they would be in less danger. One key was held by the bank manager and another by the county sheriff, in the event of an emergency. The bank manager also held a key to the safe, as did the head clerk. In a world populated by Baby Face Nelson, Pretty Boy Floyd and a host of others, Andre Nicolson had refused to take chances. Still, Josephine chafed at the thought of not having her own key to the bank.

She wished Martin a good morning and went straight back to Daniel Robertson's office and knocked on his door. The bank manager greeted her with a lowered head. He wore a black armband in mourning for her father.

"I wasn't expecting to see you for a while," Robertson said kindly. He was a small, older man who still wore Edwardian attire and a full beard. His hands constantly fidgeted whenever he wasn't working on account sheets.

"I need to discuss some business with you," Josephine said, looking around the office where she had spent so many hours as a child. After her mother had died, her father had gotten into the habit of bringing Josephine to the bank when he was working.

"Of course. I'm at your service," Robertson said sincerely. He'd worked for the bank almost from the day it was founded in 1911 and felt a strong attachment to both Josephine and her father.

"First, I'd like to have a key to the bank," she said, watching as Robertson leaned back in his chair and took another look at her.

"Miss Josephine, you know why your father didn't keep a key. I think it would be very unwise…"

"I can take care of myself." She opened her purse and showed him the Colt revolver she kept with her. "I assure you."

Robertson blanched, even though he knew that she could handle a gun. She'd gone dove hunting ever since she was a child, but he still wasn't comfortable with the thought that she could be forced to face down a hardened criminal. These days, even he felt nervous as he opened the bank in the morning. He would let his eyes roam suspiciously over anyone standing within a hundred feet of the bank whenever he put his key in the door.

"I know you can handle a firearm. That's not the point," he protested.

"I insist."

At issue wasn't just her ego. Josephine knew how easy it would be for the men who ran the bank on a daily basis to take her for granted. If she showed any weakness at the start, she would be at risk of losing control of the business. She'd thought long and hard about her new role since she'd learned she'd inherit the bank in a matter of months instead of years. Her choice was to sell her shares or to exercise control. She'd decided, at least in the short run, to keep control of the bank. Eventually, she'd have to decide if she wanted to continue to chair the bank's board of directors, but that decision could wait.

"Of course. We have another key in the vault. I'll get it for you."

Robertson stood up stiffly and walked out of the office, his posture telegraphing his unhappiness with the situation. *That's fine*, Josephine thought. She wanted everyone to know that she was not going to conform to anyone's ideas about how she should act.

When Robertson came back, he laid the key on his desk in front of her with a scowl. "Is there anything else I can do for you?"

Josephine held up the key. "I don't want you to think that this is because I don't trust you. Father had a great deal of faith in you and I do too."

"I appreciate that. I would never let you or the bank down."

"I will be going out of town for at least three weeks, and possibly a month or more." She set the key back down on the desk. "I'd like you to put this key in the safe until I return."

Robertson's mouth opened and closed several times, and the areas of his face not covered by his beard blushed red.

"I'll be needing some cash for my trip," she told him while he was still trying to decide how to react.

"Where are you going?" he asked when he'd regained some composure.

"Romania," Josephine said flatly, as though she were taking a trip to Montgomery.

"Romania?" He stared at her as though she'd suggested a trip to the moon.

"It's a country in eastern Europe. The other side of Hungary."

"Yes! I know where Romania is… basically. But why are you going there?"

"My father asked me to take my grandfather's ashes and spread them in the Carpathian Mountains," she said simply.

Robertson's mouth made more fish out of water movements. "Why in the world would your father ask you to do that?"

"It was a promise he'd made to *his* father."

"A man in your father's condition can get all kinds of funny ideas. You can't take a request like that seriously."

"My father was in his right mind when he asked me to do this," Josephine said, not totally sure this was the truth.

"Of course, but when you're dying… you… get ideas. I remember my grandmother wanted us all to sing hymns by her bedside during her last days. A person facing death has… fears. Talk to Father Mullen, he'll be able to advise you better than me."

Josephine had no intention of going to Father Mullen. The priest's opinion that women should not do anything other than run the household was well known.

"I'll think about it," she lied. "Now, here is what I'm

going to need." She laid out a piece of paper with several figures written on it.

"Who is going with you?" Robertson asked, ignoring the paper.

"Grace will accompany me," Josephine answered, though she hadn't yet brought the subject up with the opinionated maid.

"That's one thing, but what about a proper chaperone? Grace is… black. She won't be able to enter restaurants and other establishments. You can't eat alone. Seriously, Josey, you can't do this."

"Seriously, Mr. Robertson, I *am* going to do this. This is not a pleasure trip to Saratoga. I'll be eating my meals in my room while traveling and Grace can eat with me. I have thought this out. My plan is to go to Romania by the most direct and expedient route. Once at my grandfather's village, I'll spread his ashes and return."

Josephine knew that Mr. Robertson was right to some extent. She would have to be discreet to prevent any trouble, but it was not unheard of for a middle-aged woman to travel with her servant. *Middle-aged*, she thought. *Am I really middle-aged?* Thirty-five was not old, but she *was* very close to being labeled a spinster.

"Still, that is a very long trip."

"When we arrive, I'll be met by relatives," Josephine said, hoping that it was true. She had found a few letters from distant cousins that her father had kept. She hadn't been able to read them since they were in Romanian, but she'd been able to discern that they were from family.

"Have you talked to Bobby?" Robertson asked.

Josephine sighed. Robertson was clearly floundering about for any lifeline in this argument. Bobby was Robert Tucker, a local sheriff's deputy who had courted her off and on since they were in school together. He was a nice man, but he didn't seem to understand that while she liked him, she didn't want to bind their lives together in marriage. Ever.

"Bobby Tucker has nothing to do with this," she said

bluntly, tired of humoring Robertson. "Provide me with what I've asked for, and I'll think about the objections you've raised."

"If you are determined to do this, then at least let me see if I can find someone else to act as a chaperone."

"You may do as you wish," she said and purposely slid the note with her proposed travel expenses across his desk.

ACKNOWLEDGMENTS

The usual thanks go out to my wife, Melanie, for her editing skills and support; and to H. Y. Hanna for her inspiration, assistance and encouragement.

And to all the fans of the series—thank you!!

Original Cover Concept by H. Y. Hanna
Cover Design by Robin Ludwig Design Inc.
www.gobookcoverdesign.com

ABOUT THE AUTHOR

A. E. Howe lives and writes on a farm in the wilds of north Florida with his wife, horses and more cats than he can count. He received a degree in English Education from the University of Georgia and is a produced screenwriter and playwright. His first published book was *Broken State*. The Larry Macklin Mysteries is his first series and he plans to release a new series, the Baron Blasko Mysteries, in summer 2018. The first book in the Macklin series, *November's Past*, was awarded two silver medals in the 2017 President's Book Awards, presented by the Florida Authors & Publishers Association. A member of the Mystery Writers of America, Howe is also the co-host of the "Guns of Hollywood" podcast, part of the Firearms Radio Network. When not writing or podcasting, Howe enjoys riding, competitive shooting and working on the farm.